FARLEY STREET

ZANE ZUBIN

FARLEY STREET
a fantasy fiction novel

Published by Zyloo Press, Florida, USA
Copyright © 2024 by Zane Zubin

Address all inquiries to: contact@zanezubin.com

Paperback ISBN: 979-8-9917149-4-5
Hardcover ISBN: 979-8-218-43857-9
Library of Congress Control Number: 2023915046

Cover & Interior Layout: Fusion Creative Works, fusioncw.com

Printed in the United States of America
First Printing August 2024

To order additional copies, visit: zanezubin.com

CONTENTS

1. The Arrival — 7
2. Ziggy — 15
3. The Autumn Messenger — 21
4. Friendly Banters — 33
5. The Fun Ride — 37
6. Boyhood — 43
7. Rainbow and a Pot of Gold — 47
8. Playmates — 51
9. Sudden Death — 59
10. Changes — 67
11. Unusual Signs — 73
12. A Familiar Stranger — 79
13. The Fifteenth Birthday — 83
14. Homeland — 99
15. Ezekiel and Ezra — 107
16. The Dark Lover — 113
17. The Lost Lyran Empire — 121
18. Light and Dark — 127
19. Mission — 133
20. Little Signals — 137
21. The Magic Wand — 143
22. Fall Romance — 151
23. Karmic Retribution — 159
24. The End of Fear — 173
25. The Letter — 179
26. Puzzle Pieces — 185
27. The Underworld — 191

28. N. Leitner   197

29. A Seed from the Stars   203

30. Holy Amethyst   209

31. Akash   215

32. Zeke Meets His Shadow   229

33. Lion's Gate   239

34. The Mystery Woman   247

35. The Missing Week   257

36. The Great Return   265

37. Premonition   273

38. The Darkest Night   279

39. Sunshine   283

40. God's Army   291

41. The New Wave of Change   299

42. Love and God   307

43. The Far End of Farley Street   319

Appendix   337

About the Author   339

FARLEY STREET

CHAPTER ONE

THE ARRIVAL

There are no records of Zeke Tartal's birth. The night of his entry into the world, Mackinaw City was blasted with a whiteout unlike anything even the oldest resident could remember. But that didn't stop Ben Tartal and his wife, Audrey, who was in labor, from jumping into their car and setting out for the nearest hospital in St. Ignace, just across the Mackinac Bridge. Fallen trees had blocked many roads, forcing a panicky Mr. Tartal to turn down small streets and alleyways he didn't recognize, hoping one would lead him in the direction of the bridge. The snow was seriously deep, and the possibility of another storm was looming large, worrying him to no end.

That fateful evening, Christmas Day to be exact, Ben came up from the basement of Tartal House to discover his wife in severe pain. Her water had broken, and their new baby was clearly on the way. They immediately rushed towards the hospital, but the terrible blizzard made driving conditions icy and dangerous. He found only a tiny road where he could make it through. It seemed unfamiliar, and the snow was getting heavier by the minute, making it practically impossible to see anything. He frantically drove their car along the open street, hoping to find any place that could take her in.

"I feel like a desperate Joseph searching for any open stable he can find," he chuckled, referring to the very first Christmas long, long ago.

"WHAT ARE YOU TALKING ABOUT?" his wife yelled out in pain.

"Nothing, pumpkin," he assured her. "We're almost there."

"Almost where? We're nowhere near the bridge! If the snow gets any worse, the authorities are going to close it and then we're really screwed. Oh, this is going to be a Christmas for the books," she quipped.

Mackinaw City, despite its name, was a small town, and Ben had spent his entire life there. He knew all the roads like the back of his hand, but something about this narrow road felt off to him. Regardless of his attempts to double back, no matter how many turns he took, he was clearly lost. Even in the freezing cold, sweat dripped down his forehead as he hectically made turns to avoid the pounding snow. He had no idea where he was. There wasn't a single landmark, shop, or street he could recognize, and he was too preoccupied with getting Audrey to the hospital to notice just how different everything really was. By all accounts, that small road had taken him… *somewhere else.*

"This is like being in an episode of *The Twilight Zone*," he mumbled in disbelief.

Out of nowhere, Audrey grabbed his shirt. "BEN!" she screamed. "I don't care where you take me, just please do it quickly, because this baby is coming NOW!"

"I'm trying, honey. Please hold on a little longer. We're…"

That's when he saw it, like the light at the end of a tunnel. It was a dim, indigo-blue neon sign that read, "Starlight Clinic."

"I don't recognize this place," he said under his breath.

"I DON'T CARE!" Audrey yelled. "We're pounding on that door!"

He rushed to the door to ask for help, and to his great relief, they took his wife in. It was a precipitous labor, and thankfully, there were no complications. It was a tremendous sense of relief for the Tartals.

And so, on the evening of December 25, 1999, a healthy male infant arrived on this planet, in a modest clinic on a quiet corner of a snow-covered street, somewhere on the tip of lower Michigan. Audrey knew precisely what she'd name the baby if it were a boy: Zeke, short for Ezekiel, which in Hebrew means "the strength of God."

Zeke Tartal was born with buttery brown skin, a head full of dark brown curls, green eyes, and an interesting constellation of freckles. Ben was overjoyed to have a boy who would carry on the Tartal family name and could take care of his garage business once he grew up. He wanted to go back and thank the staff at the clinic with a box of homemade goodies for taking his wife in at the last minute.

Oddly enough, he couldn't find it. He went up and down the street he suspected he had driven that night, but there was just no sign of the clinic. He called the hospital in St. Ignace, which was originally going to handle Zeke's birth, but that got him nowhere. Nobody had ever heard of Starlight Clinic. It was like that entire part of town existed for one night and then disappeared. He even went to the local police station and the Mackinaw Township office to check if there were records of it anywhere, but they couldn't come up with anything. Ben was at a total loss.

"What on Earth is this supposed to mean? How could that place just vanish into thin air?"

The clinic's disappearance left him baffled. There was only one logical explanation and that was he had somehow driven to a nearby town in the storm, but that just wasn't possible. He wondered what it meant, and for years he would drive down random roads, wondering if he would ever see the "Starlight Clinic" again or if he could ever find that mystery enclave where his son was born.

• • •

Zeke was conceived earlier that spring, just two years after his parents were married. The Tartals moved from their small apartment in the center of town to a bungalow-style house at the far end of Farley Street, just a stone's throw from the shoreline. Mackinaw City was a charming lakefront community surrounded by nature. The Great Lakes Michigan and Huron meet under the impressive Mackinac Bridge, known by locals as "The Mighty Mac." The area was covered with orchards, woodlands, and nature reserves, all surrounded by smaller lakes. A large U.S. Coast Guard ship called *Icebreaker* stood, and stands proudly to this day, on the eastern docks near the departure point where ferries leave for famous Mackinac Island. Further west on the peninsula lies the Headlands International Dark Sky Park, which had a strange, otherworldly feel to it. It was reputed to be a cosmic portal — lazy, aloof, immensely mystical, and attractive as if lost… *somewhere in time.*

Ben was a tall and sturdy young man who owned an auto repair shop on Straits Avenue, just a short distance from Farley Street. He had great ambitions, working on expanding his garage business to include a dealership, which left him with little time for his simple and demure wife.

Audrey was a pale and petite yet beautiful young woman who spent most of her time reading, tending to the tiny garden outside their house, or working on stained glass projects inside during the cold winter months. Cooking wasn't her strong suit, but she enjoyed sewing and knitting. The Tartals didn't have much money, so they spent much of their free time walking along the shore and watching the massive freighters pass each other under the Mighty Mac. They frequently talked about starting a family.

"Let's get a dog first," they both laughingly agreed.

Ambitious Ben had big plans for his future son or daughter, though he decided to keep that information under wraps for the time being. One day on a whim, he brought home a small, white, Teacup Maltese because he knew his wife craved company while he was at work. She fell hard for the pup and lovingly named him Coconut, but Ben always called him "Coco."

A few weeks later, Ben had to drive to the western tip of the peninsula for some urgent business. Audrey always loved Headlands Park, so he decided to take her along. He dropped her off so she could explore it for a while, then he would pick her up on the way home. She thoroughly enjoyed roaming around the pristine woodlands. It was a magical afternoon. Sunlight kissed her soft cheeks, playing hide and seek with the leaves of the trees. A soft breeze suddenly blew over her, caressing her long, flowing hair and rustling her coat.

The silence of the woods was only broken by the feet of some wild turkey or coyote occasionally trampling on dry leaves or by the sound of a lonely bird twittering somewhere up the trees. As she walked about, she noticed a bald eagle flying high right above her head. She discovered an osprey and a whitetail deer roaming lazily near a brook. She even spotted a small black bear resting under a tree.

This made her feel like she had entered a magical world where time stood still. She fantasized about what it would be like to be Snow White or Alice in Wonderland. In this enchanting stillness, it seemed as if the whole world went on a pregnant pause, resting and nesting, waiting for something new and special to be born. This feeling of anointed magic stayed with her from that moment on.

By the time Ben finished work, it was already quite late in the day. He was in a hurry to get home, have dinner and relax. Audrey wanted to wait for the sun to go down so they could see the Northern Lights for the first time. The Headlands Dark Sky Park was a mecca for skywatchers and stargazers. She really wanted to witness the myriad of colors dance across the sky, and especially for her husband to be with her. Ben didn't want to waste time just sitting around and looking at the sky, but Audrey had made up her mind.

"Please, Ben. Can't we just stay for a little while? I've heard so much about the Northern Lights and I saw on TV that the conditions are perfect tonight. They're supposed to be phenomenal, and I really want us to enjoy them as a couple."

"But Audrey, it's already so late," he protested. "Plus, I've seen the Northern Lights as a child, and I didn't think they were that big a deal."

"Please, Ben," she pleaded.

He couldn't say no. This was the first time his wife had asked him for something with such urgency. Even Audrey didn't really know why she was insisting, but something was telling her he needed to be there. They sat together on a warm blanket, gazing at the stars for what seemed like hours. The Northern Lights danced around the sky in a vast array of cosmic colors, circling in on themselves like a vortex — a divine painting upon the canvas of the sky. It looked and felt surreal. Even Ben was impressed.

Suddenly, Audrey perked up. "Ben, did you feel what I just felt?"
"Huh?"
"Something just blew over me and touched me in a special way."

"Audrey, you're reading too many fantasy novels and you're spending way too much time in church."

"No, I'm serious. It's a different sensation altogether. Absolutely different. I can't explain it. It's strange yet comforting."

"I think you've been staring at the lights too long and it's affecting your already overactive imagination. You want comfort? Let's head home and I'll comfort you the way you like." He winked at her with a naughty grin. "Besides we need to check on Coco."

"Sounds like a plan." She smiled at him lovingly. She knew very well that Ben knew how to make love to her and tonight would be no exception. Ben wasn't an outwardly affectionate person, but he certainly was a great lover behind closed doors. The stage was set for a night of passion unlike any other.

They didn't say much to each other on the drive home; they just held hands the whole way. Nevertheless, something was conceived that night — something had forever changed. Somewhere in the deepest, secret corner of her mind, Audrey sensed a little magic wand had touched her, yet the following morning and thereafter, she didn't give it much thought. The couple returned home quite late, just approaching that magical moment when the dark of night suddenly turns to dawn.

CHAPTER TWO

ZIGGY

Zeke didn't walk or speak until he was three years old. He was always different from other children. There was always something "peculiar" about him, odd and distinctively different. His expressive face portrayed an almost animal-like sensitivity toward sights, sounds, and smells. He would squint suspiciously or smirk if he came across something or someone he didn't like. He would sit on the back porch of Tartal House and gaze at the sky and the stars for hours. His mouth would move as if he were communicating with some invisible someone or something, yet no audible words came forth. Coconut loved sitting beside him, occasionally making strange noises and looking up at the sky, too, as if waiting for instruction or guidance from some hidden source.

Ben was distraught with his child's weird behavior. He had expected a son who would run all around the house, learn to speak quickly, and show signs of growing into a capable heir to his garage business. That child had turned out to be the exact opposite of all he had hoped for.

"There's got to be something wrong with him, Audrey," he would often say to his wife. "I've seen other kids his age. People bring them to the garage all the time. He should be active and screaming like a parrot by now."

Audrey was a little more understanding. She loved her baby unconditionally. "All kids learn at their own pace, Ben. Our little boy is not like the others and is just taking his time."

Zeke didn't seem to like his father, either. He would cry and howl if the poor man tried to hold him in his arms. From the looks of it, Baby Zeke wasn't very fond of his father's unkempt hair and long, rough beard, nor did he like the smell of his skin. He cringed at the sight of him, raising his eyebrows and twitching his nose, making a strange face whenever he came near. Ben was left startled by the child's blatant rejection of him. He was completely unable to decipher the reason behind this apparent disdain. He began avoiding his son altogether as a result. He was a simple, material man, after all. Contrarily, Zeke loved his mother's company and seemed to enjoy the fragrant, flowery smell of her skin. He would smile adoringly at her, which only served to unnerve Ben even more.

One night, Ben returned home from his garage a little tipsy to find his son sitting on the porch, gazing at the stars. He became so upset watching his son just sitting there, it reminded him of the evening he and his wife had wasted at Headlands Park. "It looks like you invited an alien into your womb that evening at Headlands. I certainly wasn't a part of that 'immaculate conception,'" he muttered to her in contempt. Although he was clearly not in his senses, it hurt Audrey terribly.

Zeke evidently picked up on this. He was still quite young at the time, yet he didn't cry or make a fuss. He simply turned and kept staring at his father awkwardly until Ben was forced to back up and walk away. Ben would always carry the memory of his son glaring at him with rage burning through his eyes at being called an alien.

One fall afternoon, Audrey suddenly heard him laughing and clapping his hands. She came running out of the house, thinking he had begun talking. He was pointing his finger up at a distance and laughing. Audrey tried to discover what he was pointing at, but there was nothing. All she saw was him laughing happily, clapping his hands, and pointing in the same direction, repeatedly calling, "Ziggy! Ziggy!" These were the first words Zeke ever spoke, marking the beginning of his communication with mere mortals. There would be much more that he would impart upon humanity, but it all started with "Ziggy." He eventually began calling Audrey "Mommy" but continued to show no interest in his father.

Zeke attended his first playschool in January 2003. Ben wanted to throw him into school as soon as he began talking, hoping it would bring him up to speed with the other kids on Farley Street. He was extremely fond of his teacher, Mrs. Rosskopf, but he really didn't make an effort to socialize with the other kids. He much preferred just observing the sky. The new year brought many ordinary and extraordinary events occurring simultaneously. Audrey was pregnant again, and in late May, twin sisters entered Zeke's otherwise peaceful life. Whether they would add to the peace, bring some zest to his life, or create ripples was yet to be seen.

The girls were named Maya (after Audrey's mother) and Leia, after Princess Leia Organa (Ben really liked *Star Wars*). They both had the same curly, brown locks and green eyes as Zeke. Audrey became busier with the two babies and had less time for him and Coconut, so Zeke took on the responsibility of giving the dog company. At age four, he began babysitting his infant sisters when his mother was occupied with other household duties. He was a responsible child and adapted to the changes his sisters brought to his home with common sense and an uncommon maturity for a soon-to-be five-year-old.

One summer day, Audrey and her neighbor, Lydia Copeland, planned a play date for their kids. Mrs. Copeland had a daughter named Nora and two sons named Gael and Kai. Nora was the oldest of the lot at nine years and was almost as quiet as Zeke. She had sparkly blue eyes, long auburn hair that she often tied in braids, and a few cute freckles on her cheeks. Zeke grew quite fond of her over the years. Gael, on the other hand, was a husky, quarrelsome boy, always picking fights with other kids. Both Zeke and Kai understandably avoided him. Kai preferred spending time with Zeke over his own brother, even though Zeke was three years younger than him and the same age as Gael. The day of the outing, the women agreed to make sure their kids would be on their best behavior and would try to get along. The group was also joined by Eleanor Braganza, an older Portuguese woman hired by the Tartals as a nanny for the twins and a guardian for Zeke. Now that Ben's car dealership had taken off, there were extra funds to afford help. She was charming, told great stories and had a funny accent. Zeke enjoyed being around her as she made him laugh and would play silly games with him.

The next morning, the group set out for historic Mill Creek State Park, which had beautiful forests, wildflowers, scenic views, and a treetop discovery tower from where they could look out over the entire park. While the children played, the mothers and Mrs. Braganza sat there, laughing and gossiping. Zeke's first full-fledged introduction to the captivating beauty of Mother Earth was both awe-inspiring and overwhelming for him. Water gushing through streams and morning birds chirping in the conifer forests sounded like music to his tiny ears. Multi-colored butterflies flying over lush green fields, wildflowers blooming in the meadows, and the soft, golden sun kissing his face all wove an extremely mystical experience for a reticent little boy his age.

A few minutes later, lost in this beauty, he fell a little behind the others when a sudden shrill caught his attention. It was a hemlock warbler hunting for insects among the green branches of a tree nearby. He stopped, saw the treetop tower in front of him, and felt an instant pull towards it. Its hypnotic charm had cast a spell on him, forcing him to climb the stairs. Little Zeke wasn't scared at all. Up he went climbing, and whoa, an all-engulfing magical view awaited him at the top. All around him were birds, as far as his little eyes could see – birds of every imaginable color chirping around the feeders, alongside the creeks, and poking through the leaves littered on the forest floor. He could even hear the woodpeckers' rapid staccato cutting sharply through the trees. The Mill Pond was stunningly beautiful, with ducks floating regally on the mirrored water, delicate butterflies hovering above the wildflowers, and a bald eagle flying right above his head. It was a magical moment indeed.

Right then, he heard a familiar sound from a nearby tree. "Ziggy Zig zig, Ziggy Zig zig, Ziggy Zig zig!" Little Zeke instantly recognized the sound and turned around to look at the tree. A tiny and bright multi-colored hummingbird came chirping towards him. She sat on his shoulder and sang again, "Ziggy Zig zig, Ziggy Zig zig, Ziggy Zig zig!" Not only did the little bird hum, but now she happily sang a couplet, too: "Ziggy Bird, who is always on the seek, has finally found her friend Tartal Zeke!"

Zeke was so excited to hear her sing, he ran straight down the treetop stairs back to his mother to share it with her. "Look, Mommy! It's Ziggy. Ziggy Bird is back!" he screamed in joy, pointing at his newfound friend who accompanied him and parked herself on a nearby perch. "Ziggy Bird is singing a song, Mommy, and she knows my name! Sing, Ziggy, sing!"

He was so excited to introduce his new friend to his mother, but the bird showed no interest in sharing her secret singing skills with her or her friends. Instead, she flew away to a shady Eastern redbud a little further away. Zeke wanted to show everyone he had made friends with a magical, singing hummingbird, and the little bird's arrogance in choosing not to oblige ticked him off. Ziggy didn't fly that far away from him, though. Instead, she maintained a safe distance while following and chasing him wherever he went. When they drove home that evening, she stayed with them, following their car till they reached Tartal House. She sat on a tree branch near his house for three long days. Ziggy would go silent the moment she saw another soul around, but whenever she found him alone, she sang the same song, "Ziggy Bird found her friend Tartal Zeke! Ziggy Zig zig, Ziggy Zig zig, Ziggy Zig zig!"

She eventually flew away but kept coming back whenever she wished to see him. Little Zeke could not convince his family and friends that his new friend could speak. Mrs. Tartal ignored his behavior, thinking he was calling some random bird "Ziggy." She was convinced he had seen a similar bird when he was three.

CHAPTER THREE

The Autumn Messenger

Little Zeke Tartal was growing quickly into an intelligent, charming, and polite young lad. He had just turned nine years old and was very comfortable living in his own little world. He still wasn't very fond of his father but had started to tolerate his presence. He spent most of the time just playing by himself and reading. He loved stories about outer space and faraway lands the most. He loved going for long walks in the evenings with his mother, his little sisters, and Coconut. He also enjoyed exploring the woods and was fond of collecting different colored stones along the Straits of Mackinac.

Audrey had always noticed something distinctive about Zeke and his behavior that made her increasingly concerned. There were two very different sides to him, and he kept oscillating between the two extremes, trying hard to fit in and yet always remaining an outcast. He tended to go from a happy-go-lucky and playful boy to a brooding, lonely, and closed-off little creature that even his mother could barely recognize. At times he enjoyed being sociable. He would laugh, play, and make jokes, then suddenly retreat into his shell like a crab for no apparent reason.

Zeke's twin sisters were growing up, too, and he started noticing them both individually and collectively. The more time he spent around them, the more he realized his sisters were like night and day. Leia would screech at the top of her lungs and stomp her feet at the slightest annoyance. She hated the very sight of both Zeke and Maya and never even smiled at them. Maya, on the other hand, was a much more sensitive child. She had a calm demeanor and always giggled at the people around her.

She would often whisper into his ears, "Zeke, I have secret wings and can fly sometimes!"

"Yeah, sure," he would always answer, with apparent sarcasm as any brother would, but deep down, a part of him believed her.

Ziggy remained a loyal and regular visitor during those formative years. Zeke had come to terms with her choice not to speak around others. She would always come back at odd times, uninvited yet always welcome. She would sing and talk to him, giving his lonely soul some company as he fast approached his tenth birthday.

· · ·

It was autumn in Michigan, a season of magical colors. Michiganders loved all their seasons as each one brought a distinct flavor and spirit, but they loved fall the most. Driving across the state in October was a real treat to the human eye. Nature would bloom in all its hues around the little towns, the countryside, and the immense shoreline. The leaves on the trees would change from their usual summer greens to yellows, oranges, reds, magentas, and pinks, making all of Michigan look like a colorful canvas painting come to life.

A wealthy local man named Max Wheeler signed a four-car deal with Ben that year and was quite satisfied with the services he received at Tartal's Garage and Dealership. He was so happy that he invited the entire Tartal family over for a week-long stay at his orchard estate in Traverse City. The kids would pick cherries, apples, and the last of the blueberries while Mrs. Wheeler taught Audrey how to make preserves out of them.

Mr. Wheeler also owned a sleek, yellow speedboat named Bananadana, and the Tartals were treated to long boat rides along with wakeboarding and jet skiing on majestic Grand Traverse Bay. Zeke particularly loved cruising at top speed on Bananadana. He held on tightly with all his might and begged the driver to go faster and faster so they would lift up out of the water and fly straight to the moon.

It was the last day of their stay in Traverse City. They were planning to leave the next morning when Zeke suddenly noticed Zig hovering around him quite unusually, singing a new song: "A single friend had Tartal Zeke. Now he'll make two within the week!"

Ziggy's mysterious declaration left him confused. He had always ignored many of her rhymes, but this one felt different. He asked the bird, "What do you mean?"

But the only answer he got was, "For that riddle, you must wait. You'll meet a newfound friend at the broken gate." Zig's answer only served to make him more skeptical.

In the spirit of the season, Ben planned an overnight stay at a friend's empty cottage near McGulpin Point Lighthouse so they could celebrate a bigger Halloween in the city than just little Farley Street. The cottage had a beautiful view of the Mighty Mac just above the tree line. Once they entered Mackinaw, they noticed the festive Halloween decorations: glowing candles and lights, hanging rubber bats, pumpkins, scarecrows, overflowing cornucopias, and the traditional yummy snacks like kettle corn, candied apples, and monster-shaped cookies. The twins and Mrs. Braganza needed to rest for a bit before the evening festivities, and so did Mr. and Mrs. Tartal.

Zeke, however, was still high on energy. He had no plans to sleep or rest at such an early hour even though the sky was getting darker by the minute. He slipped into his boots and snuck out of the house so he could roam around a bit, enjoying what he could before the evening festivities began. He walked towards the lighthouse. The woods were generally dark, but that evening some of the trees were decorated with lights because of Halloween, making them much easier to navigate.

He had no idea how far he had come from the cottage when he saw an old house right next to the lake. Curious, he crawled into the house and checked every room, but it just seemed like an empty, abandoned barn house. Zeke was thrilled to have discovered a deserted place he could return to at will.

"Maybe I can create a little hideout and come back here from time to time when I want to be alone," he said to himself.

He wanted to walk in the lake for a bit, so he wasted no time, removed his boots, tossed them in one of the rooms, and ran barefoot towards the shore. The water was cool, and nobody was around. He dipped his feet in the water. The moon was just huge that night, almost blood-red in color — something he had never seen before. There weren't many stars, and the sky looked much darker than usual. He couldn't take his eyes off the giant red moon against the black sky which made it look almost ethereal. It was a "Blood Moon" night for sure — a night of a total lunar eclipse.

• • •

It was a while before Zeke realized it was getting late, and he needed to be back at the cottage before the others left for the festival. He hurried back to the room where he had kept his boots.

The place looked even darker, with only moonlight entering from a corner window. The moment he stepped into his boots, he felt something scratching his right foot.

"Whoa!"

He jumped, pulled his feet back, and almost freaked out as he saw something fly out of his boot. At first, he thought it was just a frog, but on second glance, he found it to be an ugly, freakish creature. The creepy little monster stood right in front of him, bold and unfazed. In the bright moonlight, he could now clearly see a tiny old man, the size of a thumb, wearing a little green coat, standing in the middle of the room. The creature was bald and had big cone-shaped ears, a bushy unibrow, a fat nose, and a reddish-brown beard. The moment Zeke's eyes fell on him, the man bowed in reverence. Before he could react any further, the imp jumped up and sat right on Zeke's shoulder.

Smiling at him, the little man said, "Happy Halloween, little Mr. Tartal!"

"Ahhhhhhhh!" Zeke screamed and started running for his life.

A screechy, high-pitched, equally scared voice screamed, "Ahhhhhhhh!" right back into Zeke's ear, clutching his shirt collar as they took off.

Finally, the little imp fell off Zeke's shoulder and bolted. Zeke ran aimlessly until he reached the cottage where his family was staying. The moment he saw his mother, he passed out. He regained his senses when a splash of water hit his face, and he found himself lying on his mother's lap. Everybody thought he just got spooked confronting one of those Halloween figures roaming the streets in freaky costumes meant to scare the kids. On the other hand, he thought he must have had a perfect Halloween experience: meeting a real ghost inside a haunted house on an ominous Blood Moon Halloween night.

Much later, Zeke came to know there was indeed a haunted house near the lakeside, according to local lore. "Oh yeah," a farm kid told him. "I've heard about that place a lot. My dad mentions it from time to time. He says there's this abandoned old house down there. It's supposed to be haunted. People say they see weird stuff, so you'd best stay away." Zeke knew it to be true, and he never dared to share this story with anyone. So naturally, he decided to avoid the lake house from that point on.

Children across the country happily enjoyed this festive time of the year, and the kids of Farley Street were no exception. Folks weren't really wealthy in this part of the state, but there were vast lands covered with fields and orchards, and children knew little ways to keep themselves happy and occupied. One Saturday morning, a few days after Halloween, the sun was high and the weather was unusually pleasant. It was that time of year known as "Indian summer."

The kids were still in a festive mood, and they would play in the fields around the neighborhood. As they were running from one field to the other, they suddenly came upon a corn maze — a secret farmer's corn maze, a magical corn field that came alive only for the children of Emmet County. They called it "The Amazing Maize Maze." Gael, Kai, Nora, Zeke, Maya, Leia, and even Coconut all had such fun running around this magical labyrinth, playing hide and seek and scaring each other. Zig was in a leisurely mood, too. She flew idly over the maze, never taking her eyes off Zeke.

During a game of hide and seek, Zeke was about to catch Nora hiding behind the crops, as he could see her shiny, long hair from one of those turns in the labyrinth. Just then, something popped out of the crops. He instinctively knew what it was and froze to death, watching the creepy little creature pounce on him again.

"Good morning, Mr. Tartal! Remember me?" With record speed, and before Zeke could even react, the little creature crawled up Zeke's leg, past his torso, and sat right on his shoulder, grinning from ear to ear.

"Ahhhhhhhh!" Zeke screamed before passing out.

Luckily, Nora heard him and found him lying unconscious in the cornfield. She called the other kids, and they picked him up and brought him back home. Zeke told his mother everything about the lake house and the corn maze when he woke.

"It was so small, Mom, barely bigger than my thumb." Audrey worried about her boy more than ever, fearing that he had even started seeing ghosts in broad daylight.

Throughout fall, Zig had a new song to sing. She kept humming into Zeke's ears, "Tartal Zeke lives on Farley Street. He has a newfound friend to meet. Ziggy Bird's now happy to tweet, 'Zeke's life's about to get really sweet!'"

This wasn't making him happy at all. Zig had sung a new song in Traverse City, and he chose to ignore it. This time he was more cautious since her last message came true. He realized she was a messenger from the animal kingdom.

"I have got to start paying more attention to you," he confessed, but Zig just ignored him and flew away.

Zig's song continued to ring like a warning bell in Zeke's ears. It scared him even more. He was in no mood to make an ugly little ghost of a friend, so he avoided sneaking out of his house or visiting lonely, abandoned places after dark. He chose to stay close to his family, especially his mother. The experience he had at the magic maze was no ordinary encounter. It was a meeting that was going to change everything. That encounter, paired with Ziggy's little rhyme, meant that life was about to change for Zeke Tartal — *really* change.

Now, Audrey started to notice something different about her son but assumed it was just an aftereffect of the scare he faced on Halloween night. Halloween marked the beginning of the holiday season which was always bittersweet for Zeke. Thanksgiving was a big event at Tartal House. The televised parade from New York City with the giant balloons and marching bands followed by a lavish turkey dinner paved the way for the buildup to Christmas. Zeke was fast becoming aware that he had to share his upcoming birthday with a certain someone named Jesus, and it was beginning to bother him. He noticed that his birthday and Christmas gifts were more or less combined whereas other kids got separate gifts for their birthdays as well as Christmas.

"Why do I get gypped just because I share the same birthday with this dead guy who hangs on a cross at Saint Anthony Church… and just who is Saint Anthony anyway?"

• • •

The next several months passed without much ado except Zeke being occasionally triggered by the thought of the little old man. One day, he chose to confront his fears. He skipped school and returned to the haunted house to deal with the little munchkin once and for all. *"There are no ghosts. There are no ghosts,"* he continuously declared to himself, trying to keep up his courage. He snuck out of his house wearing the same old boots and headed for the haunted house. He placed his shoes in the same place in the same old room. This was all a trap to catch the little goblin.

The shore was dry and desolate on a lonely spring afternoon. There was no wind blowing, and there was pin-drop silence all around. He could even hear his own footsteps. He walked along the shore for some time, occasionally throwing stones in the silent lake water, creating circular ripples that seemed to fade into obscurity. As he bent down to pick up more stones, he suddenly felt an invisible hand upon his back. It felt freakishly small, yet it pushed him with an unfathomable force straight into the frigid lake. Luckily, he was still close to the shore and didn't go too deep. He pulled himself out of the water immediately. As he was coming up to the sand and trying to catch his breath, his eyes caught something on a tree branch – the same tiny old man, smoking a little pipe, smiling at him and swinging his feet. Only this time, he wore a long, tall hat covering his bald head, which made him look a lot wiser than he was.

"Good afternoon and a happy spring to you, sir!" He tipped his hat and bowed his head.

Shivering, Zeke headed straight towards the tiny man and was going to tell the creature to leave him alone. As soon as the imp saw him coming, he jumped out of the tree and darted in the opposite direction, as if they were playing a game of Tag and Zeke was "it."

After a couple of minutes, he turned back and saw Zeke standing in the same position, not chasing him. Instead, he rested his hands on his waist and looked curiously at him. Zeke was an intelligent kid, and this prank had told him that the little gnome was only toying with him.

"Are you making fun of me?" he curiously asked the creature, as by now he was sure the tiny man could converse.

"Oh no! Good sir, I was simply trying to lighten the mood. I thought you would scream again, so I got scared and ran to save my life… and my poor little eardrums. It is surely not for the faint-hearted, that noise you make!" speaking in a thick, Irish brogue.

"Who are you?"

"I'm your loyal royal servant, sir!"

"Why do you call me 'sir'?"

"Your lordship had received a knighthood in his last life, and I was your loyal butler, sir!"

"Knighthood? Last life? That sounds made up," Zeke quickly countered. "... and even if it was true, why would a knight have a butler as small as you?"

The little man winked at him, his eyes twinkling, and a naughty grin appeared on his face.

"You are correct, Master Tartal. You've seen through my words and recognized my hidden talent. You see, sir, I am quite good at making up stories."

Hearing the tiny man's lies and the blatant admissions felt fun to him. "Okay, I'll play along. My name is Zeke. What's yours? Are you a ghost?"

"My name is Zag. I'm a leprechaun, and that answers your last question, too, little Mr. Tartal. I am no ghost, sir. I am only your humble and loyal servant."

"A leprechaun? What's that? Where do you live, Zag? In that haunted house?" He wanted to know more about this *leprechaun*.

"That was my temporary address, sir — that is, until I could find you. Now I live in your cellar."

"What??? You mean, you live in my house?" He thought about it for a second. "Ah, now I get why Coconut is always tugging at the bottoms of my trousers, trying to drag me down there. He wanted me to find you."

"Forgive my words, sir, but that scary little monster of a dog often wants to bite me, chew me up and spit me out like a chicken bone!" His bouncy, singsong accent fascinated Zeke.

"Hahaha!" Zeke chuckled, feeling more at ease with the little creature now. "By the way, why did you jump out of my boot last time?"

"The little cobbler that lives inside of me was mending your shoe, sir. Don't you see your shoe has a hole the size of an asteroid?"

All his fears seemed to have faded away, and Zeke laughed out loud, reaching his hand out to Zag for a warm handshake. A happy Zag jumped onto one of Zeke's shoulders instead. Ziggy Bird suddenly came flying out of the woods and landed on the other shoulder.

"Mr. Zag, have you ever met Ziggy before? She's been a loyal friend to me since I was three!"

"Dear Mr. Tartal, how can I not know her? Zag gets to do all the things Zig only wishes she could do. You see, Zag is Zig's alter-ego. We are two, and we are one — both parts of a whole."

Zeke now had two magical and mysterious friends, but he was still very much an ordinary child. Nevertheless, fate had a different plan for him, and he would need both Zig and Zag if he had any hope of fulfilling his destiny.

CHAPTER FOUR

FRIENDLY BANTERS

Zeke returned home that afternoon with Zig and Zag sitting on his shoulders. Just as nobody else could ever hear Zig talking, nobody but Zeke, Zig, and Coconut could ever see a little leprechaun living in the cellar of Tartal House. Naughty little Zag would always end up creating some nuisance that would then need immediate attention and resolution. He would merrily drink from Ben's jugs of homemade moonshine and call it his "medicine." That would, in turn, trigger his mischievous acts even more.

He considered Coconut his greatest enemy, and Coconut ferociously barked at his sight, too. One day, Zag threw away Coconut's dog food, and another day, he let ants inside the doghouse. Coconut was a nice dog, but Zag left him infuriated. He would chase Zag forever, and the little leprechaun had to run for his life.

Zig didn't stay too far behind, either. She and Zag had a love-hate relationship. They would always pull each other's legs, even literally at times. One morning, Zag was sitting on the branch of a cherry tree near the Tartal's house, whistling and enjoying the soft, summer sunlight while feasting upon some delicious red and ripe cherries. It was Zig's favorite branch, and she wanted to taste some of those cherries, too. She pulled one of Zag's legs with her beak so hard, he fell flat on the ground.

Zig flapped her wings and chirped, "Naughty little Zag fell from a tree. He broke a leg and fingers three. Zig will now have all the fun, and to the doctor, poor little Zag will run!"

Zag was furious with Zig for throwing him out of the tree. He rubbed his hands, dusted off his coat, and stood up. He didn't break a leg or his fingers. He was a magical leprechaun, after all. But, as Coconut came running towards him from the porch, chasing him and barking, he had to run again to save his life, which only added to the fun.

"Oh, Ziggy. One day I will throw you in front of this little monster Coco and let him chew you up like your favorite red cherries, you cherry pecker!" he jabbered in a single breath.

He nagged and complained to his master Zeke, though he lacked the creative and poetic flare Zig naturally possessed and fell a little short of his own expectations. "What pleasure do you achieve out of letting a raging dog loose? Why do you let him out of that useful noose? Can't you tie him tight with a buckle, so he doesn't chew my tiny knuckle? Oh poor, wee me. Is this to be my destiny? To die the death of a trampled ant? Only for being your loyal servant?"

Zeke had a hearty laugh at Zag's honest, yet comedic, efforts with poetry.

Unlike Zag's eternal enmity with Coconut who couldn't stand the sight of him, Zig and Zag loved each other's company and their friendly banters. They often had little one-off expeditions together. One evening, they saw Gael pushing other kids around on the soccer field. Gael even pushed Zeke away as he tried to intervene.

Zig and Zag couldn't hang back anymore. They had to do something about Gael's nasty behavior. They were so angry that they decided to teach him a lesson.

"It's game time!" Zag proclaimed.

"I'm with you. Let's roll!" Ziggy chimed in.

Zag used his abnormal strength and pushed Gael into a mud puddle. He fell with a massive thunder, his t-shirt and jeans completely drenched in muddy water. Then, Ziggy went to work pecking on his fat, exposed belly until he screamed. He made such a big fuss about it, whining like a baby. The other kids on the field held out as long as they could and then just burst out laughing. Mrs. Copeland came to her son's rescue and tried to find out who had the courage to push her boy to the ground. She obviously failed in her investigation. Who could ever imagine a thumb-sized leprechaun and a tiny hummingbird as the culprits?

Zeke was a much happier child now. His two friends had made his life much more interesting with their friendly banters and playful activities. Zig and Zag often sat beside him, stargazing. One night, he finally asked them the question he always wished to ask.

"Guys, will you honestly answer a question, please? You don't speak to or play with other kids like you do with me. What made you choose me as your friend?"

Zag responded, "It's because you are so special to us, sir."

"More than you know!" Ziggy chirped.

Zeke had no idea what he meant to those magical beings. They had so much to teach him, but only in time.

CHAPTER FIVE

THE FUN RIDE

It was a chilly December evening, and the sun had set early. Zeke was tucked in bed when he suddenly heard Zag's screechy voice, crying for help.

"Mr. Tartal, dear little Mr. Tartal, can you hear me? Help me, help me!"

Zeke was still just a child. He got scared and became worried about Zag. He jumped off his bed and ran towards the cellar. The sound wasn't coming from the cellar, though.

"Help me, help me, little Mr. Tartal!" the voice screamed from a distance.

Zeke followed the sound and realized it was coming from outside the house. The family had an early dinner, and everyone was in their rooms, already tucked in their beds, either reading, playing games or watching television, waiting with eager anticipation for Christmas and Zeke's birthday the following day.

"Sir, please save me. Please save me, sir!" Each time the call for help got louder and more desperate.

Zeke bundled up, flew out of the house and raced towards the sound. He entered the huge, dark cherry orchard near his house. A bright indigo light glowed in the distance. For a moment, it made him think about turning back, but Zag's calls for help made his feet move on their own.

"Come fast, Mr. Tartal! I need your help. Come and save me, please!" Zag's screechy voice could be heard from the same direction where several indigo lights seemed to be moving in all different directions.

Zeke ran faster. He reached a place he couldn't recognize. There were human-like figures wrapped in streaks of indigo lights dancing all around him. They looked at him, and he at them. A moment later, he looked up and was stunned to see Zag laughing, swinging from a tree branch. Before he could utter a word, Zag just flew down towards him, grabbed him by the coat, and with his mighty mite pulled him up — way up into what was now a spinning tornado of indigo light. For a few seconds, he felt as if he couldn't breathe.

The luminescent beams merged into this one huge pool of radiant energy as Zeke and Zag circled higher and higher. The motion of the whirlpool slowly shifted to wispy streaks of rainbow-like colors. But these colors were unlike anything Zeke had ever seen. There were millions of them, and they went on into infinity. At that moment, he could clearly feel like he was being sucked out of the Earth's atmosphere and into space. As they continued to rise higher and higher, all the colors eventually faded, and so did the tornado.

He realized he was traveling along countless galaxies and star systems. It was a magnificent journey. Every dot of light in infinite darkness represented a billion worlds, and the sheer beauty of it was almost more than he could bear. He had forgotten all the tensions and worries that had pulled him out of his house in the middle of the night as he flew past the stars with Zag at his side. Zag's solid form had now changed into what appeared to be a hologram, but it was still the same old Zag.

Just then, Ziggy came flying right beside them, though her dense, earthly animal body had given way to a much lighter and transparent cosmic one. She sat on Zeke's shoulder, humming a heavenly tune he had never heard before. He suddenly felt he was not inside his physical body anymore. It was some other astral form he inhabited instead. He felt lighter, like he had just come out of a heavily-weighted suit. He had no limbs; they were like wispy, indigo-colored streams that seemed to fade into space like a comet's tail. He could still identify as Zeke. His mind was still there, but there was nothing human about him anymore.

"This is so freaking weird!" he thought.

Then, he suddenly felt his heavenly body transform into a crystalline light. He discovered he could make this light as bright or as dim as he wanted. He could squeeze into a tiny, concentrated pinpoint of light one moment and then expand himself as far as the universe could take him the next. He had no idea how he was doing this, but it felt completely natural. It felt like he was riding a bike after many years — rusty, but he knew exactly what to do. He could become omnipresent at will and was filled with a joy he didn't even know was inside of him.

"Wow! This is awesome! It's like I'm everywhere and nowhere at the same time. Is this what heaven feels like? This is NUTS!"

He was having the time of his life. He felt his heart beating faster, overflowing with peace, love, and happiness. He knew this place; he had been here before. It felt so much like home to him, he forgot he had ever lived on Earth. He glided past the planets and the stars, then saw a strange palace-like structure made of solidified light far off in the distance. The gates were made of crystal and had two lion-like beings acting as sentries on both sides. He noticed the figures had the heads of lions, but their torsos were quite human-like. Then, out of nowhere, he saw a figure wrapped in indigo light slowly coming towards him. He knew this being, too, and immediately started running towards it.

• • •

"Zeke! Wake up, wake up, honey! Happy birthday, my boy!" He felt his mother kissing his forehead.

"Mom? What time is it?" He was still lost somewhere among the stars.

"It's midnight, dear. You know I wish you a happy birthday at twelve o'clock every year."

"Where was I? How did I get back into bed?" He was completely disoriented.

"I don't know, honey. I tucked you in and closed the door to your room, but when I came to wake you, I found your door and the front door open." After a brief pause, "Did you sneak out of the house?" Audrey was worried about her son. He had been so happy these past few days. Why would he possibly sneak out?

"*Did* I leave the house tonight?" he questioned. His adventure through the glowing portal and the galaxies had felt so real to him that he wasn't sure if he was coming or going. His heart was out of control, and it rattled against his ribcage.

"I'll ask your father to be more careful when locking the door. He can't seem to manage a single thing once he gets drunk," she grumbled reluctantly. "Let's go cut the cake. Everybody's waiting in the living room. I woke the kids and Nanny, too. Let's just have some fun, and then you can return to bed."

Ben, Maya and Leia, Mrs. Braganza, and Coconut were all waiting for him in the living room. They had secretly decorated it with balloons, streamers, confetti, and candles. They sang the birthday song and then Zeke cut his cake. Coconut ran happily around him, but then he suddenly froze. His ears perked up, and his dark eyes strictly focused out the window of the front door. He raced for it as if he had sensed something foreign, a stranger in the night.

Zeke knew the reason behind his sudden change of behavior. He, too, made his way towards the door. Zag stood outside, out of everyone else's sight, happily clapping his hands and singing the birthday song, or so Zeke could gather by reading his tiny lips. Zag's little green eyes met Zeke's as he smiled and winked. At that moment, he knew in his heart that his dream adventure had been real. He knew those stars, that palace, and that indigo being. What a great birthday gift from his cosmic friends! It was his first wild ride through the universe, and there were many more to come.

CHAPTER SIX

BOYHOOD

Zeke was getting older, and Ben's expectations of him had started to grow. He was becoming more and more disillusioned with his son. Zeke had no interest in cars or garages or anything that was even remotely considered macho. In Michigan, hunting is commonplace, particularly deer and elk, but he was not fond of such typical manly activities that he termed "barbaric," which was an odd choice of words for a child his age. He preferred looking after plants, caring for animals, and feeding birds, and he didn't like the idea of anybody hurting them. He loved planting seeds and trees and caring for his little garden, a quality he undoubtedly inherited from his mother.

The Tartal's neighbor, Lydia Copeland, often visited Mrs. Tartal with her one-of-a-kind analysis of Zeke. "You have a strange little boy there, Audrey. He never ceases to amaze me. A unique and sensitive chap, I'll say. He'll cry over the littlest thing. He must have been a buddha in a past life."

Audrey had also realized by then that her son was an extremely fragile and sensitive soul. Leia, on the other hand, loved the smell of car paint and motor oil. She would often open containers of automotive grease and smudge her face, or she would hide in a stack of tires. She hated being with her siblings and spent nearly all her time at Tartal's Garage, watching the mechanics repair damaged cars or detailing them.

Maya, who wasn't as fond of the garage and its smells, had a different view of automobiles. She looked at them as works of art. She would collect pictures of cars, especially antique ones, and try to learn about their different styles. She was growing into an eloquent speaker, and whenever her mother, her schoolteachers, or even her friends asked her what she loved doing the most, she said, "watching different cars drive on the road." She happily announced she would become a car dealer like her father one day. The older she got, the more eloquently she began describing colors, features, and models of cars.

Mr. Tartal was upset about most of the things happening in his house. He was a man of rigid beliefs and a singular dream. He had no interest in becoming a part of Zeke's little cosmic revolution. He had nurtured a simple wish to name his garage and his dealership "Tartal and Sons" one day. He would cringe at the thought of naming it "Tartal and Daughters" of all things. He felt as if the whole universe was conspiring against him, trying to sabotage his dream. Why else would the women in his house end up behaving like men and the only little man act like a woman? Sometimes he just felt like running away from his own home.

• • •

Leia and Maya did love cars differently, but Leia had begun to develop some strange quirks that worried her parents. She often ended up picking up fights and beating up neighborhood boys. One day, she even tore off Gael's shirt and beat him up. For some strange reason, Gael feared her and would not fight back. Mrs. Copeland, always warned by others to keep her son in check, finally had a chance to complain about someone else's kid for a change. She told Mrs. Tartal to get a grip on her daughter.

Audrey had to apologize on her daughter's behalf on more than one occasion. Seven-year-old Leia managed to earn herself an ironic title. Kids started calling her "Princess Leia," or just "Princess" as Gael would call her, even though she looked or acted nothing like a princess. This had the makings of a love-hate relationship from the beginning, and everybody knew it.

Gael and Kai's sister, Nora, was in high school now and had no time for the neighborhood kids. She was mostly busy with her studies and her high school friends. Zeke thus had little company left in his neighborhood. It only left him more time to think about his purpose on Earth and his childhood crush — Nora Copeland.

CHAPTER SEVEN

Rainbow and a Pot of Gold

Zeke could never forget the overwhelming experience of traveling to space with Zig and Zag that night on his eleventh birthday, but he started to question his experiences with them. It often left him thinking and wanting more cosmic trips and curiously questioning everything around him.

One warm summer night, Zeke sat on his porch watching the stars by himself. Everybody at home and in his neighborhood was asleep. Even Coconut was peacefully tucked inside his doghouse. Zeke was awake, wide awake. Zig flew towards him, and she found a comfortable place on his lap.

He lovingly stroked the back of his little friend. "Ziggy, you're always here when I need you, right?" he asked the bird. "Well, I need you now. Please tell me who I am. I know I'm not like other kids, but why? I know you can help me, Zig. Please tell me where I come from and what I'm supposed to do."

He always carried these questions inside of him, and now, they were finally out. Ziggy Bird's response left him perplexed. "The truth shall come to Tartal Zeke when it's time for him to seek. The truth is often stranger than fiction. That's why he needs a ton of conviction!"

It was a full moon night, and the sky looked much bluer than usual. There was something unique and beautiful about that night. Zeke realized he often felt melancholy on full moon and new moon nights, as if the moon had some sort of hold over him. He also felt a pull towards the indigo sky as if it were calling him, inviting him to an unknown, mystical place.

"Why do I feel like I don't belong here? It's like I'm a visitor or something," he said to himself.

Picking up on this from the cellar, Zag came running. "Master Tartal, you are on this earth, but not *of* this earth. Think about it," the little leprechaun firmly declared.

Zeke turned to him. "Look Zag, I didn't go chasing after you with a butterfly net. You came to me. There are so many other kids around here, why did you choose me? Don't tell me it's because I'm special, or you're my loyal servant, or you love me, blah blah blah. Can you be honest with me this one time, please?"

"I always do, sir. I'm always honest. It's my poor luck that you don't trust me or my answers."

Zeke thought he had made the conversation too emotional, so he decided to change the subject. "Now, do all leprechauns really have a pot of gold? If that's true, where's yours? Why do you hide it?" he jokingly asked.

"I don't hide it, sir. I keep it where it's meant to be," Zag answered evasively.

"Oh, so you mean you *do* have one! Where is it, then? Will I ever get to see it?" he inquired.

"You are an intelligent young man, Master Tartal. You won't have what we call Irish luck. You will have very real Mackinaw luck! The day you reach my leprechaun garden and see a rainbow smiling at you from a mountainside, my little hat lying on the grass beside a glitzy flower by an indigo lake near a glimmering wood, you'll know: the pot of gold is right there! Oh, and I almost forgot to mention, there should also be a star shining up in the sky – luminous and bright, just like you!" Zag said with a impish grin.

"Zag, Zag, Zag! How many more lies can you weave around a little myth? Can't you ever be just a little honest with me? How can you have a shining star in the sky during the day, along with a smiling rainbow?"

"You will know for yourself. You are special and intelligent, sir. You are meant to find your pot of gold, and I will gladly help you!"

It was infuriating. Zeke wasn't getting any answers, but that's how life works. Sometimes you just have to play along. So he did just that. "If you're a magical leprechaun like you say you are, will you grant three wishes for me?"

"That's a myth, sir! And three is just a number. All your wishes will come true the day you know who you are. The universe has your back, after all!" Zag sounded quite pragmatic this time.

Zeke had no idea what that meant. "And that's because you think I'm special?" he coyly asked.

"You are special, and so is every soul. We are all little parts of the puzzle whole. Our heart needs to open with a crack, for the universe always has our back!" Zig intruded with her little pearls of wisdom.

This conversation was going nowhere, and he was tired. So, he just got up and left. Zig and Zag didn't stop him. He needed rest. The next morning, strangely enough, Zeke saw an upturned, smiling rainbow by the hillside. Of course, there were no glimmering woods, no sparkly flowers, no indigo lake, and no shining star in the morning sky. Yet a faint voice inside him said, *"Zig and Zag weren't lying this time."* The rainbow was the little sign showing him that "the universe really does have our back!"

CHAPTER EIGHT

PLAYMATES

The early 2010s brought profound joy to the children of Farley Street. It was a particularly happy time for Zeke. He expanded his trust in his friends and his belief in Zig and Zag's wild tales. Zag, too, grew closer to Zeke, telling him fantastic stories and feeding his fancies. When Halloween finally rolled around, Zag told him the origin of the famous jack-o'-lantern.

"It comes from my homeland, you see. People used to carve faces on turnips back in Ireland. So, when Irish immigrants brought this custom to America, they started using the much more abundant and tasty pumpkin, placed a lit candle inside, and thus, the jack-o'-lantern was born!"

Zeke absolutely loved Zag's funny stories. He also loved Halloween. The Halloween tradition loved best by the children of Farley Street was dipping apples in hot caramel sauce and rolling them in crushed peanuts which made for a yummy fall treat. Another ritual they enjoyed was bobbing for apples. It was a fun game where children leaned over a huge barrel of water with several apples floating inside. They were blindfolded, with their hands tied behind their backs, as they tried to bite an apple and pull it out of the water. The child who picked the most apples would be announced as the winner. Among the Farley Street kids, Kai was the best apple picker.

One time, during the apple bobbing game, Leia got into a fight with Gael and threw him into a barrel full of cold water. The barrel was so small, and Gael was so fat, he got stuck and couldn't get out. He felt breathless and began panting. He was almost brought to tears. After a short while and a few good laughs, Leia pulled him out. Nobody knew where a small girl found such immense physical strength. Another time she forced Gael to help her with target practice by balancing an apple on his head while she shot at it with a BB gun. Poor kid.

• • •

Mothers are a perceptive bunch, and Mrs. Copeland knew her child had a crush on Leia. She was concerned about him, though, as there was something about Leia that she secretly suspected went beyond that tomboyish persona. Nevertheless, Leia loved the turkey shooting farms, the way she liked the smell of grease in the garage. She loved the sound of guns and the shrieking turkeys. The children were told the turkey that was shot would be their actual Thanksgiving Day turkey, though it was never the case. Zeke, an incredibly gentle soul and a die-hard animal lover, always avoided these farms and their brutality. He politely declined any and all invitations to go to the turkey shooting farm and proudly announced he would be a vegetarian.

It was during the fall that Maya, too, began to experience her first crush, and it was none other than Kai. Even though he was six years older than her, Maya grew infatuated with him. She would want to hold his hand and plant kisses on his cheeks. Kai, too, thought she was a cute kid, so he let her hang around him — up to a point.

Love was in the air. All the changes in the lives of these children affected Zeke in ways he couldn't really put a finger on. He could smell the fragrance of love everywhere he went. It increased his pining for something unattainable, something he could not explain. Maybe that something was love, maybe not. Though she was five years older than him, he had always been fond of Nora, the proverbial "girl down the street." She was just like him — unassuming, dreamy, lost in her own world. He always loved her company, which had now grown into a longing he simply couldn't understand.

Naturally, these years of innocent felicity did come to an end as Zeke entered adolescence — that time of a child's development when his or her full understanding of life changes. He had never even tried to fit in with children outside of Farley Street. He was always the outcast, the pariah. The neglect of his peers made him feel like he was an alien, a stranger in his own world.

It was during these years that he really started to hate the idea of Christmas. Though he had always been a very spiritual and sensitive boy, he began to loath December 25th, the day of his birth. He hated how millions and millions celebrated that day, yet there seemed to be no one who cared about him that day outside of his mother. As mature of a child as he was, he still could not shake the feeling that he had to share his birthday with what he learned to be the Christ Child, the Light of the World, whatever that meant.

"So, wait. Jesus isn't Jesus? Jesus is Christ and Christ is a light? I'm totally confused."

In a way, having his birthday on Christmas traumatized him. Seeing other children get love, admiration, and presents on their special day made him bitter at the idea of having his own happiness overshadowed by the spirit of Christmas. His feelings toward

Christmas would ultimately lead to great changes in his life, but he was still unaware of that.

Zeke was never a great student, but he had a profound insight, a universal presence, and a pleasing personality which made him a favorite of most of the teachers at school. He triggered a maternal instinct in them. They cared less about his marks and more about protecting his innocent, fragile, and vulnerable self.

Around the same time, he began having very bizarre dreams. He could see strange places and figures as if he were traveling to different places in time and space. While in that twilight state between dreaming and being fully awake, he often heard chirping sounds behind his ears, as if giggly little fairies were gossiping around him. An ordinary person would go insane. In one such dream, he saw himself flying above the clouds early in the morning when he could suddenly hear Nora's voice. She was calling him and asking him to play with her. He looked down and saw the corn maze near his home, where he'd often played as a child. He searched for her, trying to follow the laughter that led him there. He soon found a much younger version of her running and hiding behind the crops. Her hair fell over her face and blew in the wind like waves in an ocean. Her beautiful, angelic face shined like a star as soft rays from the morning sun kissed her skin. He could see a beautiful rainbow-colored halo around her. Then he would wake up.

"How is it my dreams never end? They always leave me wanting more…"

At night, he would still look up at the sky, wondering where he had come from. He still felt a connection to the stars. He also loved the smell of books. His thirst for knowledge beyond his regular schoolbooks led him to more interesting and unusual topics. He searched for books that could tell him about the stars, galaxies, and other planets. He knew he was searching for something he wasn't fully aware of, something that was hidden in the unconscious layers of his mind. He went to the city library and opened a random book. On the front page of the book, the following lines were written in bold:

"When the student is ready, the master will appear."

• • •

A few years had passed. Now in her late teens, Nora had turned into a grown-up young woman. Not only did she shy away from the neighborhood children, but she also avoided the company of her parents and her brothers. She was growing distant from everything and everyone by the day.

Zeke, on the other hand, was now entering his teens and didn't know if all the hormonal rush he felt every time he caught a glimpse of her could be termed "love." He was going through so many internal changes and was quite pensive about them. He was often found sitting alone near a boat docked in the harbor or roaming around Fort Michilimackinac.

Mrs. Copeland would often come to Tartal House to share her two cents. "You have a strange little boy, Mrs. Tartal. Does he plan to become a cloistered monk?"

Audrey also noticed the changes in her child but chose to keep quiet about them. She was reeling from her own troubles. To deal with the stress from the garage and the disappointment at home, Ben started drinking heavily, which was taking its toll on Audrey. They often had fights, and she had begun to think her husband now loved his moonshine more than her.

"Audrey, you're pissing me off catering to Zeke the way you do. He's a pansy. I'm going to have to rough him up a bit."

"Like hell you are!" Audrey was clearly coming into her own and not the demure and deferring wife she once was. "You lay a hand on that kid, you'll be pulling back a bloody stump!" She was very protective of her prodigy and was willing to do whatever it took to keep him safe.

"Don't you sass me, Missy! I'm the head of this family and this kid is making me look bad."

"Oh no, you do that plenty well on your own — the way you drink, cuss and stumble all over the place. If anything, you make *us* look bad!"

Then they both would storm to opposite ends of the house and not speak to each other for days. The cycle just perpetuated itself with no end in sight.

· · ·

Northern Michigan was always a thriving, four-seasons playground. In spring, the blossoms bursting on the cherry trees were a sight to behold. In summer, the myriad of lakes, beaches, and golf courses would all come to life, along with the magnificent shoreline encompassing the state. Everybody knew somebody who had a boat. Fall was magnificent with the changing colors, pumpkin patches, hayrides, corn mazes, "haunted" houses, and of course, Halloween. Every year, in anticipation of Christmas, there were numerous tree farms where one could board a hay tractor, scour the fields for the perfect evergreen tree, chop it down, load it onto the truck bed, head to the lodge to have hot apple cider and cinnamon doughnuts, then return home to decorate the tree for Christmas.

Christmas Eve turned into a memorable event for Zeke as he could see, meet, and speak with Nora for an entire evening. It was his birthday the next day, but Nora's presence always made it bearable. The following day, Boxing Day, wasn't quite the same, though. Nora disappeared with her friends and would often go missing for days. Christmas and New Year's thus often felt meaningless and miserable to him. Nora stayed away from her house for most hours of the day throughout the year anyway. Zeke pined for her, eagerly awaiting a glimpse of her, even if just once a day. He would stay awake all night just to see her open the gates to her house in the middle of the night and silently sneak in. It was turning into an obsession for him.

Zeke enjoyed watching the New Year's Eve celebrations on TV, but he wasn't too impressed with people getting drunk and acting stupid. There was enough of that at home. In early February, the entire nation was glued to their TV screens for America's favorite annual pastime, the Super Bowl. Zeke enjoyed football somewhat, mainly for the strategic aspect of the game, but he felt the sport was too rough overall. He loved playing and watching soccer, however, and one of his favorite moments in the game was "Sudden Death."

CHAPTER NINE

SUDDEN DEATH

For the next year, the Farley Street families were all plagued by their own issues – troubled homes, difficult children, marital discord, and more. The following winter, the Tartals and the Copelands decided to put all their issues behind them and planned to spend the Christmas holidays at Boyne Mountain Resort, a year-round vacation destination and the perfect getaway not far from home. The resort was dressed in full holiday style with lights, candles, the most festive decorations, and all the traditional goodies. There was an ice-skating rink and miles of ski, sleigh, and snowmobile trails in and around the resort.

Coconut and Mrs. Braganza kept each other company, and the twins were having a blast building an impressive snow fort. For the first time in years, Nora agreed to accompany her family on the trip. The kids of Farley Street had finally been reunited after years with Nora's return to the fold. This brought some of Zeke's childhood joy back. He was beyond happy. In fact, all the children were happy to be in each other's company — laughing and carrying on, playing different sports, and ringing in the holidays. They even threw Zeke a surprise birthday party on Christmas Eve. For him, life had never been better.

He was turning fourteen and wanted to feel what it meant to be an adult. He and Nora spent a lot of time together, drinking hot cider and talking for hours. He could see a deep sadness in her eyes, and he wanted to help her. Like it or not, Zeke was becoming a child of light. He could not bear to see others in pain. Thus, he felt drawn to Nora and her pain.

As they became closer, Nora confided in him that her father, Nigel, was in a relationship with another woman, and it badly affected her life as well as that of her brothers. Gael's aggression and anger stemmed from watching his parents quarrel at home, and Kai tried to find an escape by simply ignoring everything.

Nora's experiences resonated with him. They had very similar lives. He, too, had a dysfunctional family. Ben Tartal, who was always upset with his children and his wife, turned to alcohol for respite. Zeke could see the growing distance between his parents and the pain it was causing his mother. Leia's aggression probably stemmed from their marital discord as well, while Maya turned her anger inward. Nora disclosed how much she hated being at home, and Zeke could relate to the frustration and anger. He felt her sorrow, yet at the same time, was happy to be in her company. Little did he know, the Fates had much darker plans.

For the first time in his life, Christmas didn't bother him. The Christmas party at Boyne Resort was the best thing he had experienced in years. Ziggy found herself a perfect cozy branch on a snow-covered cherry tree nearby, while Zag had the opportunity of a lifetime to get royally snockered with the free-flowing champagne.

For the next few days, the Tartals and the Copelands took advantage of all the amenities of the resort. The boys played hockey and the girls practiced figure skating routines. Audrey, Lydia, and

Nora relished a full spa day with massages, facials, and mani-pedis. Ben and Nigel tooled around on snowmobiles, and everybody took to the slopes to ski and snowboard. They dined on venison and elk, and since Michigan was fast becoming a reputable wine-producing region, they drank only the finest local wines. There was an old grand piano in the lobby, and everybody sang Christmas carols with carolers all decked out in traditional Charles Dickens costumes.

On New Year's Eve, everybody was in the mood to party. Zeke was looking forward to the evening. He would finally ring in the New Year with Nora, a secret wish he harbored for years. Dressed in his only suit, he entered the ballroom and saw Nora in a beautiful evening gown. Her sleek, auburn hair was flowing in beach waves and her skin was as soft and delicate as an English rose. She had an ethereal smile on her face, and he was beyond thrilled to see her. He tried to talk to her, but all she said was, "We can always talk later, Zeke. Look how beautiful everything is. Let's dance." She grabbed his arm and pulled him onto the dance floor. They danced for just a little over ten minutes before Nora excused herself and scurried out, but for Zeke, those ten minutes were a lifetime.

• • •

It was well into the evening, and all the guests had joined in the merrymaking. The party hall was heavily crowded, but Nora was nowhere to be seen. She had left Zeke on the dance floor and just vanished.

"I have a hunch she ditched me on purpose," he said to himself.

He looked for her in every corner of the ballroom. He ran out and began searching for her all over the resort, but there was no sign of her. Nora had disappeared without a trace. At the stroke of midnight, when the world was happily cheering and ringing in the New Year, he was gripped by a sudden sense of fear that left him frazzled.

He rushed back to his hotel room to compose himself, and after a few minutes, Maya burst into the room, hysterical.

"Maya, what's wrong?" he asked, rushing to her side.

She buried her head in his chest and sobbed. She couldn't utter a single word, but then she motioned for him to follow her. He grabbed his coat, and with one arm wrapped around her shoulders, he guided her through the hotel and out the side door. They started walking towards the snowmobile trail when a flash of color grabbed his attention. He recognized his mother's long, emerald-green coat and he immediately felt a lump swell up in his throat. Something was wrong — horribly wrong. He could sense it.

As he hurried across the parking lot towards the commotion, a bitter, winter wind blew snow crystals into the air that stung his face like sharp, poking needles. He pushed his way through a crowd of people who were chattering in silent whispers. "Mom!" he yelled, but his voice was choked in his throat. "Mom!!" he tried again, even louder this time. She turned towards him, and even at a distance, he could see the tears streaming down her face. She held up both hands as if to stop him from coming any closer, but a bright stripe of yellow propelled him forward. The entire area in front of them was cordoned off by the police while EMTs rolled a gurney out of the back of an ambulance with the lights still cycling.

"What's going on?" he questioned, looking from the officers to his mom and back.

"Please, Zeke, go back inside. This isn't something you need to…" her words were cut off by an ear-piercing wail.

"Nooooo!!!!!" A woman tried to force her way beyond the policemen. Her blood-curdling shriek was the most gripping, horrifying sound he had ever heard. It was Mrs. Copeland collapsing into a police officer's arms; her legs simply gave out in the deep snow.

"Zeke, I don't want you to…" Audrey tried to say.

But, for the first time in his life, he disobeyed his mother and pushed past the onlookers. There, half-hidden by the ambulance's open door, was a huge splash of red bleeding fast into the dry snow, a pile of shattered glass, and the twisted carcass of a snowmobile.

"Don't look," a familiar voice said, and a soft hand landed on his shoulder. "You don't want to remember her this way."

It was too late. He already understood what lay before him. It was Nora. Amid the twisted wreckage of metal and glass was a clump of auburn hair he had once wished to touch.

"Oh, God." His legs started to shake, and his knees buckled. He had gone into shock. One of the security guards lifted him up out of the snow and escorted him back to the lodge. Lydia was beyond hysterical and Audrey not that far behind. Nigel tried to hold it together, but after a while, he couldn't contain himself any longer and broke down in tears, his face buried in his gloves. Ben immediately came to his side to comfort him. Kai and Gael were nowhere to be found.

Everyone was dumbstruck. What in the world happened? It wasn't until much later that the truth came out, and things started to make sense. Nora had sneaked out of the party to spend the night with her new boyfriend. He was a few years older than her, the friend of a friend. She had a bad habit of getting carried away by what people like to call the bad-boy persona: foul-mouthed, bike-riding tough guys with muscles and tattoos that made her feel more like a grown-up than she actually was. This time, however, it proved fatal. They'd gone to a rave at a warehouse nearby and had gotten high on drugs and alcohol when the boy decided he wanted to go snowmobiling in the middle of the night. In a loaded state, the boy thought he was going over a snow mound but instead drove straight into a parked car buried under a thin blanket of snow. They both died instantly. The impact was so destructive that Nora broke her neck, and the boy's spine was severed.

Nora's sudden death pushed Zeke into a state of complete shock. His soul felt trapped inside a body that had forgotten all its functions. His senses were totally numb. Even after watching blankly as her body lay dead on the snowmobile trail, he couldn't cry. He couldn't feel anything. It was like everything had frozen in its place, and his heart wasn't beating anymore, but he was still alive — and a part of him did not want to be.

• • •

When the shock finally receded and he started to somewhat understand what Nora's death had meant, he went into a state of severe depression. He started to perform badly in school, turned into an absolute social recluse, and began spending hours at Lakeview Cemetery where she was buried. He would simply stand by her headstone and not say anything. He didn't even cry.

It was during this period of darkness in his life that he began to question everything about life. He started to question his own sanity, and he began thinking about the possibility that Zig and Zag were just figments of his broken mind. He questioned himself, too. He would spend hours wondering who he was and what his purpose in life was. He lost touch with his spiritual self and was taken in by doubt and confusion. Why did he feel all these things? What did all the signs around him mean? Why had Zig and Zag chosen him of all people? These questions took hold of his mind, and their answers would come through revelations and trials that would make him so much more than just an ordinary boy.

As May rolled around, he had the dream again. He was flying above the clouds early in the morning when he heard Nora's voice. He leaned forward and looked down from the sky to take a full panoply of the miles and miles of apple and cherry orchards, along with the maize and wheat fields around his city. He plainly saw the cornfield near his home where he played as a child. He could see the magical maze from where Zag had once popped out and pounced on him. Only this time, Nora wasn't hiding inside the labyrinth anymore. She was flying beside him. They both had wings like angels. Her hair fell over her face and blew in the wind like a wave in the ocean. As he looked down from the clouds, he could see a strange sign that read 'Z' carved out of the corn maze. They flew down to get a closer look. Just then, Zag popped out of the Z, waving his hands. Zeke turned around to look at Nora. As she smiled, he could see a beautiful rainbow-colored halo encircling her. She was at peace.

• • •

The next morning, he woke up feeling fresh and light, as if a heavy load had been lifted from his chest. Nora's death had triggered a deep longing in him to know more about death and what came beyond. He sat there, pondering his vision for what could have been hours, until finally an answer came to him. It was as if this was all meant to be. He understood what his dream meant. She was safe. She was happy. She was home.

That evening, he felt pulled to Lakeview Cemetery again. Only this time, he wasn't driven by a sense of despair, hopelessness, or loneliness, but by an inner knowing of something special he was about to see and learn. His intuition was right. The sun had set, and it was slowly getting darker. He sat there for a while, watching the flowers and birds and noticing the epitaphs written on the different tombstones. A soft breeze blew over him. He could suddenly feel someone touching his shoulder. He looked around and saw Nora standing beside him. She wore the same gown she had worn at the New Year's Eve party, and she was smiling at him.

"Nora! Is this really you?" he inquired, wanting confirmation that his eyes weren't tricking him.

She didn't say anything. She simply smiled and nodded. Once he became aware of the wings of light emanating from behind her, he knew this dream wasn't just a dream. He had met her on a different plane. It existed in a higher dimension, only seen and experienced with the cosmic mind. In that moment, he knew he wasn't responsible for her death. It was just a story playing out in the physical realm to help him come to terms with the deeper truths of life — truths people either shy away from or fail to see and recognize. Triggers are often sent to us by the universe to help us on our journey, so we can expand our hearts and open our minds.

Nora did not say a word, yet he heard her voice. "Death is nothing but a catalyst, my dear friend. We come to the Earth plane to experience the pains and the hurts so we can transcend them and perfect our souls."

"It all makes sense in my mind, Nora, but I miss you terribly, and I'm lost without you," he replied.

Nora looked at him intensely, then she finally spoke. "I have a message for you from the Source: 'Your mission has begun. You will need to go out on a limb to find the truth you seek.' That truth for you is now, Ezekiel. Good luck and may God speed you on your journey."

Then she vanished.

CHAPTER TEN

CHANGES

It was one death and many lives. It was like a splash that sent ripples through multiple consciousnesses. Nora's death had touched the lives of everyone who lived on Farley Street, each in its own, unique way.

The Copelands had to come to terms with a total breakdown of the structure so fondly called "a family." Nigel left home almost immediately after Nora's death and began living with his girlfriend after filing for divorce. Lydia Copeland, who had been happy to remain a stay-at-home mom all her life, had to learn to take the blow of not only losing her only daughter, but the man she promised to love until death.

She had to stop licking her wounds and go out into the real world to get by. She began working at the local library to sustain whatever was left of her family. There was no time or space left for her to nurture the sense of pride around the so-called "happy family" paradigm she had spent years building. Paying her bills was more important at this stage.

Gael's life was the most affected by Nora's death. To cope, he began working odd jobs like mowing lawns, raking leaves, and shoveling snow every day after school to get his mind off Nora's death and to feel productive. Like Zeke, Gael became a far more mature, albeit fractured, fourteen-year-old. He had been a silent sufferer of a serious mental health condition for about a year, and after Mrs. Copeland forced him to go to therapy, his bipolar disorder was finally identified. Nobody in the Copeland family noticed the early signs, but Nora's death made his condition much more prominent, so much so that therapy and medication were clearly necessary.

He was full of energy one minute and unusually irritable the next, often confronting his mother. The mood swings were affecting his sleep and all his activities. His judgment, behavior, and even his ability to think were lost. He was rapidly losing a lot of weight, too. Slowly these episodes began occurring multiple times a year. From the chubby, ignorant little boy he was, he turned into a frail, mute teenager, disconnecting himself from everyone around him — even his childhood love, Leia.

To make matters worse, Leia was now showing a blatant disinterest in boys, and Gael took it personally. The loss of Nora and the subsequent developments in his life triggered a strange feeling of depravity, an inferiority complex, making him feel he deserved nothing good in life. Zeke saw what Gael was going through, and it made his heart ache. He wanted to help his friend, but his own life wasn't even on track.

Zeke's parents always had their differences. Nora's death and the divorce of the Copelands only brought the gaping holes in their relationship to the forefront. The stark difference between the two was staring them right in the eyes. Zeke and the twins were simply too young to help. The turmoil and torment in Zeke's life made him look inward. He had come to terms with Nora's death, but he could see how the people around him were still broken and hurt. He felt an instinctive and benevolent urge to help and to heal them. Nora had told him his mission had begun, and her words rang in his ears day in and day out as he awaited his destiny.

The Tartals had started out as the perfect couple, but time had been against them. Ben had turned into an alcoholic quite early in life and began turning away from his family. He spent most of his days sleeping in his garage, wasting money on betting, and drinking with the other mechanics at the local dive bar. He had no time for his wife and children. Life had disappointed him, and now he had abandoned his dreams. No rehab could change him, and no amount of counseling could save his marriage. His family would never be the same.

Audrey was aware of her own emotional fatigue and the trauma her children were facing but didn't exactly know how to handle them. Her children were different and were reacting to the growing crises differently. Leia had her own set of issues, and her mother didn't know what to do about them. She decided to accompany Mrs. Copeland and took Leia for counseling along with Gael.

The two emotionally exhausted mothers had immense respect for each other, sharing the burden of their children's issues. As a result, they developed a deeper friendship, which they both desperately needed. Lydia Copeland had no choice but to evolve as a person. Faced with an impending divorce, the collapsing psyche of her son and her daughter's death, she became a much stronger woman. For her to become that woman, she had to lose her only daughter.

Zeke and Kai stood with Gael as he fought his condition, and once he began therapy and medication, he learned to handle his mood swings much better. Zeke would often sit with Gael, not saying anything, so that Gael would know that he wasn't alone, and that was enough. Gael and Leia bonded over their mutual issues, and although she developed a sense of mutual respect for him, she continued to show no romantic interest in him whatsoever.

Kai also realized he needed to be more responsible towards his family and friends. He secretly harbored internalized guilt for his sister's death, but it shaped him into a different person. He was the closest to Nora in age among the neighborhood kids and knew how attached Zeke was to her. He realized he needed to be with Zeke more to help him deal with the pain and the changes he was going through. In doing so, he could better manage is own pain and confusion.

• • •

Coconut and Mrs. Braganza were both aging. Coco was mostly found resting in his doghouse now, and Mrs. Braganza was simply too old to continue working. She finally decided to return to her ancestral home in Portugal, leaving behind the family she had grown to love.

Meanwhile, Maya developed a brand-new crush for a new teacher in school, and her habit of dwelling in her little dream world continued. She loved the idea of being in love and had been struck by a common childhood syndrome: hyper-romanticism. This was probably the easy escape route she needed, as she was unwilling to face the harsh realities around her.

While she became an absolute escapist, the same problems turned Zeke into a seeker. He began delving deep into his core, his innermost being, which was helping him find his true voice and become his true authentic self. All the rapid changes around him in less than a year had turned him into an ardent observer of life. The death of Nora came as a profound and life-changing experience for him. It brought a deep sense of realization and awoke something that was lying deep in his subconscious. Her physical death and the metaphysical presence that followed suddenly created a ripple in his quiet life, stirring him, shaking him up from a deep slumber, and transforming him from an innocent, vulnerable, lovelorn child into a wide-eyed young man of wisdom.

"He is strong. He is wise. Look how my friend Zeke flies!" Ziggy was always around to give her two cents.

"Beware, Master Tartal, as your wisdom grows, and your enlightenment draws near, so do the trials that shall come with the answers to your many questions," Zag warned.

Zeke was used to Zig's songs, but Zag's words did more than just concern him. It brought him to a realization. Ziggy Bird and Zag the Leprechaun weren't just his friends anymore. He understood they had been sent to him with a purpose and carefully listened to their words of wisdom. He also recognized the sign 'Z' carved out of the corn maze in his dream as a sign for something bigger that was to come. He realized he needed to be more vigilant, aware, and observant. He didn't want to miss the point, and he certainly didn't want to miss the lesson.

Changes come as a gift, a virtue, as preparation for bigger battles in life. One death triggered many conscious and unconscious journeys for each member of Farley Street. They were all making a trip towards evolution in their own, unique ways. Zeke was making his way, too, and he had just now started to realize that.

CHAPTER ELEVEN

Unusual Signs

A few days after he met Nora at the cemetery, Zeke was walking down a quiet street when his eyes fell on a strange sign at the end of the road. At first, he thought it was a road sign, but then he realized it was a sign that read 'Z' with an arrow pointing in a direction that didn't make sense. He followed the sign out of curiosity and discovered a narrow, broken lane that ended in an open field in one corner of the city. It was a cornfield with a wooden fence all around. He was instantly reminded of the magical cornfield and the secret maze with the sign 'Z' he had seen in his dreams. A hand-painted board hanging from a small wooden gate read, "Welcome to Zekeland." He couldn't help but feel surprised to see his name on the board as his brain tried to think of all logical possibilities.

"Maybe it's a dream," he thought. *"Or maybe someone's just playing a prank."*

He quietly stood there for some time mulling over the word "Zekeland." He didn't care if it was real or not. He loved it. The word had instantly resonated with him so much that he felt there was indeed a special place for him — a place he had come from, a place he belonged to... *somewhere in time.* It was as if the universe was showering him with pleasant surprises, constantly trying to communicate, assuring him that it was always there for him. Whenever he needed guidance, he received unexpected help from unexpected sources — from the pages of random books to number plates on cars or some strange street name. He had developed a habit of walking miles and miles alone. He loved finding new places within little Mackinaw City. He would be guided to strange places or drawn to strange situations at certain times.

One day he saw a bumper sticker on a car that read, "Are you still sleeping?" Zeke was so confounded by the question that he kept asking himself all day, "Am I still sleeping?"

As usual, his answer came in the strangest of ways. That night, as he silently sat on his porch stargazing, he saw a barn owl sitting on a tree branch in the orchard next to his house. The moon was right behind its head, creating a strange and mystical halo around it. The moon and the owl, together with the silence and the wind, made the night look very mysterious and even eerie to a certain extent.

Zeke had read a lot about the spiritual symbolism of barn owls and bald eagles by then. Different cultures and religions have always interpreted the presence of owls differently. Some consider it a bad omen, while others think of it as a sign of prosperity. Zeke knew as much. The mysterious barn owl stared him right in the eye. A few moments later, it flew towards the porch and sat on the edge of the guardrail not far from him. He wondered if it wanted to say something and was waiting for the right opportunity to speak, making him feel uncomfortable now.

He made up his mind to ask the owl the question that had been bothering him the whole day, "*Am* I still asleep?"

Utterly amusing him, the owl answered in rhymes like Ziggy, only it sounded more like a wise old man with a cracked voice.

"You've been awakening from a thousand years of slumber. This long and dark night, too, shall pass. Remember, dear boy, age is just a number!"

Zeke felt utterly confused by the words of the owl. He eventually convinced himself it was just his imagination and went to bed. The next afternoon his father was home after many days of being away. He was in his room playing music on an old radio. Zeke didn't recognize the song, though. Someone with a cracked, masculine voice sang, "You're still awakening from a deep slumber. When it's dawn, this long night shall pass. You see, my friend, age is but a number; age is but a number!"

The singer's voice and words were so like what the barn owl had said the night before that it sent a chill down his spine. A little part of him said that the song, too, was a sign from the universe, but his growing skepticism made him decide he had heard the song before, and the owl had simply been a figment of his imagination.

One day, while in school, Zeke was looking out of one of the windows in his classroom, lost in his thoughts. His mind was wandering; he was thinking about life, and thus, strange questions struck him. "*Is this world in which we all live just an illusion? Where's the real world then?*" These questions were all fueled by the original question, "*Am* I asleep?"

With each passing day, he thought more about life, and he had new questions. But there were no answers. Then one day, he was at his study table when he powered up his computer, and a little message popped up on the screen. It read, "You are protected." It was a message from the antivirus software on his computer. But his mind told him it meant more than that.

While he was sleeping that same night, he felt someone standing right next to his bed and watching over him. In his dream, he could see the silhouette of an angel with beautiful wings and a sword in its hand, almost encapsulated in an indigo-blue light shining all around him. He felt like he was safe… and protected.

• • •

The next evening, he walked around the city alone, which had become his habit. The sun had just gone down when he noticed a small store he had never seen before. It was named Indigo Children. It instantly caught his attention. He loved the color indigo and always felt drawn to it. He entered the store, thinking it must be a new children's store. It wasn't.

It was a store that had a collection of wonderful crystals, beads, statues, paintings, and countless other items that were completely new to him. It also had a section for books on higher knowledge. In one corner of the store, he saw a crystal statuette of an angel with beautiful wings and a sword in its hand. The figurine appeared to have a sparkly indigo light oozing out of it, almost like a halo encompassing the entire body. He was shocked to discover it was the same angel he had seen in his dream the night before.

He went to the storekeeper, a warm and pleasant old man named Mr. Leitner, and asked about it. He said, "It's the statue of Archangel Michael, who is in charge of the angels protecting and looking over all the Indigo Children."

Adrenaline shot through Zeke's body. "Who are the Indigo Children, sir?" he asked.

The old man smiled at him, handed him a book, and whispered, "Dear child, they are the chosen ones." Zeke just stood there with his mouth open.

Mr. Leitner told him the book contained everything he would need to know about Indigo Children. Zeke purchased both the book and the crystal statue, which he knew were clearly waiting there, only for him. He spent all the money he had saved up, but he had no regrets. That night, he sat at his study table, fully prepared to read the book, but out of habit switched on his computer instead. A strange indigo light came out of the screen illuminating his face, and the same message popped up again, "You are protected." He chose to ignore it a second time.

Zeke opened the book and there was information not only about the Indigo Children, but also about the Blue Rays, Crystal Children, starseeds and other lightworkers, all of which he knew very little about. Inside the book on the first page, someone had handwritten:

Wisdom is like pearls hidden in shells beneath the sand and water on a sunny beach. They are found in abundance and yet open only to the ones who wish to find them.

Zeke declared to himself, "I guess this means I have to get to work."

CHAPTER TWELVE
A Familiar Stranger

It was August, the dog days of summer, and the overall energy around him felt strange. Zeke told himself he must be going crazy because of the heat. By now, he had enough experience to realize that the world and the entire cosmos were made of energy and were inextricably connected, but somewhere deep down, a part of him still questioned the signs. He simply couldn't come to terms with his own significance, his own validity.

By the second week of the month, he noticed the signs and synchronicities around him were unusually high, almost blasting him with new information, trying to draw his attention to something he couldn't decipher yet, but he knew it was coming. He would be nearing his fifteenth birthday in a few months and was keen to leave the impact of Nora's death behind and look forward to the next chapter of life.

One evening, he sat at his desk and tried powering up his computer, but the screen remained blank. He tried it a couple more times and just assumed the motherboard had died. He decided to find a local repair guy, left a voicemail and waited for a return call. Not wasting any time, he opened the book Mr. Leitner sold him.

His mother asked him to come for dinner, but he was so absorbed in his reading that she had to leave his dinner on a side table next to him. He eventually fell asleep with his cheek pressed against the keys of the keyboard. He woke to a loud bleeping. The screen flipped on and off a couple of times while it blared like a siren. Then it finally switched on, and he saw the following message written in bold:

Knock! Knock! Are you there?

Then he heard Zag's shrieky voice. "Little Mister Tartal, can you hear me? Please help me! Please help me, sir!" Zeke was immediately reminded of the same experience he had years ago.

"Zag must be up to mischief again," he thought.

Ziggy pecked on his windowpane. She looked worried. "Zag isn't in his bubble. He must be in some silly trouble. Where is he? Where is he? How stupid can he be? He's merely the size of a fig. Ziggy Zig Zig." Ziggy wasn't the usual mischief-monger.

"Her concern about Zag must be genuine," he thought, and so it began worrying him as well. Zag's distressed sounds were coming from somewhere close. *"Maybe Zag climbed inside the computer tower and got stuck inside? That's probably the reason the computer wasn't switching on in the first place."* He searched around and banged the unit a couple of times, trying to get Zag out.

"Mister Tartal, help! Help me, please!" He heard the weepy voice again. It was very close to him, almost right in his ears.

"Where are you, Zag?" he frantically asked.

"Come closer, look inside, sir. Oh no! I can't breathe. I'm strangling!"

Zeke realized the sound was coming from inside his computer. But that wasn't possible. There was no way in and no way out. He leaned close enough for his forehead and nose to touch the screen. A powerful indigo light flowed from the screen and flooded the room. Zeke squinted his eyes against the glow of the bright light.

The next thing he knew, he was sucked into the screen and straight into a whirlpool of indigo light. A crystalline silhouette held his hand twirling right up along with him. It had a long, flowing cascade of hair.

Are you Nora?" he asked. "Are you taking me somewhere up in heaven?"

The entity didn't respond. He was delivered to a pool of light outside the same palace he had seen in his childhood dream. The lion-headed gate guards bowed in reverence the moment they saw him. He walked in but turned around immediately to look at his companion, who had taken him this far.

The figure simply walked away, leaving him behind. Her long cascade of blonde, almost white hair fanned out behind her. She was unusually tall, and she wore a crown and a long, flowing gown like an empress. She turned back to look at him and smiled lovingly. Then, just like that, she was gone.

Zig and Zag sat on his shoulders, smiling and whistling in joy. He was immediately surrounded by many lion-like creatures, all equally tall, with lion heads and human bodies. They came up and hugged him as if he were a long-lost friend. He was totally bewildered, but his heart was overflowing with love and joy. One of them gently caressed his hair, kissed his head, and said, "You've finally come home. We're so happy to see you again, Ezekiel!"

Zeke was stunned to hear his birth name. *How could they possibly know that?* Still, everyone and everything felt strangely familiar. The one who had kissed his head had such motherly affection; it really reminded him of his own mother. Zeke felt he was indeed back home. He thought about the soul who brought him into this strange kingdom and wanted to look for her, but they wouldn't let him go, all wanting to embrace him and celebrate his return.

• • •

"Zeke honey, go to bed or you might wake up with a sprained neck tomorrow," he heard his mother say as she lightly nudged him. Zeke jumped off his seat and looked all around. The room looked normal, and the computer was powered off. Zig and Zag weren't around, either. Everything around him appeared normal, as if nothing had happened, except the moon outside the window looked unusually big and blue.

He looked at the calendar lying on his desk. It was 08/08/14. Nothing made sense, so he let himself believe that this, too, was no more than a dream. These dreams of his had become more frequent, and as such he had stopped paying much attention to them. But, unbeknownst to him, they were not mere dreams, and it was going to take some time for him to understand what they truly meant.

CHAPTER THIRTEEN

The Fifteenth Birthday

Zeke spent many sleepless nights tossing and turning in bed after the incident. He developed a deep connection with that mystical place and the being that took him there. An unstoppable desire to meet her haunted him and kept him awake for days and weeks. In his heart, Zeke knew this wasn't just another dream. It was an altered state of consciousness and the reality of another world. The physical and the metaphysical side of life had been overlapping for him since childhood, and it was becoming clearer than ever to him now.

The holiday season came and went without much ado, except maybe the unusual annoyance Zeke felt around Christmas. But this year had been somewhat different. Christmas was justifiably ignored by all the families of Farley Street, as they were all reeling under their own pressures. Everybody was in a sad and pensive mood, knowing New Year's Eve would bring back all the painful memories of the previous year.

Nevertheless, Zeke's fifteenth birthday passed uneventfully despite all that grief and lament. Even though he was a teenager, still inexperienced in the ways of the world, he was far beyond his years in wisdom and acuity. As silent as he was on the surface, the stir within him had turned into a storm. That day of all days, he felt an extreme urge to be somewhere, to do something he instinctively knew he needed to do. Yet, in sharp contrast to the restlessness he felt within, the whole day passed by with him basically doing nothing.

His mother had been sick for a while, so her doctors ran numerous tests. She had always been a delicate and fragile woman, and the stress in her life had finally started to take its toll on her health. The doctors still couldn't figure out what was wrong with her, so they just told her it was fatigue and all she needed was rest. He needed to stay by her side and take care of her regardless. It was nearly evening when she had fallen sound asleep. She had taken an early supper, and he knew she wouldn't wake up till the next morning. He asked his sisters to watch over her while he took Coconut out for a walk.

As he passed the Copeland's house, he found Kai and Gael patiently waiting for him and waving from the front window. They knew he took Coconut for an evening walk around this time and wanted to surprise him. They lured him inside where they held a surprise birthday party for him in their basement rec room. There were decorations and balloons everywhere along with a personalized cake. It was totally unexpected, and he was simply overwhelmed by this thoughtful gesture.

"You didn't have to do this, guys…"

Gael cut him off. "Oh, come on, Zekey Boy. Of course we had to do this! Look, we both know you hate your birthday, but you're fifteen, man. It's a big deal. Enjoy it."

"You do so much for us," Kai added. "You listen to us, and you're there when we need you, so we just wanted to show you that we care."

"I know you do, but…" Zeke didn't have any words. He just wanted to hug his friends, so he went in for the 'bro hug.' He was a simple kid. He didn't understand grand gestures, but he knew how to express love. He blew out the fifteen colored candles and cut the cake. They played pool and air hockey and laughed hysterically for the first time in a long time. After months of dealing with trauma and personal loss, the three of them finally got the chance to spend some time together, joke around, and really talk things out.

It was time for Coconut to relieve himself, so the three headed out together for a walk into town to see all the Christmas lights. Naturally, all the stores were closed, and people were in their homes winding down for the evening. As they approached the town, Zeke heard a crash and immediately a chill ran up his spine. All three boys followed the sound to see what had happened. It was dark as some of the streetlights were down, so they had to look hard, but it wasn't long before they heard the moans of someone who was injured. When they arrived at the site, they noticed a snowmobiler had crashed into a tree, and spun what was left of the machine and its rider into the middle of the icy road.

Kai pointed out, "It's a girl!"

"Oh no, not again!" Zeke exclaimed. "I can't go through this again. It'll kill me."

Thankfully, she was alive and not severely injured, but her foot was stuck in a twisted mess of metal. Together they tried to pull it out, but it was no use. It only made the situation worse.

"Gael," Zeke directed. "Call 911. We can't get her foot out. They'll have to cut around it."

As Gael called for help, Zeke tried to calm the girl down. "It's okay, kid. Everything's going to be fine, don't worry."

Just then, a pickup truck going much faster than it should down a dark road in icy conditions was headed straight towards them.

"Zeke! Look out! There's a truck and he can't see us!" Kai yelled as he saw it speeding down the road towards them.

Before he could even register what was going on, Zeke sprang into action, fueled by nothing but pure instinct. With herculean strength, he lifted what was left of the heavy machine and dragged it to the side of the road. "Stay with her!" he shouted at Kai as he ran straight for the truck. "STOP!" he screamed with every ounce of air in his lungs and waved his hands like a maniac. The driver slammed the brakes, and his truck skidded, then spun around on an ice patch and finally stopped, just barely missing the girl. Zeke ran up to the driver and was ready to kill him, but something held him back.

"What are you doing driving so fast on a dark road at night? You could have killed this girl — and us!"

"Oh man, I'm sorry. I was just having a little fun with my girlfriend in my new truck," the guy answered nonchalantly. "Isn't it cool? It's the new…"

"WHO THE HELL CARES?" Zeke interrupted. "There are designated places to do this — like a *racetrack*, but I'm not about to argue that point with you now. There's an injured girl here!" After a brief pause, "You know what? Just get out of here," Zeke snapped at him.

"No problem, dude. Again, I'm sorry if we scared you." Then the guy and his girlfriend took off.

Zeke just threw his hands up in the air and shook his head from side to side. "What's the matter with people? Absolutely clueless. I just don't get it."

After a few minutes, the police and the fire department arrived at the scene. Zeke and the boys explained the situation and were told, "You boys are incredible. You really saved this girl's life."

"Not us. It was Zeke here. We don't know where he got the strength to move that sled in time, but he did," Gael explained.

"It was like second nature to him. He knew exactly what to do," Kai interjected.

"Any one of us would have done the same," Zeke countered.

"I don't know about that," Gael responded. "You're stronger than I am, even though you don't look it." Gael gave Zeke a quick wink.

The girl was visibly shaken but mustered enough composure to express her gratitude. "Thank you, Ezekiel. You're a prince among men."

Zeke bowed his head slightly and tipped his hat in a cute and gentlemanly way. "Happy to oblige, my lady," he replied in a charming mockney accent.

Kai cocked his head and gave Zeke a look. "Who do you think you are, the Artful Dodger???"

"Yes, and you can consider yourself — part of the furniture."

Gael offered, "I think I hear a song coming on! That's from last year's school play." The three boys just looked at each other and burst out laughing. They really were the best of friends even under the most difficult of circumstances.

The police told the boys they could take it from there and sent them on their way. As they headed back towards Farley Street, Zeke questioned, "Who was that girl, and how does she know my birth name? Even my mother doesn't call me that. Does she go to our school?"

"Never seen her before," Kai admitted.

"Me neither," Gael confessed.

Just then, Zeke heard a voice, a familiar yet unknown one, and it said, "You have passed your first trial, Ezekiel. Congratulations. The next step in your journey begins now."

"What? Who said that?" Zeke was totally confused.

"Said what, Zeke?" Kai asked.

"That voice, didn't you hear it?"

"No. Are you okay?"

Zeke looked around, searching for the voice. He was completely baffled.

"Are you sure you're okay?" Kai was starting to get worried.

"Oh God, he's going back into space mode," Gael said with a grimace.

"What? Oh yeah, I'm fine," Zeke interjected, trying to deflect the moment. "Let's get Coconut home. He's probably frozen stiff by now."

They continued on their way, processing in their minds what had just happened. After a few moments of silence, Gael blurted out, "A prince among men, eh? I guess we're going to have to start calling you 'Prince Ezekiel' from now on." He bowed deeply before Zeke as if greeting royalty.

"Knock it off, Gael."

"I've also never heard you swear before!" Gael said in shock.

"Well, normally I don't, but this one just came out of nowhere. That guy was such a jerk."

"You know, what you just did back there was nothing short of amazing. You're a hero, Zeke," Kai offered.

"Guys, I'm telling you, I have no idea how I did that," he tried to explain. "My dad says a sled that size weighs at least 500 pounds, not counting the rider."

Gael went off, "Yeah, well I do. You did that because you're a good person. You're brave, you're smart, and you're strong. I always knew that, but today you proved it. You saved that girl's life." After a brief pause, "… and don't try to be modest. I know I could never be that brave, but you are, so accept it. Happy Birthday, bro."

Once Gael and Kai went into their house, Zeke headed home with Coconut, trying to recall the voice in his head. Just then, Ziggy flew towards him. Zeke's heart fluttered a bit. He wondered what funny little pearl of wisdom the bird had brought him now. She flapped her wings and flew to his shoulder. She didn't even bother to tweet or greet him for his birthday. He felt a bit upset with her strange and quiet behavior, but rather chose to ignore it.

He was still reeling from the events of the past hour. He looked up at the sky which was crystal clear and filled with distant twinkling stars. The moon was unusually bright and had an orange hue to it, making it look more like a soft sun. He recalled that tonight's moon was a Super Wolf Moon. He returned home, went immediately to his room and slid into his soft, comfortable slippers, not realizing Zag had set up shop there. He immediately pulled them off as something scratched one of his feet.

Zag shot out of Zeke's slipper like a circus clown out of a cannon, landed on his shoulder and screamed, "A very happy birthday to you, Mister Tartal, and many happy returns of the day!"

Zig started to sing, "Happy Birthday to…" when he cut her off.

"Knock it off, you two." Zeke couldn't help but smile at their gesture. "The day is almost over now. It's too little, too late," he said mockingly. Then he turned to Zag. "Weren't you busy drinking in the cellar the last time I saw you?"

"Ya don't take good care of me nowadays, sir. The bottles in the cellar have been dry for months — no magic potion left for me. I suspect your daddy's on to my shenanigans," he said with a gleam in his eye.

"I have an idea. Let's party it up, or even better, let me grant three of your wishes, Mister Leprechaun and Miss Birdie. Tell me, where do you wish to go? What do you wish to do? What do you wish to have?" Zeke was now in a jovial mood.

"The Lights," Zag wasted no time answering. "Mister Tartal, I wish to see the Northern Lights. I've heard they are a visual treat tonight. We don't even need to go to Headlands. I see they are bigger and brighter than ever over the Mighty Mac — and see if you can scarf up some of your daddy's hooch so I can really enjoy them. Does that answer your question about what I wish for?" he asked smugly.

"I suppose it does, Zag. I suppose it does."

• • •

They reached the Mighty Mac about 9:30 pm, just in time for the visual dance and lighting spectacular. For some reason, it wasn't especially cold, and people were scattered all around in small groups, ready to take in Aurora Borealis. Zeke was about to sit comfortably on a bench, but then Zag jumped off his shoulder and began running all about like a child. Zeke had to run after him like a parent trying to stop a naughty toddler from getting lost in the crowd, but Zag just wouldn't stop. He kept singing and dancing, clapping his hands and running around in joy. "I love the Northern Lights, sir! I wish to dance with them."

Zeke relented as Zag could clearly outrun him. "You two have fun playing in the lights. I'll go for a walk and enjoy them on my own. It's been a heavy day for me." They followed him, but at a safe distance.

The silent woods, the Northern Lights, the mystical wolf moon, and the twinkling stars made him feel as if he had been transported to another dimension. He was once again lost in time. After about thirty minutes, he realized he had strayed too far from the crowd. It became dark and foreboding. He also realized Zig and Zag had disappeared, leaving him alone in the darkness. He decided to head back. Just as he turned around to leave, he heard Zag's voice.

"Here I am, sir. I see you! Follow me… no, this way. This is the way, yes. Walk a little left, then just a little to the right, and then walk straight ahead towards these woods where you'll find me dancing with the stars and the lights."

Zeke felt a bit relieved and began walking faster in the direction where he could hear Zag's voice. Then he saw Ziggy flying right above him.

"A little more, a little further, sir, just a bit more." Zag kept calling him and guiding him, and Zeke kept walking. He didn't realize how far he had come, but when he stopped, he couldn't hear Zag's voice anymore, nor could he see Ziggy. Instead, he saw something else that simply blew his mind.

A gigantic tornado of light spun down from the sky above and was heading towards him, trying to find a perfect place to land. The tornado constantly changed colors, and sudden thunder and lightning roared in the sky as it descended. A few moments later, the tornado slowed its rotation. Eventually, it settled on some open ground near him. Once it stopped, Zeke could see a structure that looked like a half-open oyster shell made of shining, what appeared to be, metal. It was reflective yet had a luminescence of its own. Zig and Zag still were nowhere to be found.

Zeke felt an immense attraction to the spot where the tornado of light landed. It was a strange magnetic pull he couldn't resist. He neared the shell-like structure. The top was almost fully open. As he came close, he saw a soft, peachy light radiating from it. He inched closer and could now see someone sitting inside. The being appeared to be a young woman, but he couldn't make out her face, only her hair — a long, blond cascade draped down her back. His heart skipped a beat.

"Nora?" he thought.

He came as close as he could before the young woman suddenly looked up at him. Before he could even think or react, she held out her hands and pulled him in. The lid snapped shut, and the shell rose into the sky with the tornado of light surrounding it once again, spinning at a phenomenal rate. Zeke was so overwhelmed he couldn't utter a single word. He just sat there, looking all around and trying to process everything that was happening.

He felt like he was in the space capsule of the movie *Apollo 13*. The clear sky, the wolf moon, and even the stars were visible through the window-like openings. The inside of the shell was a circular room, which was mostly white, but there were peach-colored panels with some alien pattern etched into them. All Zeke could see and feel was a pool of soft, warm light all around the shell, constantly glowing and changing colors, making for a real visual treat and a cosmic experience way beyond his wildest imagination.

"Who are you? Where are you from?" he finally mustered the courage to ask her.

"Hello, Ezekiel! You can call me Zoom. That's my earthly name. I'm called by a different name in my homeland, though." She reached out a hand for him to shake.

"Your homeland, where's that?" Zeke asked. "Is it the land of the lion people where I have been before?"

She smiled but didn't answer. He finally had the first chance to have a proper look at her, and he was absolutely awestruck by her otherworldly beauty. She was unusually tall and remarkably feline. Her porcelain-like skin looked so pale and smooth, as if she had no blood running through her veins at all. The pupils of her catlike eyes constantly changed from blue to yellow to fiery red and were insanely hypnotic, bright, and glowing. She had an extremely mysterious air about her and an equally mysterious smile on her face.

He was instantly reminded of the Catwoman he had seen in comic books and in the Batman movie he saw with Kai and Gael. There was something so magnetic and magical about her that it was almost impossible for him to take his eyes off her. What attracted him the most was her soft, wavy hair that fell past her waist, exactly like Nora's. He also noticed Zoom looked about Nora's age as well.

"You look like someone I used to know. What connection do you have with Nora Copeland?" he couldn't stop himself from asking her.

"I look like her because it's easier for you to relate to me."

"What do you mean 'relate to you?'"

Zoom gave an endearing chuckle, and the childlike innocence about her literally took his breath away. Her resemblance to Nora made him feel like he had fallen for her, but he was still unsettled by the situation.

"I'm neither she nor he, neither this age nor that, but I'm appearing as primarily female right now because you will understand me better and it won't frighten you," she answered mysteriously. Changing the subject, "Have you noticed your friends here?" She turned her head from side to side. To his delight, Zig and Zag instantly appeared like magic and took their respective places on each of Zoom's bare shoulders.

"Oh, you traitors are here. Was it your plan all along to bring me here? You knew about her then, didn't you?" Zeke scolded and scoffed at them with mock anger in his tone, yet he was feeling overwhelming relief on the inside. He trusted Zig and Zag, and their presence put him at ease.

Zag winked at him, and Ziggy whistled. "Oh, la la, Mister Tartal. Of course, we knew you were supposed to meet your new cosmic friend Zoom this evening. Now that you've turned into a dapper and debonair young man, she's our birthday present to you. Isn't that just grand?" Zag explained, grinning from ear to ear.

"A happy heart sings Chakalaka Boom! Zig Zag Zoom! Ziggy Zag Zoom!" Zig chimed in.

"Zig Zag Zoom will always be at your service from today on, sir. The trio is now complete, and we wish you many happy returns of the day once again!" added Zag.

Zeke felt extremely embarrassed at the idea of this mystery girl being his present. His cheeks went red as he blushed. "What do you mean 'present'? She's an actual person, you know… uh, I think." He turned to her and said, "You *are* an actual person, right?"

She just smiled brightly and gave a quick chuckle. Zeke admitted she was beyond beautiful, and he was smitten by her, but he didn't know her and certainly didn't trust her. He was still extremely curious to know more about his new cosmic acquaintance. A few minutes later, Zig and Zag disappeared, leaving the two of them alone. He wanted to know more about her, so he mustered all his courage and sat beside her. "What made you say you're neither he nor she?"

"I'm here to share everything about me with you, Ezekiel," she softly pressed his hands and whispered. He sensed a strange feeling deep inside of him, but he held it down.

"We aren't bound by your earthly understanding of gender, age, and time. We can become what you want us to become. We can present ourselves in the way you wish to see us, so you can easily relate to us and feel comfortable interacting with us. It's one of the advantages of being made of pure light."

He suddenly felt confused and on edge. The idea of having no constant shape or form didn't seem to go down well. His deeply conditioned human mind instantly reacted to a truth it couldn't recognize. He felt so triggered and disturbed, so uncomfortable and upset with her answer, that he instantly pulled away.

"I can read your mind, Ezekiel. I know your human mind has its limitations and has been conditioned to think a certain way for thousands of years, but the time has come when the junk stored in your cellular memory and your human DNA needs to be purged."

She gave him his space. It took him a while, but Zeke tried to get over his initial fear and confusion. He wanted to know more about this mysterious woman, so he declared, "You're an extraterrestrial, androgynous shapeshifting alien then, and this flying oyster shell is a UFO, is that right?"

Zoom smiled at him once again with a lot of affection. "Yes, if that's what you choose to call me."

"What do you mean by that? Am I wrong in saying it?" he inquired. The truth still felt quite unnerving and left him feeling anxious.

"No, you aren't. You're just trying to analyze and judge your experience a tad too much. Not only are we androgynous, but all human beings are androgynous in some way as well. We're all made of energy. The whole cosmos is a blend of masculine and feminine energies, and so are you!" Her insight and words put him in deep thought.

"Tell me something, Ezekiel. Do you call your next-door neighbor an alien? Let's presume someone lives a little further away from you, say in another city. Would you call him or her an alien, then? Go farther away and think of people living on another continent, far, far away from you, say Africa or Asia. Would you still call them aliens? Why do you call beings living in other star systems, galaxies, or planets aliens, then?

"We are all cosmic neighbors. Earth is just a planet among many in the neighborhood. There are so many galaxies and star systems out there. We're all galactic beings, and yet, we're still neighbors living in a cosmic neighborhood. We don't think of humans as aliens, Ezekiel. We think of them as our brothers, sisters, and dear friends."

Zeke was about to say something but Zoom raised her hand and stopped him. "I'm not finished yet. Let me answer your first questions first. After all that I said, I'll leave it to you to think of me as an alien or a cosmic friend. The same holds true for the shell we're now traveling in. It's just a form of transport, one among the many we use, the way you have automobiles, motorcycles, buses, trains, planes, ships — even submarines and rockets. You come up with new forms of transport almost every day, don't you? I've even heard humans talking about flying cars these days."

He couldn't challenge her sharp logic. Her ideals were simple yet alluded to a deeper meaning. Zoom finished her monologue in a single breath. Zeke knew whatever she said was true, and his lips curled into a smile as he listened to her impassioned argument. She was quite emotional while answering his insensitive questions. He had unknowingly hurt and insulted her by pulling away from her, and so he was extremely apologetic.

"You're absolutely right, correct on every point. I'm sorry for my words and actions, Zoom, but may I ask you something else now — something I really need to know?"

She smiled at him once again, still holding his hands and reassuring him.

"Why did you choose me of all people, and why do you keep calling me Ezekiel? I know that's my birth name, but no one ever uses it — not even my mother when she's crazy angry with me. I heard someone else call me by that name recently, too, and I know I've met you before in my dreams. What does this all mean?"

"It's because you're one of us, Ezekiel. You are from Lyra, and I am from Vega, which is an extension of Lyra. We are the 'Lion People,' and we've helped human beings in every stage of their evolution. From the time they first walked on this Earth, we were always with them. We held their hands and guided them. Human beings are going through the next stages of their evolution now, and so our visits to Earth have increased. They need our help — now more than ever. Some of us are here to help them indirectly, and some among us have incarnated as human beings to help them directly. That's what we have always done. You are the one who chooses that path. You chose to incarnate on this planet because humanity needs you, now more than ever. You, Zeke Tartal, are… a Lyran Starseed."

CHAPTER FOURTEEN
HOMELAND

The journey to Lyra was a spellbinding experience for Zeke. He and Zoom flew through the stars and past galaxies, traveling from Earth to the enchanting Lyran Kingdom. Sitting inside a flying saucer that looked like a beautiful oyster shell, he felt like a bird in space. He had been freed from the cage of his physical body. Zoom held his hands, and he kept looking into her eyes as she shared with him all the wisdom and knowledge his soul was desperately seeking.

Even though he knew she was telling him the truth, the idea of his true identity felt strange to him. In fact, it made him anxious. "Did you ever really notice how different your life has been from that of everyone around you?" she questioned.

He smiled and silently nodded his head in agreement, thinking about his dreams, visions, signs, and above all else, Zig and Zag. He always knew the answer. He was *very* different from others.

"Have you ever felt like an alien walking on Planet Earth with a different identity? Have you ever felt ubiquitous and omnipotent just gazing at the stars? Have you ever longed to go back to your true home?"

"Why, yes. Only I never knew where that true home is — or was."

"You do realize, Ezekiel, we have met before in several previous lifetimes. We have taken many forms but have always known each other. We have been family, we have been friends, and we have been lovers. We have been a male-female couple, we have been a male-male couple, and we have been a female-female couple."

"Well, why not double or even triple the fun?" He was becoming more comfortable around her now, so a little joke here or there seemed fitting.

He thought her explanations were mindboggling, but he believed them. He also realized his attraction for Nora must be a manifestation of his connection to Zoom. He recognized her, not because she looked like Nora; it was the other way around. He had felt connected to Nora because she reminded him of some past version of Zoom.

"Who exactly are you, Zoom, and who am I, for that matter?" he suddenly asked, looking deep into her hypnotic eyes.

"Like I said, you are a starseed and…" She was going about her pithy statements, but he raised his hand, abruptly stopping her.

"Look, Zoom. I need to know the truth and nothing but the truth."

"That you will know soon enough. Voilà! We are home," she announced as the tornado of colors appeared around the ship again as the shell slowly descended and docked. They were in Lyra.

• • •

They had finally reached the gateway to the great Lyran Kingdom. The lion-headed guards bowed in reverence and opened the gates to the same crystalline palace Zeke had seen in his dreams. Many lion-headed people came running towards them with unparalleled enthusiasm. They were crystal blue beings who hugged and embraced him warmly, as if he were one of them, like a long-lost friend or family member. A lion woman came ahead and kissed his forehead.

"It's so good to see you back home, Ezekiel." She hugged him tightly, and he instantly recognized her as his own mother of all people!

"How could this be?" he wondered. "My mother is still alive on Earth!" He was beyond perplexed. "I'm going to need some answers pretty soon, y'all."

Nonetheless, he felt a deep connection with this community and had a strong inner understanding that he belonged to the people Zoom fondly introduced to him as the Lyrans or "the Lion People." It wasn't an unknown place for him anymore; it was his homeland, and these lion people were all his friends and family. Yet, he still felt he needed to know more. Everything was happening exactly the way it had before. He experienced all this in his vivid dream just a few months earlier on August 8th. The only thing he didn't know was the significance of the date.

After his homecoming and the warmest reception imaginable, Zoom took him into the palace. She played the perfect hostess taking him around every corner of the vast Lyran estate. She took special care to share with him all the intricate details of the hallways, the chambers, and the gardens they visited. It really was a place beyond time and space. It existed neither in the day nor the night. It was neither on land nor in the air. Perhaps somewhere in the ether, he thought.

Zeke noticed something peculiar and unearthly about the architecture. There were no windows, doors or ceilings — just transparent, crystalline walls. There was no gravity, either. These beings could just glide and didn't have to float like spacemen in those old movies. The flowers in the gardens were the kind he had never seen before. Moreover, they possessed specific and hypnotic fragrances that gave him a sense of euphoria each time he smelled them.

"My God, this is like catnip!" he exclaimed. "This is just too good to be true."

All his senses were heightened. Streams, lakes, ponds, and rivers all around provided a musical tinkling. Tiny celestial melodies came out of every flower, every leaf, and every blade of grass. There was no bark on the trees, no dirt, mud, or cement, although the roads were paved with gold. Everything he saw reminded him of the description of Heaven and the Garden of Eden he had read about, yet it was nothing like the traditional imagery imprinted on his mind.

As they walked around holding hands, he was told that the Lyran capital wasn't simply a palace or a kingdom. It was the legacy of a vast and expansive empire. There were tales of love and loss, war and victory. Sexuality was forever fluid here, and all Lyrans took pride in their androgynous nature. They could morph their sexuality at will, much like humans change outfits to suit their moods. They understood the balance between their masculine and feminine energies, and that their true strength and wisdom stemmed from putting those energies to the right use as needed. Zeke wanted to discover everything about them. He was told about the Galactic Wars and was particularly interested in the Lyran warriors, a sect of the otherwise peace-loving race. He was eager to hear about the role of heroes and heroines in the shaping of galactic history.

They reached a massive chamber inside one of the many palaces. The huge hall looked more like the throne room of some ancient emperor. A white and golden throne sat on a raised platform at the far end of the hall. Two separate rows of smaller thrones lined both sides of the hall with a long, lush carpet and table-like structures.

As they reached the chamber, Zoom whispered, "This is where it all began. The mission… do you remember?"

The room looked familiar as if he had been there many times before. Still, he couldn't fully recollect. The empty thrones on either side of the main throne were slowly being filled by royal lion people taking their respective seats as each one of them walked into the hall. Finally, a very old lion-headed man entered and walked up to the dais. His face was one of kindness and wisdom. He had a white mane, and his skin was milky white. His jeweled headpiece of pure gold shined like the sun and sported an interesting harp-shaped emblem.

All the members present in the chamber stood up and bowed their heads before him. He sat on his throne and began presiding over the meeting of his council members. Zoom motioned to Zeke, "This is the Lyran High Council, our eternal guides who constantly think about and work towards the betterment of the entire galaxy. They consider the evolution of all galactic beings in every star system, planet, and universe. Do you remember them? Do you remember the mission they chose for you for when you volunteered to incarnate on Earth as a human being? Do you remember your mission now, Ezekiel?" she whispered again, desperately trying to help him remember and wanting the veil to fall so he could remember his true identity.

He felt utterly lost. There were flashes of recollection going off in his mind like fireworks, but the only thing they brought was confusion. He could not recognize the old lions, and trying to do so only made his head hurt. She took his hand and led him to Izar, the council head, to inform him of Zeke's arrival. The kind, old Lyran smiled at him and welcomed him home.

"Ezekiel, my boy, how I have missed you and that brilliant mind of yours, but I suppose the weight of my words is lost on you. You don't even remember who you really are yet. Well, I'll let you deal with that." He turned to Zoom and said, "Make it so that he remembers himself, Ezra. We are all counting on you."

"Did he just say Ezra? I thought her name was Zoom!"

Izar blessed Zeke and Zoom and embraced them like a loving grandfather, bestowing them with honor, calling them his cherished warriors, and wishing them success.

• • •

Once their meeting with the High Council was over, Zoom brought him to a private chamber — a room where they were supposed to spend some time together. Before he could say anything, a group of young male attendants carried him off. They took him to a bathing chamber, spoiled him rotten, then dressed him like a prince before bringing him back to her who had been dressed similarly like a princess.

Zeke felt terribly uncomfortable, but Zoom saw through that. "Worry not, Ezekiel," she pronounced. "I know you have questions. Ask, and I shall answer."

"You still didn't answer my question. You still didn't tell me the whole truth. Who am I right now, and who are you, Zoom?" He was restless again, desperate to get to the bottom of everything.

"Well, I wanted you to experience the truth rather than for me to simply explain it to you," she replied and then sat with him to share her many stories.

"You are and always have been 'Ezekiel,' the handsome and charming Prince of the Lyran Empire, and among the few great warriors we have ever had." She fervently tried to help him remember who he was. His memories did return slowly, but they gave him more pain than comfort — the pain of a past life, of a past love.

Then, in an instant, it clicked. He had been a warrior, a leader, and a lover. With Zoom's help, he finally knew who he was, and he knew who she was. "You, you are Ezra, Princess of the Highest Order, the Lady of Light, and Keeper of the Legions of Vega. And I... I know you."

"Yes, my love. Now let me show you." Saying that, she connected her mind with his and showed him the story of the eternal love between the timeless lovers, the Warrior Prince Ezekiel and Ezra, the Princess of Light.

CHAPTER FIFTEEN

EZEKIEL AND EZRA

Once upon a time in the ageless expanse of the cosmos, there existed many planets in a small constellation of stars known as Lyra. On these planets lived many humanoid species, the celestial ancestors of our modern-day humans on Earth. Lyra held one of the most significant places in the evolutionary history of life in the galaxy. The Lyrans were lion-like humanoids, much taller than modern-day humans, with extreme feline traits. They were one of the most advanced races in the galaxy, with a vast, expansive, inclusive, and prosperous empire. They were known for their grace and strength and were a peace-loving race, yet they fought some of the most significant galactic wars in history.

Prince Ezekiel was a young and dashing warrior. He was the Prince of the Second Order in the Lyran kingdom. He belonged to the Sayvant, a sect of Lyran society dedicated to maintaining peace throughout the galaxy. He was extremely strong and bold, wise and trustworthy. Izar, the council head, was so fond of his favorite prince that he was often considered the "Chosen One". Everybody loved him. Stories of his might and valor had gained an almost mythical reputation across the entire Lyran empire, reaching as far as Vega.

He, however, was unmoved by all the praise and adulation ushered upon him. Despite his reputation as a warrior, he was a wanderer and a pacifist at heart, drawn to spiritual teachings and cosmic wisdom. He loved gallivanting across galaxies and exploring new star systems.

Vega, the brightest star in the constellation of Lyra, visible even from the furthest reaches of space, had a robust, independent, and prosperous empire of its own. Located some twenty-five light years from Planet Earth, Vega and its surrounding stars are thus often misrepresented as a separate constellation. Since Vega was a part of the Lyran heritage, the High Council decided they needed to expand their empire to include Vega.

The council members chose Ezekiel to lead the team setting out for the massive expansion endeavor. At the same time, as the Lyrans made plans to establish a colony on Vega, the original residents of Vega (known as the Vegans or the Veganites), had already begun expanding their territory and building their own colonies in the constellation of Orion. The team designated to establish the Vegan colony in Orion was headed by a beautiful princess named Ezra, who was the daughter of the appointed emperor of Vega.

When Ezekiel and his team reached Vega, they discovered another humanoid species already dwelling there. Ezekiel himself was very curious to meet the members of this new species, but among his followers, many distrusted the Vegans. The Sayvants came from a segment of Lyran society that was fiercely loyal to the empire, so tensions rose very quickly. The Vegans, on the other hand, had no concept of violence and warmly welcomed their Lyran counterparts. The Lyran team eventually began living on Vega, but there were some among them who harbored resentment for the Vegans. Ezekiel saw the underlying tensions among his people and did his best to propagate harmony between his team and the Vegans. Eventually, he became the Ambassador of Lyra and served as the representative of all Lyrans living on Vega. He became more than a warrior, though. He became a champion of peace between the two empires, and he became their leader.

With Prince Ezekiel's efforts, the two empires slowly merged into one over a period and began being called the Vega-Lyran Empire. The Lyrans and the Vegans were almost identical in nature and never practiced or propagated wars unless provoked, which was rare. Their defense strategies and techniques were unmatched anywhere in the cosmos, so they were largely feared by evildoers and left alone. Among the Lyrans, only Ezekiel's clan, the Sayvant, were warriors, and even they abandoned their violent ways over time. The peace-loving, variegated Vega-Lyran population became intergalactic explorers who eventually expanded their territory and built their empire on other planets and star systems, collectively advancing the development of the universe. These original humanoid species of the galaxy had no concepts of lust or greed. Their hearts were full of love, joy, and light. They expanded their territories to build a harmonious, cosmic community sharing love, friendship, divinity, and prosperity for all.

On Ezekiel's insistence, many Lyran warriors created families on Vega and lived there to further the bonds of unity between the two races. Yet, unlike most of his friends who fell in love with their Vegan counterparts and settled with them, Ezekiel was fully focused on building a cosmic synergy rather than on his individual life.

There was something that secretly intrigued him, though – the stories he often heard about the Vegan princess Ezra. He had heard her name countless times, and many stories of her wisdom and grace had reached his ears. Even as the ambassador of his people, he had never managed to meet the elusive princess, and this only fueled his imagination about her. A loner and a spiritual soul, Ezekiel had never felt a pull like this towards anyone before.

His fascination with her reputation was unlike anything he had ever known. The more he heard stories about her beauty, her skills with statecraft, and her love for her people, the more his secret desire to meet her was kindled. He knew she was far away from her homeland in Vega, in another star system altogether, but he still couldn't stop himself from wishing to meet her once at least. His wish was surprisingly fulfilled when it was revealed that Ezra and her team had finished building the remote Vegan colony and were soon to return home.

There was a truth carefully hidden behind her decision to return sooner than she had originally planned. Ezra had also heard a lot about the Lyran warrior from her peers. While in Orion, she had heard about his trip to Vega and how he single-handedly fashioned a new empire. She had heard about the warrior who had used words instead of force to merge two peoples into one. After hearing about his titanic reputation, she could not stop herself from secretly wanting to meet him. She had a valid excuse to support her wish, too, as her work in Orion was almost over. Both Ezekiel and Ezra were subconsciously thinking about each other. Little did they know, it was their divine destiny to meet — a cosmic plan beyond their control.

• • •

When Ezra returned to her homeland, she was welcomed with a huge banquet in her honor. Almost every important official from Vegan royalty was present there to greet their beloved princess, yet she was in search of someone else, someone special she desperately wished to meet. Finally, the moment arrived, and the Prince of the Lyran Empire was introduced. Standing right in front of her eyes, waiting to welcome and congratulate her on her success, was Ezekiel, the captivating Lyran prince. He, too, was mesmerized as he watched Ezra walk towards him in her silvery gown, like Cinderella entering the ballroom. Her fiery eyes locked with his. He found himself instantly paralyzed by her gaze, and sparks flew.

Ezra and Ezekiel had finally met, and they felt an instant connection. They already knew so much about each other's reputation, yet they felt like they wanted to learn more. It took them a while to stop talking about the empire and were finally afforded the chance to get to know each other on a much more intimate level. There was an immense cosmic force bringing them together and an intense knowledge that they were perfect for each other. The two roamed around the heavenly gardens of Vega and spent countless hours discussing cosmic concepts and spiritual harmony. They had so much to talk about and so many dreams to share.

Ezekiel and Ezra met on many occasions, working for the greater good of the empire, and over time, they grew passionately in love. The Lyran prince finally asked the Vegan emperor for his daughter's hand. The match was praised by all who came to hear of it — the greatest warrior of the Lyran race and the stunningly beautiful Princess of Vega. Their union would seal the bond between the empires once and for all. Soon after, Ezekiel took the Princess of Vega back to the capital of the Lyran kingdom, and they were welcomed by the High Council with the greatest honors. They were divine beings in love and were an inspiration for the entire Vega-Lyran population. They were both offered seats on the High Council to lead the new empire to prosperity.

The two cosmic lovers in union loved their kingdom and their people with all their hearts. Slowly and steadily, they brought many divine changes to the huge Vega-Lyran empire. They were blessed by the head of the High Council, who was fond of Ezekiel already, and as he learned more and more about her, became extremely fond of Ezra, too. They were like his children, and he trusted them with the future of his empire.

The cosmic couple nurtured another secret desire as well. They were both highly spiritual explorers at heart who loved venturing to different star systems and galaxies. Once all their responsibilities towards the Vega-Lyran kingdom were taken care of, Ezekiel sought permission from the council so the two lovers could set out on a cosmic voyage together. There was no reason left for the council to hold them back, and thus permission was happily granted. In the laws of the new empire, nobody curtailed another's freedom, for freedom was forever celebrated.

As they began their cosmic voyage, they went first to Sirius and Orion, where Ezra had earlier built an extended Vegan colony. They established great cosmic laws for the Vegan civilization to flourish, and then they moved on. From Orion, they went to the Pleiades. Ezekiel had to fight in many conflicts, and Ezra brought wisdom and knowledge to many new astral races. All across the galaxy, they became symbols of hope and peace as they brought light to all who were lost in darkness. They happily brought their cosmic dance of light to every dark corner of the galaxy — completely unaware of a constant set of eyes tracking them.

CHAPTER SIXTEEN

THE DARK LOVER

The Vega-Lyrans were beings of light. Their innocent hearts did not know darkness, and Ezra never realized she had a secret admirer, let alone a dark one. In the constellation of Orion dwelled a dark, scaly, lizard-like race long before Ezra and her team had even set foot there. The emperor of this reptilian race was called Draco, the Dragon. His empire, named after him, was one of the largest constellations bordering the territories of Lyra. The Lyrans were utterly unaware of the monstrous neighbors lurking in the darkness right next to them.

Emperor Draco and his race loved the smell of power. These power-hungry Reptilians wished to acquire and spread their influence over more and more planets, star systems, and galaxies so they could expand their territory and become the unchallenged masters of the entire universe. This scary and all-engulfing hunger kept them continuously motivated. The Reptilians had always known about the Lyrans and the Vegans. They purposely chose to remain hidden in the galactic shadows, away from the light of Lyra. Draco used his influence from his homeland of Alpha Draconus to make many lesser and underdeveloped humanoid species surrender to his control. The Reptilians forced these humanoids to work for them as they built a great empire of their own.

By the time Ezra arrived in Orion, Draco was already ruling many parts of the constellation. The news of the Vegan princess arriving spread like wildfire among the Reptilian species in Orion, and soon Draco, too, knew of Ezra's arrival. He strictly instructed his subjects to remain silent and in the dark, as he wanted to keep his empire a secret from the newcomers.

Draco was smart enough to plan his next moves. He didn't want the Vegans to know about the Reptilians. Instead, his plan was to let the Vegans build their colony and bring their knowledge and technology to Orion. He would let them think they were safe, then attack them once they let their guard down. He wanted to get his hands on the advanced knowledge the Vegans possessed and then claim it for his very own. He didn't stand in the way as Ezra and her team built their colony. The Vegans worked tirelessly in harmony and joy. After each day's work, they would all gather in the garden of Orion-1, the planet they had chosen for their colony, to sing their happy songs of light and play the melodies of their distant home. Little did they know they were being stalked by a dark, slithery race of Reptilians waiting to pounce on them.

After following them back to Vega and finding there was so much more to their empire, so much more they could conquer, the Reptilian Army reported their whereabouts to their emperor. It was now the time for the emperor to take charge and lead his army to conquer them.

• • •

Draco was ready to attack the Vegan colony on Orion-1. He took charge of his fleet and secretly landed hundreds of soldiers on the planet. Yet before the attack could commence, a sweet angelic voice reached his ears. He had never heard a song so sweet and melodious. He commanded his army to wait, to remain hidden while he went ahead.

The Reptilians were a race gifted with many abilities. They could change their color at will and hide in plain sight while still in the protection of darkness. Draco had mastered this ability, and he used it to remain hidden as he followed the song. The melody led him to the palace of the Vegans. There he stood, at the edge of the garden where he couldn't be discovered, looking at Princess Ezra, the most beautiful among the beings of light.

She stood right in the middle of the perfectly manicured garden, singing to her people in a long, shimmering gown. Her long hair cascaded down her back, and her head was crowned with a small, flashy, diamond tiara. She held a golden trident in her hand, and her eyes flashed like powerful beams of light. A halo of silver-blue light beamed around her body, brighter than the shining stars.

Draco's heart skipped a beat and many beats after that. He felt something neither he nor many of his race had ever felt. Draco's race had no concept of love. They were a species devoted to conquest and to power. Yet there stood their leader, feeling something akin to love for a being of light. His love came from his obsession with power. Ezra was the most beautiful being he had ever seen, and he wanted to possess her, to control her. He wanted her beauty to belong to him and to him alone. The Draco-Reptilians had ruled other humanoid species, but they had not yet encountered actual beings of light, so they didn't know what it was like to face the light.

When they saw the Vegans in Orion from a distance, they witnessed the true power of light for the very first time. They realized that the Vegans had the power to illuminate the galaxy, and that meant they could destroy their own Reptilian empire, built in the shadows of the stars. As such, the Reptilians grew to fear them. The

Vega-Lyrans were beings of such pure light that they could reduce the Draco-Reptilians to ash simply being in their presence. Ezra was the purest of the Vegans. They called her the Lady of Light, and light was lethal to Draco's kind.

Draco had already been informed of occurrences when exposure to light had killed members of his race, and he knew he could not fully appear before her, ever. Nonetheless, he fell in love which illuminated him from within, albeit temporarily. Still, he did not know how to rise in love as an eternal being of the dark. In its initial surge, love (of the light or the dark), did what it always does — fills one's heart with joy and ecstasy. His heart was so full of light that he felt like singing a song or writing poetry, just as all lovers do for their beloved.

Draco returned to his palace lost in love, not knowing what to do. He forgot his lust for power and his hunger to rule, and for a time, was at peace. He could not focus on his empire and his people. He could not sleep and lost his appetite. All he could think of was her. She became an obsession for him. He stealthily began following Ezra wherever she went, tracking her every move and watching every step she took in the great constellation of Orion. He cherished a secret dream to see her as the reigning empress of Orion by his side and instructed his people to aid the Vegans from the shadows so he could grow closer to possessing her.

• • •

Ezra and her team were bestowed with numerous blessings, and building their new colony on Orion-1 seemed like child's play. They had no clue who or what the invisible force was helping them, but it was nothing new. Light beings were accustomed to receiving cosmic support wherever they went. The V-L humanoids were naturally aligned with ALL THERE IS. It was such a common phenomenon for them that they couldn't smell anything underhanded. Unsuspiciously, they went about building their colony.

It was a compelling experience and quite a novel one for Draco, too. He had only learned to grab, snatch, and steal until then. He'd never experienced the power of receiving, giving, or helping others. Love taught him new lessons, helping him explore unknown territories within his heart that he never even knew existed. The more he unconsciously practiced these virtues, the lighter his heart became. It was a blissful feeling. His heart was full of hope, hoping to dwell in Orion with the love of his life forever. Little did he realize his dream would be short-lived and his hopes were waiting to be shattered.

Once Ezra and her team finished their mission and the colony on Orion-1 was established, they decided to return to Vega. This filled Draco with fear and sorrow. Darkness crept into his being once more, and he wanted to keep Ezra in Orion forever, but the love in his heart did not allow him to give in to this dark desire. He decided to let her go with the hope that he could keep track of her moves and one day invite her to return to Orion on her own as the queen.

"She has established her kingdom with her own hands. She will surely come back to rule it one day," he said to himself. For he believed that she, too, like him, wished to rule.

Draco waited for Ezra, hoping she'd return, yet eons passed, and she never did. Waiting and waiting, he lost control over his life. He turned away from his people and his dream to conquer the universe. His obsession with Ezra was slowly growing into madness. She was all that mattered to him, all he could bring himself to think about. His patience was slowly wearing out, and the light in his heart faded slowly and painfully. His faith and love turned into anger and frustration, and he finally decided to leave Orion in search of her. Emperor Draco ordered his men to collect all the information they could about the Princess of Vega. He decided to march towards Vega to meet her, but just as he was about to depart with his army, his informers returned with news that would shake him to the core of his being.

After her return to Vega, Ezra met the Lyran warrior, Ezekiel. Their relationship blossomed, and after a long courtship, they were now headed for Lyra to seek blessings from the High Council and from Ezekiel's family. She had left Vega to be with the love of her life and would soon be wed, after which they would both become leaders of the Vega-Lyran empire and would dwell between their two kingdoms.

The news of their union spread quickly, and Draco couldn't comprehend anything he was hearing. When and how did all of this happen? How could Ezra dare to fall in love with another? She was supposed to be his. He had let her go, and he had waited for her. His heart almost stopped beating for a while. Dejected and in silence, he slithered back to his private chamber and shut the door. He did not allow anyone to see his tears, to hear his heart breaking.

• • •

As was the nature of his people, Draco was consumed with anger and bitterness. When he finally returned to deal with his royal duties, he was unrecognizable to even his own people. His green eyes burned with a fire of hatred and obsession. He had no other emotion in his heart but the pure rage that now formed the center of his universe. All that made sense to him now was the idea of vengeance. The only way he could think of to make his pain disappear was to shift his focus from Ezra to the person who had snatched her away from him — the mighty warrior Ezekiel.

His obsession for revenge turned into rage. Finally, he could take no more of this self-inflicted torture and simply lost his mind.

He became the terror of his own people as he slowly became prone to violent outbursts. He would often scream as he ran out of his palace in absolute madness, shooting a salvo of fire from his hate-filled green eyes, incinerating anyone or anything that got in his way. The scales on his lizard-like body glowed like fireballs, and his sharp tail would swing from side to side like a giant knife, even shredding his own subjects.

He would trample upon everything that stood in his way, crushed both friend and foe to dust, and spewed red-hot fire over his own people. They would scream in utter horror and fear. The poor commoners had to run and hide to save their lives from their own ruler. There was sheer chaos and panic throughout the entire Draco-Reptilian empire. Even his own army would abandon him during these fits of rage. They would run and hide and wait for him to regain his senses. The Reptilian race had never seen their ruler in such manic rage, and they, too, feared what was to come.

CHAPTER SEVENTEEN

THE FALL OF THE EMPIRE

Draco had long been infamous for his cruelty, but the love he felt for Ezra had, even if momentarily, turned his heart soft. For a brief yet hopeful time, he had begun enjoying virtues like kindness and generosity. Still, once those virtues abandoned him, he fell from his place of love and, in its stead, rose the most ferocious monster anybody could ever imagine.

In his fury, he wanted nothing more than to destroy the Kingdom of Light. Yet he could not. For in his path to vengeance stood one glaring wall: his army could not survive in the light. Any Reptilian foolish enough to go anywhere near the Lyra system would perish because of its intense brilliance. Draco wanted to counter that. He summoned scientists, thinkers, philosophers, and dark magicians from every corner of the galaxy, both humanoid and Reptilian, to the capital of his dark empire and ordered them to find him a way to invade Lyra. No one had any answers. Evidently, there was no antidote for the pure light of the Vega-Lyran race.

He never gave up, though, and kept waiting for the right moment and the right opportunity to pounce. He did a lot of groundwork for his invasion, all in anticipation of the day when he would finally rain the fires of his vengeance upon the unsuspecting people of Lyra. He did have the resources and a plan to make his dream of conquering Lyra a reality, however.

"Prepare a sheet of dark metal that will cover the sky of Lyra and block out all light, so my army can enter and attack the capital," he demanded.

Unfortunately, no power in the universe could put out the heavenly light of Lyra forever. Thus, Draco forced the scientists under his control to build a temporary solution. He had them create special suits of armor with hooded covers that would allow his soldiers to survive in the light. He had an opening and a way to get his soldiers inside. Now all that remained was for him to put his plan into motion.

•••

Meanwhile, Ezekiel and Ezra were busy with their voyage through the galaxy. It was common knowledge that they would soon be the king and queen of the Vega-Lyran empire. They were loved by one and all, and everybody was happy to have them as their leaders. Vega-Lyra had turned into what humans would call "heaven." There was eternal sunshine, joy, music, love, and abundance under the loving and nurturing guidance of their loving king and queen-to-be.

The more Draco heard about the undying love of Ezekiel and Ezra, the more determined he became to destroy them and their kingdom forever. He stealthily followed every movement of the two lovers as they set out on their galactic honeymoon. In the meantime, he could very strategically plan his next moves. Finally, his patience paid off, and his golden opportunity arrived.

He reached out to his allies, the Grays, for help. The Grays were originally a humanoid race living in the apex of the constellation

Hercules who had now moved to Zeta Reticuli. An apocalyptic war destroyed its surface long ago, forcing them to live underground for thousands of years and eventually transforming them into soulless creatures with extremely short human-like bodies, enlarged hairless heads, smooth gray skin, and large black eyes. The radiation from their nuclear weapons had permanently damaged their reproductive systems forcing them to use cloning for the survival of their species. Staying away from light for such a long time, they began displaying an aversion to it. They became a violent and warring race.

Like the Reptilians, they loved acquiring power and control through stealth and manipulation. Draco had sent an invitation to the Grays to join the Reptilian Army in attacking the Lyran planets. They were happy to oblige, of course, as Draco offered them an equal share in the spoils of war. As the Reptilian Army and their Gray allies waited for the moment of darkness to spread over the Lyran sky, Draco himself followed Ezekiel and Ezra with a small Reptilian brigade of his own. Then, as the ominous moment arrived, he blew his trumpet.

Draco's trumpet could be heard across the whole universe as every Reptilian and Gray ship transmitted it. The Dark War had begun. Ezekiel and Ezra heard the gut-wrenching sound and saw the sky above them turning darker and darker by the minute. Before they could comprehend what was happening around them, Draco's trumpet had blown loud enough to serve its purpose. The Reptilians cast the metal sheet, spreading a black cloud over the Lyran sky. The Reptilian-Gray army had instantly entered Lyra and attacked the empire, taking all citizens by surprise.

Lyrans had great warriors among them, the Sayvants, but they were unprepared, and without their great leader, Ezekiel, they could not even hope to fight the combined might of their attackers. They were eternal beings of light, completely unaware of the darkness in any shape or form. There had been eternal sunshine over the Lyran kingdom, thus no one ever knew what darkness was. They were in no way prepared to fight in the darkness that the Reptilians had cast.

Draco's army took advantage of this ignorance and attacked the home planets, killing millions of the most divine, peaceful, and intelligent Lyrans. They brutally murdered Izar, the old and loving head of the High Council, captured many great leaders and dragged them to Draco's dungeons. Before leaving the most beautiful constellation of light the cosmos had ever seen, the Reptilians made sure to lay waste to every nook and cranny of the heavenly kingdom. They destroyed every palace, burned every garden, and tore down every monument. The great streams dried up, and the flowers lost their lush petals and fragrances. In a single day, the greatest empire among the stars was reduced to ashes.

Meanwhile, Draco and his forces descended upon Ezekiel and Ezra in another part of the universe. They used a special cloth made of the same metal as the dark sheet to snare them, and although Ezekiel put up a good fight defending himself and his eternal love, the darkness left them powerless.

Ezra and Ezekiel were then brought in front of the dark emperor Draco. For the first time in the galaxy's history, darkness met the light. Just the sight of the giant slithery and scaled dragon through the hood that covered her face sent chills down Ezra's spine for the first time in her life. Draco's henchmen bound and gagged Ezekiel as Ezra was forced to kneel before the dark emperor.

"Who are you? Why have you brought me here, and what do you want from me?" she demanded as soon as her mouth was freed.

"I, my dear, am your secret admirer. I am known as Draco, King of the Universe." Clearly his ego was as big as the universe itself. "At long last, you are here in front of me in all your glory, and you can't run away."

"King of the Universe, you say? How unheroic of you to have a lady bound in such a manner," she quipped.

He circled her like a shark. "It would be so much easier to kill you if you weren't so beautiful."

"You know, bloodlust is not a good look on you." Ezra acted calmly, even though she was secretly terrified.

"There is something fascinating about you. You are neither goddess, nor angel, nor siren, nor vixen. You are something far more powerful."

He couldn't contain himself any longer and slowly extended his hand to touch her cheek. The piercing, brilliant light she emitted from her eyes melted his hand on contact.

The pain was excruciating. "Ahhhhhhhh! Why you little…"

"Now, now. Mind your manners, sir. You are in the presence of a lady," she proudly proclaimed.

"Damn you!"

"Don't think I'm not a match for you, Draco."

"I was hoping you'd say that," as he pulled back his arm and studied what was left of his claw which was now dripping like hot wax. "Damn, that hurts."

"I was hoping you'd say that," she stuck back.

"Don't worry. It'll grow back. It's one of the benefits of being Reptilian."

"Lucky you."

"Why aren't you afraid of me?"

"Because I stand in my light. No creature of the dark can harm me, not while Ezekiel is at my side."

"God, I hate that name. What do you see in this little rat anyway?" gesturing to Ezekiel.

"Something you know nothing about, I assure you."

"Don't be so sure."

He studied her face for about another minute, then looked her straight in the eye. "I'm not entirely evil, you know."

"No, I don't know."

"Nevertheless, I have a plan for you."

"Is it a good one?"

"Like I said, I have a plan."

"You can see I'm trembling." She projected a fierce image of bravery and courage, but deep down she was still afraid of him and what he might do to her.

The Reptilian emperor stared intensely at the Vegan princess with his monstrous green eyes, making her feel tense and nauseated. Ezekiel was terrified, too, but also angry. He wanted to save his princess from this monster, but he was rendered helpless. Darkness had brought the two lovers face to face with evil, something they did not know existed till then, yet they instinctively knew they had to confront it and eventually defeat it. The dark race had finally revealed itself and was not going away anytime soon. And so it was that the empires of Vega and Lyra fell, the great warrior and his princess were captured, and the stage was set for the greatest conflict the galaxy had ever known.

CHAPTER EIGHTEEN
LIGHT AND DARK

Ezekiel and the other captured Lyrans were dumped into Draco's dark, dank prison cells — shackled, bound, and under constant guard. He released Ezra from her chains, forcefully separating her from Ezekiel and confined her to a separate part of his wicked mansion. The Draco-Reptilian empire did not have many natural resources, nor any source of light, so they had to create fire for everything they wished to see and do. The plants in the gardens of Draco's fortress only bore dark flowers. There was smoke and mist everywhere. It was an empty, lifeless place, and every moment spent there suffocated Ezra.

"Why is he doing this?" she questioned his servants, overcome with rage and confusion. "He is the most vile creature I have ever laid eyes on!"

The servants were instructed not to speak to her. Draco had his subjects decorate his lair with all the riches of the universe and made grand plans to profess his love. Ezra was bathed in scented water, the rarest of perfumes were sprinkled over her, and she was dressed in a golden, jeweled robe, her hair tied in plaits and pinned with diamonds and crystals.

Draco was happy, convinced he had vanquished everything that had once stood between him and his true love. He believed he had finally won over his love, even if it was through force and manipulation, but he had not yet understood the true power of the light. Once all his grand plans had been set into motion, he had his servants drag Ezra before him.

"Welcome, Princess," he spoke as his slimy, slit tongue fluttered visibly. "I hope you've been enjoying your stay."

"I enjoy my confinement as much as you enjoy my contempt for you," Ezra retorted.

"Come now, Princess, surely you have realized that any resistance is futile. You are mine now. I have won you by laying waste to that good-for-nothing empire you once ruled."

"I am no prize to be won, Draco. I am the Lady of Light, and darkness can never win over light. Our great empire of peace shall never succumb to the likes of you or your people, I assure you. We will rise again."

"Senseless dreams, hopeless ambitions — HAHAHA!" Draco's horrifying laugh made every hair on Ezra's feline body shiver with fear. "I like your spirit, Princess, and I will thoroughly enjoy breaking it. Have no fear. You will be fully mine in time."

Saying this, he came close to her and tried to profess his undying love in his own dark and evil way, but as he did, Ezra closed her eyes and thought only of pure, divine love. This, in turn, signaled every captive Vega-Lyran in Draco's dungeons to do the same, along with Ezekiel. All of these thoughts in concert evoked the light in Ezra's heart that suddenly burst from her body like a star. So powerful was this utterly blinding radiance that it burned Draco's slimy skin.

"Aahhhhhhhh!" screamed the Dragon, severely charred and blinded in pain by the dazzling light. He ran like mad from his throne room, unable to bear the heat generated by the force of

Ezra's light. Now that light emanated from her entire body. She was like a mighty star on the surface of the Draconian world. Her light reached every part of his fortress of hell. The Reptilian empire could not handle such a huge light force and began to crumble. There was chaos and pandemonium as every Reptilian ran to save itself from the destructive radiance of Ezra's glory.

The massive Reptilian empire was in shambles in a fraction of a few earthly seconds. The Vega-Lyrans had to do nothing special to bring it down but to stand united in the force of their light with Ezra as their beacon. As Ezekiel single-handedly established a kingdom of light all those eons ago, his lover now razed an empire of evil with nothing more than the power of love and the light known as Christ. Reptilians began dying by the millions. Their bodies could not withstand the light and were burned and charred by its massive heat. Draco realized that he had invited his own destruction with his ego and pride. All he wanted now was to remain alive, to breathe, and not to be burned to death.

In utter shock, fear, and desperation, he managed to escape just in the nick of time. Draco ran like hell from his stronghold. He took a few loyal followers in his royal vessel, a gigantic Reptilian starship, and took refuge in a remote Reptilian hideout in a dark corner of the galaxy.

$$\bullet \ \bullet \ \bullet$$

Once she came to her senses and realized she was free, Ezra didn't realize the utter devastation that her light had wreaked upon Draco's kingdom. She immediately ran to free Ezekiel from his chains as he took her in his arms.

"Ezra, my love! What did he do to you? If that greasy monster laid so much as a finger on you, I swear I will rip…"

"No, no, my love, he did not touch me. He could not. We both know the power of the light. It made me strong enough to thwart his advances and to lay waste to all he held dear."

"I thought I would never see you again. I just want to hold and kiss you forever."

"There will be time for that later, my love. First, we must leave this cursed place. It truly makes my skin crawl."

"Yeah, it gives me the creeps, too. I have never come across a world as dark and barren as this one in all my travels. How do these slimy reptiles continue to exist?"

"I have a feeling we haven't seen the last of them, nor their leader. He's very clever."

"Well, we'll cross that bridge when we get to it. For now, let us leave this den of darkness and return to our home. We have much work to do."

Ezekiel, Ezra, and what remained of the V-Ls, returned to their beloved homeland. Unfortunately, all that waited for them was ruin, rubble and the charred bodies of their families and friends. They found themselves standing amid the husk of a leveled empire where their mighty capital had once stood.

They wept tears of pain and sorrow as they witnessed the extent of the devastation that Draco had unleashed upon their home. For the first time in the history of their existence, they felt true grief and despair — complete despair that gave birth to anger. Then, their eyes began to fill with rage as they felt an undeniable urge to kill Draco and erase his entire race from existence.

They soon recognized that this destruction was brought about by lower emotions — emotions of darkness and evil. Ezekiel himself spoke to his people and told them that they could not allow such dark emotions to cloud their minds. In the cosmos, there is no concept of linear time, so they had the power to go back in time at will. They were beings of light after all, and light has no bounds. They could easily choose to return to happier times when Lyra was intact and all their fellow Lyrans were alive. That way, the memory of this destruction could also be erased by beginning at an earlier period, creating a new timeline free from the pain and destruction of Draco's attack. Lyra could be resurrected again, and all their friends and families could come alive simply by deleting the timeline they were standing in.

Yet they did not do so. Instead, they chose to keep this reality alive. For Ezekiel and Ezra knew that changing the flow of time was not something that would be without consequence. They taught their people to understand that. Their empire was gone, but their fallen friends and family could return. As eternal beings, the Lyran people never truly died. The light of their beings could and would reincarnate upon other worlds. Once their physical form perished, they would be born again. Reincarnation was common among their people. They could rebuild their great cities, and eventually, all who had died would return.

The Reptilian attack had taught the Lyrans a very important lesson: they needed to be aware of the darkness, which they were ignorant of earlier. They realized these dark beings had spread their influence over the cosmos, trying to take over and control it. They were moving, breeding, growing freely and needed to be challenged. In that moment, the forces of light learned of their cosmic and eternal opposites. The binary of good and evil was forged and would forever continue. It was right then and there the Lyran forces of light took the oath to guard the universe from the darkness.

"From this day forth, we Lyrans will free all galaxies and star systems from the lust and greed of the dark Reptilians and Grays. We pledge to eliminate all darkness and dispel all illusion and ignorance while spreading the power of the Christ light to the entire universe.

We will bring those who have fallen into the darkness back to the light wherever and whenever we find them and eliminate those who have been consumed by evil."

They had seen the cruelty of Draco and the Grays while they were captive, and now they sought to conquer it. They decided to let the fallen Lyran empire remain as an emblem of light, a symbol of their oath to keep reminding them of their mission. And thus, the original might and beauty of the first Vega-Lyran empire were lost. Its memory remained only in their hearts, but the empire would rise again as the fallen Lyrans reincarnated and their ruined cities were rebuilt.

CHAPTER NINETEEN

MISSION

Ezekiel, Ezra, and all the surviving Lyrans made it their mission to liberate the universe of darkness and despair. They began sending envoys to different planets in distant galaxies and star systems. They sent preachers and warriors to bring knowledge of the lurking darkness to all who were good and to vanquish evil agents. The Veganites, too, joined them in their quest. While exploring the Ring Nebula, the Vega-Lyrans came across a colony of Reptilians who had claimed the territory for themselves. They decided it was time to wage a holy war against any and all Reptilian control over the universe, and thus began the Galactic Wars.

The forces of light from other star systems and galaxies, too, joined the war against the Draconians. Great humanoid races from Andromeda, Alpha and Proxima Centauri, Hyades, and many other civilizations came to the aid of their fellow beings of light as the war became more destructive and all-consuming. Ezekiel, Ezra, and the V-L armies, along with their allies, fought an all-out war against the Draco-Reptilians in the Ring Nebula.

It was a devastating series of battles, and the death toll was in the millions. The Reptilians had created weapons that allowed them to withstand and combat the divine light of Lyra, whereas the Lyrans had found new ways to harness their light and turn the dark beings into dust. After a gruesomely long battle on the planetoid called Zildan-Alpha, the Legions of Light finally defeated the Reptilians and broke their might in the Ring Nebula. But they could not find their emperor, Draco the Dragon.

Both Ezra and Ezekiel knew he was hiding somewhere in a concealed stronghold, but they had no clue as to where that could even be. Nonetheless, they pledged to continue their holy war whenever and wherever they encountered these dark beings. Since then, the Lyrans have fought numerous battles against the Reptilians. These skirmishes initially started in the Cradle of Lyra, but soon spread to the constellation of Orion, where Ezra had built her Vegan kingdom and so had Draco.

Ezekiel and Ezra were desperately searching for Draco to end his tyranny when Ezra finally realized the truth. Their black-hearted emperor could only be hiding in the darkest regions of the Orion System, where the Draco-Reptilians had once held great power. It was time for her to take the war to the wicked monster who started it. Thus, she decided to return to Orion with the full force of her people, to find and face Draco, and to slaughter him with her own hands.

"I wish to accompany you, Ezra," Ezekiel professed.

"No, my love. This is my battle, and I wish to fight it without involving you in the horrific madness that is to come. Don't worry about me. Remember, I was a commander long before we ever met, and the greatest warriors of our race stand behind me. Fear not for me, but for that evil monster who shall face my wrath. Yes, it means we will have to part for some time. How long, I do not know, but our eternal love will always bring us back together."

By now, Lyrans had lovingly seeded the first souls of human civilization on Planet Earth. They happily inhabited the planet, honoring Mother Earth, the heavens, and nature. They enjoyed abundance and prosperity without any knowledge of greed or power. Like their Lyran forefathers, humans had initially been divine beings of light who could communicate with the Source and nature, but that did not last.

Soon after the conception of the human race, the Lyrans and their allies realized that they had gone down a darker path and turned into different beings than their divine ancestors. It took the beings of light ages to realize that their dark counterparts were to blame here as well. The Reptilians and Grays had found a new way to invade and infest every planet and star system they came across.

They had begun incarnating in huge numbers as humans on Planet Earth and similarly on other planets, aping and cloning the original inhabitants. This way, they could easily merge with the light beings and begin to corrupt their minds, control their thoughts, and inject dark ideas of greed and lust into their consciousness. The Reptilians had begun manipulating humans from within their numbers to keep them in a state of deep slumber, away from their true and divine nature.

• • •

Ezra returned to Orion to fight Draco while Ezekiel discovered his own calling, a true divine mission. He was the Chosen One, after all. He and some of his fellow Sayvant warriors volunteered to incarnate as humans on Planet Earth and other planets as their original inhabitants to counter the Reptilians. Their mission was to rid humanity of this darkness and liberate human minds from Reptilian control by way of divine consciousness. The war that had started in the heart of the Ring Nebula and had spread to the farthest reaches of the universe was now being fought on Earth, yet it was not fought with weapons and ships but with words and minds.

Meanwhile, Ezra and her legions were still fighting an actual war against the Reptilians in Orion and desperately searching for Draco. Unbeknownst to her, Draco had already managed to escape from Orion after encountering her forces. He did not have the courage to face her light after what it had done to his once mighty fortress, and thus he ran. He knew if he tried hiding again, she would find him anyway, so he chose a different path. He was among the Reptilians who volunteered to incarnate on different planets, and Draco had chosen the perfect one – Planet Earth.

While on one hand, Ezra and her allies continued to fight a never-ending series of wars in the constellation of Orion that would later come to be known as the Wars of Orion, Ezekiel and his fellow lightworkers kept incarnating on Earth at several periods of human history, slowly guiding humanity away from the Reptilian control and towards the light. Throughout his countless incarnations on Earth, Ezekiel had no knowledge of the fact that Draco, too, had been incarnating among his beloved humans… at least not until now.

CHAPTER TWENTY

LITTLE SIGNALS

When Zeke woke the next morning, his mind was a blur. He was dazed and confused. "Where am I? How did I end up in my bed?" he kept wondering as he looked around his room.

His mind was fractured, and ancient memories of another life flashed like fireworks in his brain. In a few minutes, he came to his senses, and his human memory returned. He jumped off his bed and ran to his mother's room to check on her. It was very early in the morning, and she was still asleep. Zeke went to Maya's room and found her sleeping as well. Finally, he entered Leia's room, and she was busy trying to repair some broken parts of a toy car.

"Hey, Leia. Didn't I go out last evening? Didn't I ask you and Maya to take care of Mom for a while and take Coco for a walk? Didn't I…" Zeke began bombarding her with his queries.

"Yeah, you left. What's the matter with you? Don't you remember — and can't you see I'm busy?" She was trying hard to fix her toy car and was already on the verge of freaking out on it and Zeke.

"How did I end up in my bed this morning, then? When did I come back home?" he inquired again. Zeke was so obsessed with figuring things out that he completely ignored her lack of interest in him or his questions.

"Hey, hey. Back the truck up, bro. Have you gone nuts or something? What do you mean, 'How did I end up in my bed?' Where else were you supposed to be? You came home late last night and went straight to your room. We asked you if you wanted dinner, but you wouldn't answer. It was like you were in some kind of trance, dude. Mom was worried you might have been drinking like Dad. Go get your brains checked and stop bothering me, will ya?" Leia dismissed him with a snarky look and was as rude as she could possibly be for a ten-year-old.

"Leia, I know you're trying to fix that car, but there are other things you need to fix first. Could you please watch your words before you speak to someone older than you next time? You're my kid sister and I love you, but you're growing up now, and one day I expect you to act like a responsible person. Why don't you try practicing a little kindness and politeness from now on?" Zeke reacted in a calm, poised, and mature way, yet there was a seriousness in his tone that Leia could not ignore.

His message was loud and clear. She was astonished to see her brother behave like an adult for the first time in her life, so little Leia shrugged her shoulders along with a "My bad."

Frustrated, he countered, "Could you please try saying, 'I'm sorry' instead? Our words are like little magical signals that we push into the universe. Leia, you should know by now that words have the power to hurt. They also have the power to heal. A half-hearted 'sorry' isn't enough, either. It has to be honest and sincere. It's the intonation. People want to feel it from you. They need to know you have a contrite heart and that you really mean what you're saying. Words are like a secret magic power. You should try using that power sometimes. It may come in handy one day," came Zeke's instant and spontaneous reaction.

"Intonation? Contrite heart? Where does he come up with this stuff?" she wondered.

He didn't know exactly where such wise words had come from either, but he surely had woken up to a different reality. Wisdom and knowledge were seamlessly flowing out of him. He had gained an immense sense of strength, inner power, and courage. He had just returned from the stars, after all. His homeland had not sent him back without a magical gift. It was the gift of power that comes from learning to find his voice and, of course, from a bigger and higher truth of his own existence shown to him.

He had never bothered to care much about how his sisters spoke or behaved with him in the past. He was a shy, timid boy who never tried to correct or guide anyone, but right then, he realized something inside him had snapped, like a switch turning, like a light bulb had illuminated, allowing him to stand in the presence of his own power and be his true authentic self.

His senses felt heightened, and he could listen to people's words more carefully than he ever did before. He could understand, analyze and respond to every action around him. He could almost feel the vibration of every word. He had begun reading between the lines and noticing that the power of spoken words was slowly revealing itself. He could also feel the vibration of unspoken words as if he had suddenly gained the power to listen to other people's thoughts. From the day he returned from his homeland, Zeke had begun understanding the weight of both spoken and unspoken words.

Along with his heightened senses, he had also returned with the recognition of darkness. The flashes of his ancient memories reminded him of his mission – a mission to raise the consciousness of humanity. The control of the Reptilians and Grays over human minds, which had kept them in a state of deep slumber, had to be broken.

Humanity needed to be brought back to its true divine power and purpose: the purpose to embrace and spread light across the globe. The light did not need any language or words, but the human world was still under the pressure of words creating negative thoughts and vibrations, something the dark Reptilians relished and thrived on.

As fragments of his past lives returned, Zeke realized that the human ideas of heaven and hell, good and evil, were simply manifestations of the original struggle between light and dark that humanity had inherited from its divine ancestors. These concepts were the embodiment of the Lyran memories, hidden deep within the human condition, forever coded onto their DNA.

• • •

Zeke became so sensitive to words and actions of his family, neighbors, and schoolmates that he began watching his own words and actions. He instantly grew up and started acting like an actual adult. He was preparing for his final exams at school while learning and discovering new things about himself at the same time.

Mrs. Tartal's health was deteriorating, and it was revealed she was suffering from Multiple Sclerosis. He stayed home most of the time now to take care of her. His mother was a very pure soul, and he was more like his mother than his siblings or his father. Zeke and his mother had been similar souls ever since he was born. They clearly belonged to the same soul group. The concept of soulmates is too often romanticized by humans, but in its trueist sense, Zeke's mother was his real soulmate.

Zeke had begun utilizing his time at home while reading and learning more about his mission as a starseed. He was especially trying to learn about the secret power of words. He thought deeply about the right and the wrong use of words as a tool. Words had power, he knew that, and it took him time to understand what that power meant and represented.

"Words should have the power to express exactly what we feel," he thought. *"If we use bigger words for smaller thoughts, we might express more than we mean. If we use smaller words for bigger subjects, we might fall short of the right words when we wish to speak about a bigger subject."*

Zeke's inherent wisdom from his ancient lives told him, "If each word vibrates at a certain frequency, then that means innumerable words spoken and thoughts invoked by innumerable people are sending innumerable frequencies out into the universe with every passing second. Positive words and thoughts sending out positive signals must then be colliding with negative words and thoughts sending out negative signals."

It was so much fun to think that words fought and countered each other in the ether. The science behind words influencing our lives appeared much simpler to him now. If negative thoughts and words outnumber positive thoughts and words in our environment, the world at large would begin thinking and creating negative experiences for itself. But what if positive thoughts and words outnumber negative ones? If so, a larger picture of how this world functions could magically change in an instant.

CHAPTER TWENTY-ONE
THE MAGIC WAND

Zeke often visited his favorite bookstore in town, The Bookworm, so he could learn more about the world and discover hidden truths. The memories of Draco, the Reptilian Army, and the destruction they had wreaked upon the Lyran kingdom would return to him as flashes that haunted his young mind. Nevertheless, they kept him focused on his mission.

One day, when he was at the store looking for more books to read, he saw an old man sitting silently on a bench near the street across from the store. The man was wearing a dull, white robe that looked old and shabby. He had snow-white, unkempt hair, and a long, equally white beard. The wrinkles on his face made him look a hundred years old. He held a long string of brown beads in his hands. The man was sitting with his eyes closed, murmuring to himself as if he was chanting a mantra or meditating upon something.

Zeke was intrigued by the presence of this old man, so he walked out of the store and positioned himself at a safe distance from the bench. He didn't expect the man to look back at him at all. Yet right then, and to his utter amazement, the man opened his eyes and looked straight into Zeke's. His eyes shined with a wonderful light that reminded Zeke of the divine light of his homeland. The old man looked like the very embodiment of wisdom. He had a strange smile on his face as if to say, "I know who you *really* are." The man then closed his eyes and went back to his meditative state.

Zeke felt a strong urge to talk to him, to ask him questions, but he did not want to bother him, so he decided against it. But just then, the old man opened his eyes a second time. He motioned for Zeke to come closer, he reached out his hands and took Zeke's hands in his own. He smiled at him and pronounced, "Healer, heal thyself. Seeker, seek the truth!"

His words sounded like some sort of prophecy. The man then released Zeke's hands and returned to his trance, leaving Zeke utterly confused. Taken aback by the strange encounter, he practically ran back home. That night, Zeke went to bed early and, once again, had a strange dream. In his dream, a distant voice said, "Healer, heal thyself. Seeker, seek the truth!"

Zeke opened his eyes to find that his dream had taken him to a sandy beach on a tropical island. It was early evening, and the sun was just about to go down. He was sitting on the sand and saw the same old man sitting a little further out. As Zeke stood up, the old man did the same and walked towards him. He looked at Zeke with kind eyes and lovingly asked, "Won't you participate in this evening's prayers?"

Zeke looked at him as if his words had hypnotized him and began following him without a word. The old man guided him nearby where a large group of people had gathered in a circle. They looked like tribal men and women in traditional regalia who seemed native to the island. They had torches burning around them that lit the entire beach as the sun went down. Then, the nightly ritual began. There was a large fire at the center of the circle. Zeke looked around and could see little huts in the light of the torches.

He was in a clearing inside a tribal village. Zeke realized he wasn't anywhere in today's world; he wasn't in the present. He had somehow traveled into the past, yet the old man still looked the same. Zeke and the old man joined the group, taking their place in the circle. They all held each other's hands and sang a soul-soothing song, more like a chant. It consisted of a single word, "Ho'oponopono," that they kept repeating and singing as if they were all chanting a mantra.

"Ho'oponopono, Ho'oponopono, Ho'oponopono."

• • •

Zeke suddenly woke up in his bed as the morning sun kissed his cheeks. He could hear Ziggy twittering from his window. She was singing "Ho'oponopono" as well.

He looked at her and smiled. "Good morning, Ziggy Bird. Where have you been all this time, and just how do you know "Ho'oponopono?"

Just then, something scratched his chest. Zeke almost screamed only to find Zag sitting there, bouncing like a ball. "Ahem!" The second their eyes met, Zag laughed and winked at him and began doing somersaults up and down his chest. After a few moments of this tomfoolery, he rendered, "I am sorry, Mister Tartal. Please forgive me, sir."

Just when he was about to speak with Zag, his eyes fell over Zoom, standing by his bedside. She gave him a small kiss and pronounced, "Thank you. I love you."

"Zoom, Zoom! Is that you? I need to talk to you!" Zeke rubbed his eyes and jumped out of bed.

But as soon as he did, he found his room empty. No one was there. Zig, Zag, and Zoom had completely disappeared. He was alone. "Were they part of my dream?" he asked himself.

Whether just a dream or something else, everything that had happened was pointing towards these questions: "Who was the old man? Where did he come from? Where did he take him? What was the song those men and women were singing? Why was Ziggy tweeting the same song? Why was Zag asking for forgiveness and Zoom saying thank you? What were Zig, Zag, and Zoom trying to convey to him by appearing in his dream?" All these questions and more rang through his mind, and he would soon have the answers.

The unexplainable dream made Zeke feel extremely restless. He was unable to sit in one place for more than a few minutes that day. He didn't know what to do or where to go. He had no idea how to find the answers he needed. After a while, he went to his mother's room to check on her. She was awake and lying on her bed, blankly looking up at the ceiling.

"Mom, there's a word I just heard about. Can you tell me what it means?" he asked her.

"What word, my boy?" She felt weak, and it was hard for her to speak, but she knew her son well enough. She wanted to answer his question, so she endured the pain.

"Ho'oponopono. Do you know what it means?"

His mother smiled at him and said, "Where did you hear this special word, Zeke? It's a lovely word. Yes, I know it. I learned about it years ago from a book. It means 'to correct.'"

She was very sleepy and dozed off soon after telling him that. Much of Zeke's interest in books and his wisdom had come from his mother. She, too, had been an avid reader and was drawn to higher truths. She had a lot of answers and was a wise woman, though life had been unjust and cruel to her.

She always said, "If you want to know more than others about the world around you and how it works, read books, Zeke. Books hold magical secrets."

Zeke let her sleep and went straight to The Bookworm where he had met the old man last evening. He went to the store manager, Miss McDowall, and asked her if she had seen an old man sitting outside her store. The manager said the man had been sitting there on the same bench every evening for the past seven days as if he were waiting for someone. Nobody knew where he lived or who he was.

That fateful evening, he asked the manager to give Zeke a string of beads and a book he wished to leave for him. Nobody had seen him again since. Zeke instinctively knew the book would have all the answers he was looking for, so he wasted no more time. He went straight home and opened it. The book was about healing techniques practiced in different parts of the world. It was an ocean of wisdom from ancient cultures and traditions. Everything he had been searching for was right there in front of his eyes. The book had all the information about the magical healing powers of the word "Ho'oponopono."

The word had come from the Kānaka Maoli, indigenous Polynesian healers of the Hawaiian Islands, who originally practiced Ho'oponopono within extended families in Hawaii as a method of reconciliation and forgiveness. It was considered a cleansing process for putting things right and rectifying mistakes. According to the book, a man maned Dr. Ihaleakala Hew Len, a Hawaiian therapist, miraculously cured an entire ward of criminally insane patients by simply using this technique.

The incident marked the official entry of the traditional practice into the modern world. The book told Zeke everything about the way this technique worked. The age-old practice was perhaps the simplest yet most amazing of the magical power of words he had discovered. It used the concept of taking responsibility for everything negative happening within and around oneself and not passing the blame.

He continued to read, "Everything begins with us, within us, and hence, the course correction must begin with none other than ourselves. Once we start, our vibration shifts. The universe reads this positive shift within us and begins responding accordingly. Four simple steps help us achieve this highest state of positive vibration: showing repentance for all our previous conscious or unconscious mistakes, asking forgiveness for them, expressing gratitude for being forgiven, and sending out love in return."

"I am sorry. Please forgive me. Thank you. I love you," used in this practice, denotes these four steps. All we need to do is recite them repeatedly, aloud or in our minds, really meaning them from the bottom of our hearts, so we address each of these emotions within us. This simple practice, used as an everyday morning or nighttime ritual, can magically transform our lives. The true healing power lies in feeling the words and the willingness of the universe to forgive and love.

Zeke read through the chapter with a smile on his face. The real reason behind Zig, Zag, and Zoom's appearance that morning, and the words they had uttered in his dream, were clear to him now. They were bestowing upon him the secret power of this magical practice. He smiled, looking at the string of beads he held in his hands. Like a lightning bolt, something he had read in a random book years ago flashed through his mind: "When the student is ready, the master will appear."

The old man's prophecy, "Healer, heal thyself. Seeker, seek the truth," made sense to him now. No wonder it was a tool used by ancient Hawaiian healers. Not only did they heal themselves before they healed others, but the secret wisdom they carried was "to heal themselves, to heal others." The string the old man gave him contained a hundred and eight beads, a number that, when simplified, adds up to nine, signifying the completion of the cycle of spiritual enlightenment. The wise old man had left it for him so he could count the number of times he practiced the healing technique he had just learned and to keep focused on his goal.

He began his practice by saying "Thank you" to his cosmic friends Zig, Zag, and Zoom, who appeared whenever he needed guidance and protection on his earthly mission. He said, "Thank you," to the wise old man. The master did appear when the student was ready to learn. He had come to visit him from a faraway land, from an ancient time, to hand him over the powerful magical healing tool Zeke could use to heal himself, so he could heal the world around him. This was the first magical gift of wisdom he had received after his return from his homeland, Lyra. Ho'oponopono. It would become a magic wand, a tool he would use to heal many, the first of his many gifts.

CHAPTER TWENTY-TWO
FALL ROMANCE

Zeke was being introduced to the power of simple things, within him and around him. His senses were awakening, and a higher force was guiding him through the experience. It was all that was needed for him to turn into an enlightened being. His dreams and visions had increased in number. He was able to hear more, and he understood the intent of words instead of just their meaning. Thoughts and words weren't mere tools for him anymore; they were cosmic forces that held the power to change the world. He was listening and listening carefully. He learned that to heal others, he had to first heal himself. It was now time for him to begin his journey as a guide, and he would start off the course by helping the people around him.

At the same time, he was still busy with his studies. He wanted to get the best grades in school, so he could make his mother happy. He knew he couldn't live up to his father's expectations, but he wanted his mother to feel proud of him. Ben had grown so distant from his family and was so disillusioned with his son that he now only came home once or twice a week, choosing to spend his time at Tartal's Garage instead. Audrey's deteriorating health didn't appear to be a cause of concern for him, either. The doctors said she had a weak heart and needed plenty of rest, but no one, except Zeke, noticed the emotional pain her lonely heart was experiencing. He devoted most of his time to his mother and utilized the remaining hours to study. He learned about his origins, his mission, the tools, and the powers he would need to change the world, all while trying to make it through high school.

The dynamics around the neighborhood were changing as well. Zeke's friends were coping with their own problems. Gael was trying to manage his bipolar disorder along with school and his yard work. Mrs. Copeland was working more hours at the library, waiting for a much-needed pay raise so her family could get through its financial challenges. Kai had finished high school and was officially heading towards adulthood. On the surface, he appeared to be a mature and sensible young boy, but was secretly dealing with a crisis, a wound that had never healed. It was a wound of loss. He had never fully processed his sister Nora's death.

Kai had nurtured a secret desire to counter the childhood pain of losing his sister, which his young and fragile mind believed was somehow his fault. He wished to grow so rich and respected that all his problems would be solved. He aspired to study at the best business school in the world: Harvard University. He fought the pain and guilt of his sister's death so obsessively that he subconsciously attached all his ideas of success and failure to getting into Harvard.

It was a challenging process, but Kai was adamant about walking down that path regardless. He had secretly discussed his dream with a friend from school who had a cousin living in Boston. He worked at one of the biggest companies in Boston and was a Harvard graduate. Kai's friend told him he would speak to his cousin and check if Kai could go and live with him for a while to learn the ropes of business before he could manage to live on his own.

After making all his plans, Kai suddenly announced his decision to leave Mackinaw City. The news came as a shock to everyone in the neighborhood. The biggest shock came for Gael. Zeke, Kai and Gael had always stuck with each other through thick and thin, but with Zeke lost in his own world now, Gael's only consistent support was his brother. He had an emotional dependency on Kai.

When Kai announced his decision to move away from home, it felt like a betrayal to him. He had an emotional breakdown, and it took him many months to completely recover from the shock. Gael had never forgiven his father for leaving home after his sister's death, for abandoning him as a child, and for letting him suffer and fend for himself at a time when he was supposed to enjoy a happy, healthy, and secure life as a child. He always accused him of all his sufferings and his mother's woes. Gael also accused him as the main cause of Nora's death, and he was partially correct.

While she was alive, Nora had turned away from her family due to the daily fights between her parents. Mr. Copeland had borrowed a lot of money from a lot of people and then suddenly decided to leave home with another woman. After his daughter's death, he literally ran away from home, leaving Gael, Kai and their mother behind to face life on their own terms. All the hate and pain were hurting Gael more than anyone could have known. He was falling apart, and Zeke saw that.

It was time for Zeke to step up and take on the role of a friend and a guide to Gael now. The challenge was to help Gael without making him dependent. As a lightworker and a healer, he needed to begin with healing his home, his friends, and his neighborhood first.

• • •

Zeke was still in the habit of wandering in the woods every evening. It was autumn again and the leaves were changing colors all around Mackinaw City. The weather was crisp and invigorating. The whole town was blanketed with fall colors and harvest scents. Everybody loved the pleasant weather and the festive mood. Even Coconut was more active than usual. He loved autumn in Michigan.

During that wonderful time, Zeke couldn't stop thinking about Zoom. He still hadn't understood how she felt about him. He knew he loved her, as he had in his life as Ezekiel of Lyra, but he still wanted to talk to her. He wanted her to explain things to him. More than anything else, he wanted to see her one more time. If only she could come to visit him once, just once. Then he would walk with her along the lake as she told him stories of his past lives, and they could enjoy the Fall Festival together. Like any teenager, he too craved romance, but his wish to see Zoom was much more than that. What was unknown to him was the fact that his wishes hadn't gone unheard. The universe had heard his thoughts, prayers, and secret desires. He had no idea that pure thoughts had the power to make his desires manifest faster.

One evening as he was walking near the lake, he saw a pretty girl sitting alone on a bench near the woods. Zeke's heart skipped a beat. "Is that… Zoom?" He couldn't make out her face, but her hair and the aura around her made him think it was the girl he had been waiting for. As he tried to get a better look at her, she stood up and began walking. He followed her as if he were instantly hypnotized. After a while, he lost sight of her as if she had vanished into thin air. He desperately ran towards the lake to find her. He instinctively walked into the woods, and his heart skipped a beat again. He could feel her presence, her unmistakable presence.

"The merry-go-round goes Zoom, Zoom, Zoom," he heard a sudden and soft tweet from above. He looked up and found Ziggy hovering over his head.

"And angels meet around the dome, dome, dome!" Zeke laughed as he heard the accompanying shrill, high-pitched voice of Zag, hanging upside down by one leg on a tiny tree branch.

"Where's the dome here by the lakeside, my dear Zag?" he asked lovingly.

"Master, oh no, no, no! I was wrong. I was so wrong!" as he struggled to pull himself upright. I was simply trying to rhyme with Zig and doing a very poor job, I'm afraid. Ignore the dome for now and try to see the lyrical value I added to it, sir." His explanation made no sense, but Zeke loved it. His friends were back, which meant Zoom was, too. Within seconds, she was standing right there before them. He was ecstatic. She was back, but for how long?

The next few days went by like a dream for young Mr. Tartal. Zoom had indeed come down from the sky just for him. She was as happy and talkative as any young girl. They went on normal dates, like normal teenagers, visiting his favorite places, walking in the park, and roaming around the city. He sneaked her into his school, took her to Farley Street, to Saint Anthony Church, and to Lakeview Cemetery.

While at Saint Anthony's, Zoom went immediately to his statue to pay her respects. After a few moments of deep prayer, she turned to him. "What do you know of Saint Anthony of Padua, Zeke?"

"Not much."

"Well, he was a Franciscan friar from Portugal and is the patron saint of lost items — and people. If you pray sincerely to him in times of loss, he goes to work on your behalf. That's his job."

"Oh, yes. I've heard the prayer: 'Holy Tony, look around. Something's lost and must be found!'"

She smiled at him and said, "That petition may come in handy one day."

He shrugged his shoulders not knowing what she meant, so he grabbed her hand and they continued their little tour of the city. The two walked hand in hand by the beach, along the woods and meadows, soaked themselves in the warm sun, and dipped their feet in the cold lake water. They kissed passionately under the light of the silvery moon, which was the happiest moment of Zeke's life. They took Zig and Zag along, and together the four enjoyed the hayrides, the infamous corn maze, and the autumn festival. What made it interesting was that Zig, Zag, and Zoom were invisible to everyone but Zeke. The locals who knew him only saw him talking to himself or to invisible friends, laughing out loud at seemingly nothing, and thinking he had completely lost his mind.

"Isn't that Tartal boy a little old for imaginary playmates?" one mother questioned.

"That kid is two sammies short of a picnic," a passerby remarked.

"Maybe Lydia Copeland should take him to therapy along with Gael," Mrs. Kravitz, one of the more nosy neighbors, interjected.

This time, Zeke knew it wasn't just a dream. He was far too happy for it to be a dream, and if it were a dream, he never wanted to wake up. He didn't know how Zoom survived on Earth, nor where she stayed when she wasn't with him. He didn't dare to ask her as he didn't want to upset the cosmic forces that brought her to him. He didn't care much, either. One night he managed to sneak her into his room, and they spent the whole night looking up at the sky through his window. That was when he noticed the tattoo on her upper arm.

"Cool tattoo you have there."

"It's the Lyran symbol of solidarity. Any starseed would wear it proudly." She grinned at him. "You see the stars form the shape of a lyre or harp which gives the constellation its name. Vega here is its brightest star. Legend has it the god Apollo gave a magical lyre to Orpheus, a gifted Greek musician and poet. He played the most divine music ever heard. He eventually became crazed with grief over a lost love, and he aimlessly wandered the hills until he died. The Muses found him and buried him while Apollo placed his magical harp high in the sky… as Lyra."

"Dang, you just know everything, don't you?"

"I get lucky once in a while," she replied, winking at him.

"Wait a minute! Haven't I seen this symbol before — on the headpiece of the High Council Master?"

"My, my Zeke. You are quite a perceptive lad, aren't you?"

"I get lucky once in a while," he winked back at her, and they both laughed.

They had the fall romance of a lifetime, and that made Zeke feel like he had really grown up. It made him feel happy and complete. Then, he feared Zoom might leave again once the Fall Festival and Halloween were over. One evening, she invited him to meet her at the cemetery. He agreed, went there, and sat on a bench. Soon, he saw Zoom standing exactly where he had seen Nora.

He went up to her and asked, "Why did you bring me here, Zoom?"

She smiled and said, "Do you remember flying with Nora once in your dreams? Now that I'm here on Earth with you, I thought I should remind you of that dream and fulfill your wish to fly. Let me give you secret wings so we can fly together for a while."

She touched him on his back, and he instantly felt as light as a feather. All pure humans are made of light, and as a Lyran, she could manipulate that light. As his body lifted into the air, he felt as free as a bird. Zeke was so overwhelmed by the experience he forgot to ask her where they were heading.

Before he even realized it, they had reached the Lyran capital again, flew past the crystal gate, and entered the palace. Zoom took him to a special chamber, where he could see a dome right above his head. He had a smile on his face as he realized Zag wasn't just trying to rhyme when he said, "And the angels meet around the dome!" It was a message for him.

"Now, why did you bring me here?" he asked, as he was certain there was a very special reason behind it.

"There's a lesson for you to learn here, Ezekiel. Observe everything happening before you, and you'll know for yourself," she said with a mysterious smile and a twinkle in her eyes.

CHAPTER TWENTY-THREE
KARMIC RETRIBUTION

Zeke found himself inside the strange dome-shaped chamber along with Zoom. Like all other chambers in the Lyran Kingdom, this one didn't have doors or windows, either. People could just walk through walls like spirits. The chamber had many rows of seats set in circles around a huge golden throne like the one Zeke had seen in the chamber of the Lyran High Council. The throne was on a high platform, with two smaller thrones flanking the main throne.

"What is this place, Zoom?" he inquired again.

"Don't you remember? It's the Chamber of Reviews, Ezekiel." She smiled at him, and his memories returned in a flash. "You used to joke and call it the 'Chamber of Tears.'"

Within what seemed like only a minute in Earth time, all the rows were filled with men, women, and beings of all kinds from different parts of the galaxy, including Earth. He distinctly remembered the room's purpose now, as he recognized them as departed souls from the different planets where the beings of light lived. Then, the new council head appeared and took his seat. He was just as kind and distinguished as the former, albeit noticeably younger. It was obvious he had a good, long reign ahead of him. Two other council members followed and took their respective places on each side of him. They called out the names of each departed soul and read out the events of his or her lifetime on Earth.

It was like parent-teacher meetings during the school year or employees having annual performance reviews before their directors. There was no judgment of good or bad here. All Zeke saw was absolute compassion in the council head's eyes, yet every soul had tears in its eyes. No one said a single word as their deeds were read out.

There were thieves, liars, murderers, and good souls all in the same room, standing before the same throne. Soon, the whole chamber was flooded with "tears of repentance." Every soul cried upon its sins and begged for forgiveness until even the council head had tears in his eyes. Zeke was so moved that he was sobbing like a baby. He had heard of those intense Ayahuasca purging ceremonies in the Amazon jungle, but the word "intense" didn't even come close to describing the bleeding, draining, and exhausting experience he had just witnessed.

He came back to his senses only when Zoom pinched him hard. "I am going to tell you a secret, Ezekiel. It's something that only a few mortals know, and even fewer understand. Please be very selective with whom you share it," she whispered with a mysterious gleam in her eyes.

He felt an uncontrollable sense of intrigue. "What is it, Zoom? Tell me."

"All lightworkers go to their respective worlds with a divine mission, just like you did on Earth, and it's all mapped out in the world of the metaphysical. For our purposes, let's use the example of a coloring book. An attendant then walked up to her and handed her a large, soft-covered book with the letters 'ZT' on the front. "Actually, this is your coloring book, Ezekiel." They thumbed through it together. "Do you see an outline on every page?" she asked.

"Yes, of course."

"Good. Each page represents an important event in your life that was mapped out before you were born. If we look at these pages right now, then that is your progress up to this point. The colors or crayons represent your free will, meaning the decisions you make and the actions you take along the way. You're allowed to color the pages any way you like and with any color you choose because of that free will.

"You can color within the lines, color outside the lines, use bright colors, dull colors or simply not color at all, but the end result, the last page, will always be the same because of that outline. The way your book, or the story of your life, takes shape is up to you. There are happy pages and not-so-happy ones. We don't use the words good or bad in spirit because everything is just as it should be.

"Even a murder or a fatal accident is part of the divine plan, despite the fact it doesn't make sense to you or anyone else at the time. There's only one exception to this rule, and I want you now to meet someone who can explain it to you in a way you'll better understand. This is Eric, and he's a newly arrived soul. He recently took his own life. He wants to show you his coloring book."

Eric was a young boy sitting among others his age. He, too, was crying, but upon seeing Ezekiel, he just walked up to him and smiled. "Hello, Ezekiel. I'm Eric. I just love how you colored some of the pages in your book. You're so clever! I'm afraid I wasn't so clever. I became severely depressed in my earthly incarnation, and I chose to end my story early." He held out the coloring book of his life, showing it to Ezekiel.

"You'll see the pages of the last two-thirds of my book have been torn out. I was only seventeen when I took my life. I've been meeting with the Council of Elders, and they're mapping out a new plan with me as I must return to Earth and complete my mission. I thought I'd be off the hook ending my life, but I guess it's not that easy. Only this time — this time, I'll live under less trying conditions, lest it happens again. I can't believe it. They are sending me back to do it all over again! I have no choice in the matter."

After a brief sigh, Eric continued, "Will you do me a favor, Ezekiel? When you return, please tell people suicide is never the answer. It just restarts the cycle. I know sometimes people see no other choice, but please guide them. Show them there is always hope. Show them the light, will you? I deeply regret my actions now, leaving all the people I loved behind. I left them with so much pain and confusion — more than my own, in fact. I never, ever realized the damage I had the power to create, but I'll try to make things right in my next lifetime. I must go now. Goodbye, Ezekiel, and may you always stand in the Christ light."

Zeke was left overwhelmed by Eric's words. He had tears rolling down his face. He turned to Zoom. "Why would you bring me here, Zoom? All this pain, all these crying souls — why would you put the weight of their guilt on my shoulders?" He turned to the crying ones.

"And these beautiful souls, why would they commit such sins? Why do mortals lie, steal, and kill when all that does is make their souls cry? It just doesn't feel natural, or right. And Eric, that poor boy, why would he do something like take his own life? Life is so beautiful, Zoom. Why would he end it?"

"I know. People often find the burden of life too much to carry, and they try to escape or commit what you call crimes or sins. Remember their human lives are a way for them to learn and evolve. They have a veil on their memory of the light, just like you did, but souls always cry when they go against their inherent nature. Their souls are like guiding forces, always working to bring them back to the light. Some listen to their souls and learn their lessons faster, while others go more slowly. You need not worry for them, for all souls learn eventually.

"All pure souls return in time to the light, my love. We just need to be a little more patient with the ones who take longer. That's the reason lightworkers like you need to incarnate on Earth and in countless other worlds where these beings of light make their home — to spread the love you have within you and to help them learn to listen to the voice of their souls, to help them understand the laws of karma."

He smiled in agreement. Just then, he saw a man sitting a little farther from the rest. He was the only person who did not look up at anyone, but just hung his head in shame as he kept looking down and appeared to be weeping. He thought this man was oddly familiar, like he had seen him somewhere before. Right then, the man raised his head for a moment, leaving Zeke utterly shocked. He was absolutely stunned to see the man was none other than Nigel Copeland, Kai and Gael's father! *Why is he among the departed souls? Isn't he supposed to be alive?* His heart raced out of control.

Mr. Copeland was crying uncontrollably. He deeply regretted his deeds and begged for a second chance in front of the council head. When he saw Zeke standing in front of him, he simply looked at the young man he had once known and uttered, "I'm sorry," with tears running down his cheeks. Then he hung his head in shame again. The dream ended right there.

• • •

Zeke could still feel Nigel's apology ringing in his ears when he woke up the next morning. It was like a never-ending echo. He was back on Earth now, tucked safely in his bed, with no trace of Zig,

Zag, or Zoom anywhere. He kept his vision of the Review Chamber to himself and went about the day as usual. If things were to go according to plan, Kai would be leaving for Boston early next year. Gael and Zeke were spending as much time with him as they could. The Farley Street kids had been through so much together. A small change in anyone's life had a ripple effect on all the others, changing the dynamic of the entire neighborhood.

Later that afternoon, the three boys sat silently on a bench near Lakeview Cemetery, thinking about the old days while also trying to come to terms with their changing realities at the same time. That's when they saw Leia running toward them.

"Kai, Gael…" she managed to say before stopping to catch her breath.

"Leia, what's wrong? Are you okay?" Gael asked her.

She looked up at him, and all she could bring herself to say was, "Your dad… he's home, and he can't walk. He's paralyzed!"

It took both Gael and Kai a few seconds to process the news. Gael was so stunned he couldn't move. Zeke immediately remembered the dream he had the night before. He had no idea what was going on, but he knew it was something horrible. Leia and Zeke helped the brothers snap out of the initial shock and took them back home. There was an ambulette parked outside the Copeland's house. The yard was crammed with people as the whole neighborhood gathered to see what had happened. Naturally, Mrs. Kravitz was peeking through her window taking it all in.

Watching all of this, Zeke was afraid his worst fear might have come true, but as they reached the front door, he saw that Mr. Copeland was very much alive. A male tech was offloading him in a wheelchair while another one briefed Mrs. Copeland about his condition. He had been in a terrible car accident a few weeks prior while on a diving holiday in Belize and had been in a coma. His partner, the woman he lived with, died on the spot.

He, however, survived the accident, but his spine was severely damaged. He couldn't speak and was paralyzed from the neck down. The doctors said he would probably be in a wheelchair the rest of his life. Looking at him reminded Zeke of Nora's tragic accident from all those years ago, and that thought sent chills immediately down his spine.

Gael was the one who felt most affected. He was filled with rage and sadness, but above all else, confusion. He had no intention of caring for a man he blamed for everything wrong with his childhood and the death of his sister. This man before him sitting in a wheelchair pushed him towards a miserable life. It was because of this man he had abandonment issues. It was because of this man he was forced to grow up too soon, and it was because of this man he believes he became bipolar. Kai had already decided to leave home, and his father's return had no effect on his plans. Despite his condition, Gael had nothing but contempt to offer his father. He was in no mood to forgive or forget.

"Serves him right," he concluded, trying desperately to convince himself of his own words.

It was now apparent that Zeke needed to step up for his friend, to help him understand the significance of actions and deeds and the true meaning of forgiveness. Just as words are extremely important for the world, so are actions and deeds. Now Zeke had to prove himself through his deeds. He didn't want Gael to feel broken or be consumed by hate. He couldn't let his friend shy away from his past or from his responsibilities to his father, either. He had to help him face both.

• • •

The next morning, Zeke visited Gael and asked him to go on a walk. As they strolled along the breezy morning beach, Zeke began his efforts to help his friend.

"You know Gael," he said. "Everyone creates his or her destiny by thoughts, words, and actions. You remember all those sayings we used to hear as kids: 'You make your bed, you lie in it,' and 'What goes around, comes around.'"

"Yeah, yeah. Blah blah blah. Looks like Papasan is reaping his just deserts," Gael blurted, just staring straight ahead.

"They're more than just words, Gael. We often fail to understand whatever we do to others always comes back to us in stranger ways than we could ever think of. That's the spiritual law of cause and effect that we humans like to call karma. Didn't you notice what happened in your life? What your father did to you was his karma. His misdeeds came back to haunt him in ways he never expected. You had no part to play in it, and you had no control over it. It was karmic retribution, and it happened because he needed to face everything he did. It was a lesson his soul chose to teach him." He looked straight into Gael's eyes to ensure he was paying attention.

"Why are you telling me all this?" Gael asked, frustrated and agitated.

"Because now that his part is done, it's your turn, Gael. You have two clear choices here. You can either choose to forgive him and help a vulnerable man incapable of taking care of himself, who also happens to be your father and you know in your heart is the right thing to do, or you can avenge his actions towards you and give him what you think he deserves – the pain and suffering you received from him, the sorrow you endured due to his actions.

"I know the first option appears extremely difficult, and the latter seems ideal in this moment, but trust me, Gael, what you choose to do with the situation from now on will create *your* karma.

You won't have any control over it, and neither will your father." Zeke had an air about him that made him sound like a prophet.

Gael was left speechless for a while. His mind was still trying to process Zeke's logic and the power of his words. He looked at him wide-eyed and asked, "What am I supposed to do then? You sound like you have it all figured out. Help me, Zeke. Guide me through this. Will you show me how to be a real man for once?"

Zeke smiled at him lovingly, making him realize that he wasn't alone. The light in his smile and the compassion in his voice had a hypnotic charm. "Take a step back from all of this and look at the bigger picture. In a way, your father has been your greatest teacher. When you look at him, you don't like what you see in front of you, do you? Then think about it! Why would you turn into something you don't like in the first place? He was selfish, and you hated it.

"The first lesson you learned was not to be a selfish man like him. Isn't that true? He ran from his familial duties, and you hated that. The next lesson you learned from him was to never run away from your responsibilities, right? You never liked anything about him. There's such a simple lesson in that. Don't turn into him, Gael. Don't be like him. I'm not trying to scare you, but similar actions always bring about similar consequences. Would you like to invite the same consequences he did? Would you choose to do the same things he did to you, even after you hated them so much?"

His words were like magic, and Gael was pushed to think way deeper than he ever had before. He couldn't deny Zeke's wisdom for a second.

"So, what do you want me to do? Do you want me to forgive him?" Gael finally asked.

"If you really want an answer from me, I'd say yes."

"But how, Zeke, how?"

"As difficult as it might sound now, I would still say grant him forgiveness even if he doesn't ask for it. There's no virtue bigger than forgiveness, Gael. The most important law of karma is the Law of Forgiveness. Karma is like this complex and simple concept all at the same time." He noticed how confused Gael was, so he explained further. "Many times, we try sowing a seed, and we water it every day. Yet it never grows. We don't reap anything, good or bad, out of the seed we sow. Then we grow impatient, thinking our actions aren't showing any results.

"But when a seed is sown, many factors need to work together in its favor. We can't be ignorant of those and just sit and wait for them to bear fruit. We need to check the quality of the seed before we plant it. We need to increase the fertility of the soil while we plant it, and we need to wait for the right weather for it to grow after we plant it. We have to be patient and observant at the same time, so those other factors can be aligned. Do you understand that?"

"I suppose so." Gael was trying hard to understand what Zeke was saying. After all, his words had a power that demanded attention.

"The same goes for all spiritual laws. Karma can seem tricky because it isn't always operating on its own. It's interwoven with other spiritual laws. Then again, it is quite simple to understand because the Law of Karma says we only need to correct ourselves and nobody else. All we have to do is monitor or keep a watch over our own thoughts, words, and actions. Every time we consciously try to correct those little mistakes we tend to make, we create good karma for ourselves. Every little correction goes a long way, and we start reaping the benefits before we know it."

Zeke's words slowly started hitting their mark. "When we do all that, the other spiritual laws, just like the other factors while sowing a seed, automatically fall in place and begin to align things for us. Bad karma is nothing but the negative patterns and habits we tend to create within us that manifest as external consequences. They keep coming back as triggers in our lives, to show us where we have created those incorrect patterns, but the same triggers also give us the opportunity to correct those patterns, too."

Zeke went on in a flow, and Gael listened carefully. "If you choose to do to your father what he did to you, you'll create the same pattern and thus see the same results until you choose to change it. Don't you think it's wiser for you to break that pattern forever, here and now, before it even begins?"

"But forgiveness needs to come from within, Zeke. I can understand all you say about 'karma' and the logic behind it, but I just can't feel it in my heart. How can I forgive him when I feel like I shouldn't?" His question was quite honest and simple.

"Forgiveness isn't half as difficult as you think, Gael. As I said, you just need to see the bigger picture. What if he is deeply repenting of all his actions and deeds? Won't you regret not being able to forgive him sometime later in life, then? Ask this of yourself right now," he tried reasoning with him.

"No. I don't think I'll ever regret not forgiving a man like him." Gael was very clear about it.

"Okay then. Let me show you something. Find a position that's comfortable for you. Relax, then take a deep breath and close your eyes. Now try to see your father asking for forgiveness and see yourself doing whatever you wish to do with him."

Zeke began guiding Gael through a visualization exercise, one of the most powerful forms of meditation, and Gael religiously followed each of his instructions. He saw his father sitting in front of him. He could feel all the anger he had felt for him all his life. In his vision, he made scathing accusations against his father and was as unforgiving of all his actions and misdeeds as he had always wished. Gael's hatred towards him was so obvious that he didn't even have to try very hard. Strangely enough, in his vision, he didn't see his father reacting the way he used to earlier in life. He didn't express any anger towards his son, but looked at him rather lovingly and apologetically. He had tears in his eyes as he sat in front of Gael, asking for forgiveness with his hands folded. He hung his head in shame.

When Gael's eyes met his, his father said, "I'm sorry."

Gael shared his vision with Zeke, who had a mysterious smile on his face. It was the power of Zeke's light that had created that beautiful sight. Gael didn't know this was the exact vision Zeke had about his father, too, just the night before. He knew it wasn't only a vision but a link between souls that didn't need a language. He didn't say anything about his own dream to Gael. He just continued to guide him through his vision.

"Now release this vision and think of yourself ten years later. You are sitting alone and looking back at your past. You are thinking of what you did to your father today. How do you feel?"

Gael began the journey of looking at his future and didn't even realize tears of repentance had begun falling from his eyes and soaking the earth. When Zeke's voice finally guided him out of the vision, Gael came out of it feeling peace and calm. He felt no anger towards his father anymore. All the pent-up negative emotions were released. He felt absolute love, empathy, and compassion for the weak man who was already reaping the fruits of his misdeeds and the repenting of his actions.

Gael felt a sudden sense of positivity and joy flowing through his entire body. He was clear about what he needed to do. He decided then and there to forgive his father and help him through his difficult times by taking care of him and not running away from his responsibilities.

Zeke was extremely happy to see his first success as a lightworker. He was able to plant that first seed of light within Gael. Now he also wanted him to heal further. He now had use of 'Ho'oponopono,' the magical forgiveness ritual, and felt it was the right time for him to share it with his friend. Gael was a good listener and a fast learner.

Every morning he went to the beach, and there while breathing in the fresh morning air, he practiced this secret healing ritual, visualizing and feeling the four simple sentences – I am sorry. Please forgive me. Thank you. I love you. Slowly and steadily, he could see his life-changing magically. He felt calm and positive now. The depression and bipolar disorder that used to affect him so much earlier were gradually disappearing. He was happy most of the time and felt no remorse as he was saved from committing a grave spiritual mistake. More than words, it was Zeke's guiding light that healed him.

Then, soon after, Gael's yard work picked up so much that he had to hire another boy to help with the load, and that afforded him some additional cash. Meanwhile, his mother received her much-awaited pay raise, too. As a result, most of their financial debts were cleared. All of this happened within less than two months of forgiving his father, taking responsibility for his actions, releasing unhealthy attachments, and sincerely practicing the forgiveness ritual.

"As within, so without," Zeke said when Gael happily told him all of this. He had changed his friend's life simply by guiding him, and Gael would never forget that. He grew as a person, and he became Zeke's first success, but that was not the end for Zeke Tartal. His days of healing had only just begun.

CHAPTER TWENTY-FOUR
THE END OF FEAR

Zeke was slowly turning into a guide, a hero. He realized being a hero, though, wasn't about acquiring supernatural physical powers or saving the world from some great big monster. Being a hero meant changing the world around him, one person at a time, by helping others kill the monsters on the inside and hearing the voices of their souls through his healing touch.

His first tool, the magical power of words, had helped him bring a change in a dear friend's life. Now, he was ready to learn more. He was looking forward to more cosmic experiences and guidance from his friends, Zig, Zag, and Zoom. He waited anxiously to collect more of their wisdom and to use it. Yet, there was some sadness in him, too. Zoom's sudden departure had left him feeling upset. Christmas was fast approaching, and he was slowly accepting the fact that his birthday fell on Christmas Day, and to be that closely aligned with Jesus Christ (a hero of the highest order) was something to be shared and celebrated after all.

It had been a good year for him, one of joy and plenty, which made him believe that it was God's way of telling him to prepare for something great that was about to come. His heart was growing fuller as his secret wishes were being fulfilled. Christmas Eve finally rolled around, and Kai was planning to leave for Boston early next year.

This was going to be his last Christmas spent on Farley Street, so Kai threw himself a party at home, inviting all his friends and a few close neighbors like the Tartals. Ben came straight from his garage, where he now lived almost all the time. It felt like a reunion for the whole neighborhood after a very long time. It brought back many memories, and with those memories, came pain.

Being there made Zeke feel a strange heaviness in his chest. He had started to believe that he had gotten over the pain of Nora's death, but being there at that party brought back all those memories. The whole house had been lit with colorful and festive lights, inside and out. Amid the celebrations, he suddenly saw her. It was Zoom. He saw her through the window, standing in the snow-covered backyard, smiling at him in a beautiful, long fur coat. She had Zig and Zag sitting on her shoulders. He was delighted to see her again and ran towards the back door to sneak outside.

"Zoom, I… you're here! I can't believe you're here."

"I came to wish you a merry Christmas, a very happy birthday, and to promise you a magical new year, Zeke. I can't stay for long, but I'll be back soon," she whispered, and literally vanished before he could say anything, leaving him confused but still happy.

He was glad to see Zoom back on Earth. It left him so unbelievably optimistic that he became fully present at the party and paid close attention to both Gael and Kai, who had been trying to get him to open up for a while. The next few hours were the happiest time the residents of Farley Street had spent together in years.

As they all laughed and reminisced, Lydia suggested they revisit Boyne Mountain Resort for purposes of closure. She knew it was a place that was linked with everyone's trauma, and she wanted both families to heal, especially her sons. Though Ben and Audrey were originally hesitant, they agreed to the idea after Lydia talked to them in detail, and so the plans were made.

Zeke had gained enough knowledge to look past the ordinary. He knew meeting Zoom was no mere occurrence; a higher force was at work. He knew nothing could be left unfinished in his life, not even unresolved emotions. He knew that before he could begin his mission of dealing with the pain of others, he had to resolve his own past wounds.

The next few days at Boyne Mountain were an overwhelming experience for everyone. Mr. Copeland had a breakdown. He cried uncontrollably, and although he could not say a single word, Zeke knew exactly what he was feeling. He was the only one who knew that this helpless man's tears were tears of repentance and grief.

Lydia made every attempt to make Kai understand there was still a place for him at home. She made a push for him to stay, but it was no use. He had made up his mind. He told her that he was thankful and would always remain thankful for all she had done, but he simply couldn't grow as a person if he stayed in Mackinaw. He explained to her that this was the only way he could accept his pain and move on, and she listened.

In the end, she gave him her blessing and accepted that she couldn't hold him back. Gael had a similar emotional experience. Thanks to Zeke, he learned to let go of his pain and his anger. He had evolved as a person, and returning to the place where his life began to fall apart helped him find pieces of himself. He had been slowly putting himself back together for years, and now at the resort, he reconnected with his father. He helped and cared for him, and in doing so, he learned to let go of everything.

It was a time of growth for the Tartal children, too. Maya was still in her own cocoon, and her aloofness concerned Zeke. He tried to talk to her, and in many ways, he did help her to understand that life wasn't like the fantasies in which she had chosen to live. But eventually, it was Leia who got through to her. Despite being twins, the sisters had never really been terribly close, but they understood each other.

It was the most overwhelming experience for Zeke. Every minute at Boyne reminded him of the last days he had spent with Nora. Those memories were bringing up emotions he thought he was done with. As the new year came around, everybody was back in the mood to party — everyone except Zeke, that is. That place made him relive his most traumatic memories, and it gave rise to a deep-rooted fear he had carried for years — the fear of losing the people he loved, the fear of death, and the fear of having to face another dark year ahead. Gael and Kai had to constantly force him to come out of his room, but he just wanted to run away from everything, especially the party.

Eventually, they all gathered for the New Year's gala at the same hall where he had seen Nora for the last time. That was when he saw her. Zoom was there, and she was smiling at him. He was stunned to see her dressed in the same beautiful evening gown Nora had worn the night of her death. She had an ethereal smile on her face, and her skin glowed with a divine aura. She mouthed, "I love you," blew him a kiss, and waved goodbye. Then she vanished into thin air. Zeke just stood there, stunned.

After a short while, his mind began to play tricks on him. Like Nora, he heard voices that told him she was gone for good. She had also suddenly disappeared just like Nora, and just like Nora, she would never return. Zeke's fear closed in on him as he felt his heart beating faster. He couldn't feel the air in his lungs, and a constant voice was telling him that he would lose Zoom just like he had lost Nora. He looked for her in every corner of the ballroom. He ran out of the hall and began searching for her all over the resort, but there was no sign of her.

"If I never see Zoom again, even if this is the end of our love in this life, I will meet her again in another. Ezekiel and Ezra will always meet again," he affirmed. Zeke understood the power of his own light, and thus, fear had no place in his heart.

As he rose from the shadows of his fear, he felt a hand on his shoulder, and with it came a feeling of relief. As he turned around, she stood there, lovelier than ever, with a smile on her face.

"Hi!"

"Zoom! Where have you… why on earth would you do something like that? That was NOT funny. Do you have any idea how painful that was for me?" He was furious.

"It wasn't pain, but fear. This was a test, my love, a trial of courage. You cannot be gripped by the fear of death forever. To be a true lightworker, you must transcend all fears and be free — and this test proved that." She had such a calming smile. It eased and erased all his anger. "You had to face the worst of your fears, Ezekiel. You had to come to terms with the inevitability of death once and for all, and now you have passed your trial, but there will be others."

"Others?" he tried to ask, but she cut him off.

"That is for another time. For now, let us live in this moment of joy. Let us make memories to celebrate your triumph."

And so, they sneaked out of the party, found an empty banquet room and danced all night, away from the eyes of all. They held each other's hands and were lost in each other's eyes. At the break of dawn, they found themselves walking on the same snowmobile trail where Nora had died, and together they watched the year's first sunrise as light began to rise on the horizon.

"You know, Zoom, I'm okay with all of it now. My fear of death is gone forever, and this awesome sunrise confirms it. The cycle of life continues whether we want it to or not."

She held his hands and said, "I had promised you a magical New Year, Zeke, and I have kept my promise. You know I must leave now."

"Will I ever see you again, Cinderella?" he relented with sad, moist eyes. "Or will I spend eternity chasing after you?"

"Yes, of course! How can I live without seeing you? We are eternally together, you and I," she softly spoke.

"No, Zoom, I mean, will you ever return in this life?"

"This time, my love, it's *your* turn to come and find me," she smiled with a playful gleam in her eye.

"See what I mean about chasing after you? Where… and how will I find you?" he asked, looking deep into her eyes.

"In the land where the rivers flow and the floodgates are opened. Where the body never dies, and the dead can walk. Where the sun travels towards the timeless through the sky. Wait for me, and I'll see you there."

"How am I supposed to know what that means?" He held her hands, trying his best to hide his anxiousness behind a strong face.

"Fear not. We are the lion people. We are warriors. We are eternal, and we always have been. Just remember who you are, who *we* are, and you'll find the way." She smiled at him one last time, then she disappeared.

CHAPTER TWENTY-FIVE
The Letter

The new year had brought with it the message of a brand-new life waiting for Zeke. All the hurts, fears, cares, and worries of his past had been erased. It was the promise of a new beginning, but he wasn't yet told what this beginning would mean. The words Zoom had left him with continued to haunt his mind.

"The rivers flow. Floodgates open." He kept repeating them over and over. "The body never dies. The dead can walk." Her words were like a puzzle, one that demanded his every thought. "The sun travels towards the timeless through the sky."

It was a riddle he needed to solve if he ever wanted to see her again. Every second of every day, he became obsessed with her words. Her riddle was all he could think of. One afternoon, as he was lying on the grass in his backyard, he found himself thinking about his old nanny, Mrs. Braganza.

"I wonder how she's doing now. Is she happy with her family in Portugal, or is she sad and lonely… like me? Is there anyone left to take care of her?" Once again, the thought of death filled his mind. *"Is she even alive?"* She was already so old when she left, and it had been a couple of years since she did. He suddenly realized even his

mother felt lonelier after she left. During the time when she was at Tartal House, she and Audrey would bake a special, colorful Bolo Rei (King's Cake) for him together every year on his birthday. They were friends and Zeke thought about how much his mother must miss her friend.

"Coconut must miss her, too," he thought. Coco had become accustomed to her. Back in the day, she was his favorite member of the Tartal family, and the two had a very strong bond. After she left, he must have felt separated from his mother.

"Do dogs feel the same kind of pain that humans do?" he asked Coco, and naturally, got no response.

A year ago, he was about to enter the ninth grade, just stepping into high school, when he met Zoom for the first time. This year, everything seems to have changed. She was gone, Kai would be gone soon, and Gael was too busy with his yard jobs and taking care of his father. It was like Zeke had slipped everyone's mind entirely, and as enlightened as he was, it still bothered him.

His friends had moved on. Zig, Zag, and Zoom were on sabbatical, probably with no plans of reappearing for a while. His earthly friends were too busy with their own lives, and so were his siblings. He couldn't even feel the presence of his spirit guides anymore. His father hadn't been a part of his life for some time now, and even his mother who had been his greatest support, now seemed detached from everything around her. It was as if everybody had turned away, everybody had left. It was something he had never experienced before, and he, of course, had no idea how to deal with it.

This new feeling of having to walk all alone was unsettling and unnerving for him. It felt like he was constantly waiting for something to happen — something like a new job, a new place, or a new purpose to ring in the next phase of his life. It was as if he was in a void, waiting for something new to be born, something more tangible, something he could connect with. He knew this was also an important part of the journey. He needed to walk alone for a while to explore life on his own, without the physical, mental, emotional, or even spiritual support of others.

He worked harder than ever to get good grades. He had been an average student all through elementary and middle school, but as he entered high school, he began realizing the importance of his studies. He fared quite well in ninth grade, and the next three years were crucial, after which he would be out of high school and would begin a new journey towards higher education, like Kai. Zeke already knew he was destined for bigger things. He was supposed to be a guide, but he understood that he had to live a normal, human life, too. So he focused on his studies to evolve not only as a lightworker but also as a human being.

"Floodgates are opened, and the dead can walk. The sun travels towards the timeless. Where could such a land be? Is it supposed to be here on Earth or somewhere else in the galaxy?" He kept asking himself how he could solve the riddle. He kept thinking hard with every ounce of his wisdom and skill. His life became an endless circle of school life, home life, and thinking about the puzzle. He would walk around town every day, thinking about Zoom's words, completely lost in thought.

One evening, while he was out for a stroll, he unknowingly began walking towards his favorite store, Indigo Children. It was probably the only place that could make him feel at home for a while. A fearless black cat accompanied him most of the way. As he approached the store, a sudden gust of wind came out of nowhere on the otherwise windless night. It was so strong he had to close his eyes to prevent sand and dust from getting in them. When he finally opened them, he saw the wind bringing with it a strange piece of paper.

It came flying towards him and fell to the ground, right in front of his feet. He bent down to pick it up but realized it wasn't a normal piece of paper. It seemed ancient and felt almost like a leaf when he touched it. It was torn and extremely delicate. It had a lot of scribbling on it in a language he couldn't read.

He stood there for a while, thinking if he should keep it or let it fly in the wind. Suddenly an idea struck him. He could take it to the storekeeper and ask him if it was something that flew out of the store. *"It might be a page from some ancient scripture."* Feeling excited about the prospect, he rushed to the door just minutes before closing time.

Noah Leitner, the storekeeper, loved Zeke. The boy had been visiting the store since childhood after all, ever since he had first discovered the store name and its intriguing sign. The old man had been witnessing weird things happening around Zeke for years. He had also been a crucial part of his evolution and an important helper on his journey as a lightworker.

Zeke went straight inside and asked him, "Do you recognize this piece of paper, Mr. Leitner? Is it from one of the books in your store?"

Noah looked at the paper from every angle and declared it wasn't.

"Could you at least give me an idea about what it might be?" he then asked.

Noah smiled at him and asked, "Where did you find it? This is a very rare find, kid. It's papyrus."

"What's papyrus?" Zeke wanted to know more about it.

Noah brought an old oak chest out of a cabinet hidden inside one of the walls. It looked more like a treasure trove and had a lock on it. He took a small key out of his pocket and opened it. Inside the box, there was a very old portfolio filled with papyrus. He handed it to Zeke and asked him to feel it.

"This is an ancient collection I have, and it's made of papyrus. The modern word for paper was derived from this writing material, my boy. Papyrus was a great gift of the River Nile to ancient humans. It was prepared from the pithy stem of a water plant with the same name, a reed which grows in the marshy areas around the river."

"Can you read what's written on it?"

Zeke knew Noah had immense knowledge of languages and scriptures. Noah smiled at him and took the piece of papyrus in his hands. It looked like a letter someone had written in ancient times. The ink had almost faded. He managed to read the crux of the letter and then explained it to Zeke. It was a letter written by a woman to her husband. She had mentioned the reason she needed to go to war and how much she loved him. She had also mentioned she would return to him once she had accomplished her goal. She didn't mention what her mission was exactly or what her name was, but she had ended the letter addressing herself as "the one who loves Ma'at."

"Ma'at? Do you know what that means?" Zeke inquired.

"Ma'at was revered and worshiped by ancient Egyptians as the Goddess of Truth, Justice, Balance, and Order. She represented the concept of how the universe was maintained."

"And 'the one who loves Ma'at,' is that that supposed to be some kind of title? What can you tell me about that?" he inquired again.

Noah tried to think, but he couldn't seem to remember who the woman that loved Ma'at could be. He finally handed the letter back to Zeke.

"I don't think I remember any god, goddess or being in Egyptian mythology who was referred to as the 'the one who loves Ma'at,' but I do know a lot about the gods themselves. I'd be happy to tell you some of their stories." So, Noah told him about the gods of Egypt, and Zeke listened with his natural curiosity.

He went back home thinking about it. As he walked back, he also kept thinking about all that he had learned about Egypt from Noah. He loved the stories of Ma'at, her father Ra, her husband Thoth, and their children. He felt an instant and deep connection with that ancient land and all the gods and goddesses. Every single one of those stories felt familiar, but the papyrus he held in his hand felt almost alive.

"Someone must've written it with so much love in her heart for her husband," he thought. He could almost feel the emotions running through the letter, and he so wished he could read and understand every word of it as if someone had written the letter for him and the wind was just a messenger. *"Who could this mystery woman be, who wrote such a loving letter to her husband before going to war?"* He was instantly reminded of Zoom, his galactic warrior princess. *"She must have gone to the battlefield many times, too, like Ezra of Vega, and must have left such letters for him, for Ezekiel, whenever they parted ways."*

His memories were still clouded, but her words ruled his mind. He picked up the letter again. A beautiful fragrance rose from it. He could almost smell Zoom's scent on the letter. The longing for his beloved increased like never before. He wanted to see her again, and for that, he had to find the land of the rivers.

CHAPTER TWENTY-SIX

PUZZLE PIECES

Zeke returned home lost in his thoughts. He held the papyrus for hours and thought about the letter. At the break of dawn, he left his bed still feeling restless. There was something bothering him, something he had missed that his mind was unconsciously trying to recollect. He finished his morning chores, checked on his mother as usual, and went off to school. When he returned, he was still thinking of the letter. As soon as he got home, he ran to his room and picked up the letter again.

He brought it to the porch, sat there, and stared at it like he was trying to decipher every alphabet letter written on it. He smelled it again, desperately trying to find a deeper meaning to the message it held.

"Didn't Mr. Leitner say papyrus was a gift from the River Nile?" thinking out loud. "The river… the river that flows and floods. Wait. Yes, that's it."

He felt one step closer to solving the puzzle. He couldn't wait to run back to Mr. Leitner and ask him everything he needed to know about the source of the letter. He ran and ran towards Indigo Children. When he finally reached the store, all he found was a huge lock on the door and a sign that read, "WE ARE CLOSED. N. Leitner."

Noah hadn't mentioned anything about closing his shop that evening. Zeke checked with the neighboring merchants and learned that Noah had left for his hometown because of something urgent. He wasn't going to be back for at least a month. Zeke felt hopeless and angry with frustration. He couldn't wait for an entire month. He went back home that evening disheartened. He patiently carried on with school, his chores, and his frustrating life.

Meanwhile, Kai was waiting for his friend's cousin's approval to go and live with him in Boston. He waited for a while, but neither his cousin nor the friend turned up with any news. He became so desperate that one day he just left without telling anyone. He didn't wish to face his friends or his family. He couldn't handle the weight of goodbyes. The fear of failure was so strong, he simply vanished, leaving just a note that read:

> I'm leaving for Boston, and I'll come back only after I graduate from Harvard. I don't know how I'm going to do it, but I'm doing it.
> Blessings on all of you,
>
> Kai Copeland.

Kai's mother couldn't do anything to help her son, and his paralyzed father was visibly heartbroken. No one had expected such a desperate move from Kai of all people. He had always been such a calm and mature boy. Nevertheless, his actions showed Zeke how valuable and important patience was.

Every event in his life taught him something new, preparing him for something bigger. For some strange reason, Ben had started staying at home even longer than usual, and Audrey seemed to be feeling a little better health-wise. They had started spending more time together. It was a bit odd for Zeke to believe his father, who hadn't really cared for his mother for so long, had changed suddenly, but he was happy for her. He only prayed this would help her heal.

Kai's departure created a void in the neighborhood. Zeke also began noticing a subtle change in Maya's life. She began spending less and less time at home. She was only twelve. *"Where does she go?"* He began to feel terribly uncomfortable with that situation but chose to put it on the back burner for the time being.

The days flew by without him even realizing how fast they went. He still had to learn the lesson of patience. He religiously kept going back to Indigo Children every evening to check if Mr. Leitner had returned. Finally, it was Valentine's Day, and the youth of the city was all in the mood for romance. As affection was publicly on display all around, his young heart longed to see Zoom again. That evening, he saw the bright blue light flooding the road again. The store was open — and so was Zeke's mind.

He was so happy that he almost ran into a moving car as he approached the door. When he entered, he found Noah standing on a ladder rearranging some items, only the mysterious smile he always had on his face was missing.

"Where have you been all this time, Mister L? I've been waiting for you!" he shouted in joy.

Noah turned around and looked at him. His face immediately lit up as soon as he saw Zeke. He gave the boy a warm hug. "I came back just for you," he chuckled.

"Well, I'm glad to see you again! I have a question for you. I've been waiting to ask you this since the time we last met." He was all excited to finally be able to ask all the questions he had in his mind. Noah smiled and nodded. He was all ears.

"You told me last month that papyrus was a gift from the River Nile. Tell me, did the Nile ever flood, and was Egypt called the land where the rivers flow?" As he felt closer to solving the riddle, the excitement in his voice was uncontainable. Of course, he could have looked for all the answers on the internet, but he needed to be sure, and only Noah could give him straight answers.

"Oh, yes. The yearly floods of the River Nile have been famous since ancient times, and the Nile has multiple tributaries, so yes, Egypt is called the land of the rivers."

"That's perfect. Tell me all you know about the floods, please."

Zeke had wanted to know about the ancient Egyptian civilization from the moment he touched the papyrus. He knew he had a connection with that wonderful land. He could almost see the Egyptian landscape through the eyes and words of Mr. Leitner as he described the significance of the floods to him. "Could Egypt be a place where nobody ever died?" he wondered, needing to put every piece of the puzzle together.

"You seem to know a lot about this place, kid. Where did you hear about it? Did you watch a movie or something?"

Zeke shrugged his shoulders. "Just askin'"

Noah gave him a skeptical look for a second, but then continued once he realized Zeke was seriously interested in the subject but trying to play it cool. "Osiris, one of Egypt's most important deities, was considered the god of the underworld or afterlife. According to ancient Egyptian mythology, 'the Duat' or the realm of the dead was where all souls went after they die."

"Cool, and what about the dead walking, were the dead ever supposed to walk in any story from Egypt?" he suddenly interrupted him.

Noah happily replied, "The underworld was where the other gods resided along with Osiris. It had a single entrance. One could reach it only by traveling through the tomb of the dead. Whether an Egyptian pharaoh or a poor peasant, all wanted to enjoy a happy afterlife in this underworld. The Egyptians knew that the best way to preserve a body was to mummify it, so after their deaths, the pharaohs of Egypt were mummified and buried in elaborate tombs. The dry heat of the desert mummified their bodies, and then they were buried in graves with trinkets, toys, and other precious things they wanted to have with them in the afterlife. You're right in a way when you say no one died, and even the dead could walk in Egypt."

Noah had answered two of his questions, and Zeke knew he was closer to than ever to solving the puzzle.

"I've one last question for you now, and I hope this isn't, like, bothering you or anything." He was clearly feeling more comfortable with Noah now, and he wanted him to feel relaxed, too. "Could you please tell me what the role of the goddess Ma'at's father, the sun god, was in ancient Egyptian civilization? Did the Egyptians believe the sun traveled timeless through the sky?" He needed to put a few more pieces together to decipher Zoom's message.

"Ancient Egyptians worshiped the sun as Father God, the giver of life. They considered him the one who created the universe at the beginning of time. Does that answer your question about the sun traveling toward the timeless, kid? They called him Ra or Re, who controlled the ripening of crops. He was central to the idea of royalty and kingship in Egypt. Ra played a very crucial role in their lives, representing warmth, light, and growth. He existed beyond time and was thus timeless, traveling through the sky each day to face the darkness each night," he concluded with a smile.

With most pieces of the puzzle solved, Zeke was now sure of the land Zoom had indicated through her riddle, through all the clues she had left for him to find her – it was the mystical and ever-mysterious land of Egypt! This, too, had been a test, a trial of his resolve, of his patience, and now he was one step closer to completing it. He was lost in thought and was about to leave the store when Noah called him and asked him to wait for a while. He took a book down from one of the shelves and handed it over to him.

"This book has all the little stories you need to know about the magical land of Egypt. You won't find any of these online. This is the book from where all these stories came. Take it home with you. I'm sure you'll love reading it." Zeke was happy to purchase the book and was about to pay for it when the old man stopped him. "This is a small gift from me to you on this special day of love. Happy Valentine's Day, kid."

CHAPTER TWENTY-SEVEN
The Underworld

Zeke was so happy that evening that he unknowingly overlooked the sadness he saw in Noah's eyes. He couldn't contain his excitement over solving Zoom's riddle and learning that the place she wanted him to find was on Earth. It was only later, once his enthusiasm dialed down, that he realized what that meant.

Egypt wasn't anywhere close to where he lived – little Emmet County at the tip of the Lower Peninsula in Michigan. It was a different part of the world, making it almost impossible for him to be there anytime soon. He had never traveled anywhere outside the state, let alone the country. He couldn't even imagine going to Egypt. Even if he did, how would he find her... and where? His cosmic friends Zig and Zag weren't around to help him find her, either. There were more serious issues he needed to deal with now. His mother wasn't well, and he had been looking after her for months trying to nurse her back to health. He also needed to study hard so he could maintain good grades in school.

Once again, he was reminded of the test of patience. He knew that this was probably the reason he had been taught that much-needed lesson at the beginning of the year. He figured he needed to know much more about Egypt and its connection to his mission before he could physically go there. He also realized that the test of patience was also a test of faith – faith in the unknown, and faith in the divine timing of the universe. He needed to trust that the universe would guide him back to his beloved when they were meant to be together.

After he came back home with the book that night, he began reading all the stories about that unknown land. He read all the little details Mr. Leitner had left out. He read all about ancient Egyptian civilization, its culture, its rituals, and its deities. Those stories helped him slowly tie up the loose ends of the puzzle.

Zeke already knew Zoom was referring to the underworld and the afterlife when she told him to look for the land "where the dead can walk." She had specifically meant the mummified bodies of Egypt when she said, "the body never dies in this land." While reading about Ra's journey in a boat for millions of years, he clearly understood why she stated, "the sun travels towards the timeless," for Ra himself, was the sun.

While reading the fascinating Egyptian myths, he fell asleep. He had a very strange dream that night. In it, he saw Mr. Leitner sitting alone in a graveyard. He was in tears, mourning over multiple graves. After some time, a young woman walked towards him. She had the body of a woman but the head of a black cat, reminding him of the lion-people of Lyra, yet she was unlike them in many ways. She wore many adornments around her neck and had a hat that looked like a crown on her head.

She affectionately pressed a hand to Noah's cheek and asked in a loving and soft tone, "Why do you cry? Have you lost someone, my dear?"

He was lost in his tears and simply managed to nod his head in agreement. The cat-headed woman held his hands and spoke with motherly affection.

"Do not worry, my child. I shall guide you to a place where you can search for all whom you have lost."

He looked up at her in shock and asked, "Where, Mother?"

"You shall find them where all who have passed reside now," she answered.

She helped him to his feet, and they began walking. He followed her with a childlike faith. She took him to what looked like the entrance of a tomb. It was terribly dark, yet the two went in. After a while, they came to a passage where several statues stood in unison. He stopped near one of the statues of a hawk-headed god wearing the Double Crown of Egypt. Even in the dream, Zeke instantly recognized the statue as Horus, the son of Isis and Osiris.

The cat-headed woman stood beside Noah and spoke to him, "This is Horus, god of the sky."

"Will he be able to tell me where my lost loved ones are?" he asked.

She smiled at him with love and affection in her eyes again and said, "It is his father, the Lord of the Underworld, King Osiris, who can help you."

Zeke hadn't read about any cat woman in the book of Egyptian myths, yet her energy felt very familiar to him. He knew she was an Egyptian goddess who was taking Noah to the underworld. She guided him to the temple of King Osiris, who sat on his golden throne.

Then, the god of the dead spoke. "Whom do you seek?"

Noah still had tears in his eyes as he replied, "I'm seeking all my loved ones. They've left me, and I can't seem to find them. I feel lost and lonely. I don't know what to do. I don't know how to live anymore."

Osiris lifted his arm and pointed his finger. "Seek them in that direction, gentle one. May you find what you need."

Noah ran in the direction the god had shown him. He ran for what seemed like hours past dunes of sand and wandering souls until he finally came upon a clan that Zeke could only assume were his loved ones. Noah ran towards them and hugged them in joy. Zeke couldn't see their faces, but he could make out the silhouettes of an old woman, a younger man and woman, almost his parents' age, and another young boy closer to his age, all hugging him warmly.

"Are you all happy? Are you safe?" Noah cried.

"We are. We are safe, and we are happy. You don't have to worry about us at all, Grandpa!" the young boy chirped.

"How will I live without you? Let me come with you, please!" Noah's eyes welled up again.

"It's still not your time, dear one. Don't you worry. You'll be fine. There's someone who won't let you miss us as much. You must be there to guide him. I can see you already love him, Noah," the old woman answered in a rough, broken voice.

"He'll remind you of us. He'll be your family, Father. He'll give you a purpose," the young man added.

Noah smiled at them one last time and bid goodbye. Just as he turned to leave, he saw a man walking up to him holding a scepter in his hand with three symbols, one of which Zeke could identify as the ankh, as he had already read about it in the book. The man had green-colored skin and a long chin beard, his body enveloped in a shroud. As soon as Noah saw this man, his eyes glittered with joy.

"Oh, you followed me all the way here!" He hugged the man with great zeal.

"Let me take you back to where you belong. I have so many questions left to ask you. Will you answer them?" the green-skinned man asked him.

Noah answered while still hugging the man. "Yes, yes, my child! Let's go back to where I belong and let me help you with all your queries. I was told I still have some time. Let's go, son."

• • •

Zeke woke up and found himself in his bed. His heart felt heavy. *"What was that dream all about?"*

He thought he had dreamt of the underworld, as he had been reading about it with such passion, but then why did he see Mr. Leitner searching for his loved ones there? *"Who were those people he hugged? Who was the green-skinned man? Why did he seem so familiar? Why did Mr. Leitner call him kid and son, just as he addresses me?"* Then came the realization.

"Maybe because… that's me!" he said aloud. To his utter amazement, he suddenly realized the voice of the young green man was none other than his own voice. "Yeah, it was my voice! Why was I green and…"

He was suddenly reminded of the sadness he had seen in Mr. Leitner's eyes the evening before. That evening, Zeke went back to Indigo Children. The old man was roaming around inside his store as usual. Zeke went straight up to him and said, "You never told me your first name was Noah, did you?"

Noah turned around and looked at him in a state of shock. He stayed silent for a moment, and then, with the usual mysterious smile on his face, he asked, "You had the same dream as me last night, didn't you, kid?"

It was Zeke's turn to feel shocked. "Was it me… the green man?" he asked instead of answering.

Noah smiled at him again and said, "Yes, I recognized you immediately. I'm here for you, son. I have a purpose: to help you on your journey, whatever that may be. Go back home and read the book I gave you. There's an answer waiting for you in that book."

Zeke wanted to know more. He wanted to ask Noah so many questions but listened to the old man's advice and went home. He began reading the book of Egyptian myths again. The page he opened next sent chills down his spine, not out of fear but because of the sheer amazement at what he saw. The page had a picture of a man with green skin, a long chin beard, his body wrapped in a shroud, and a scepter.

It was the image of the creator god Ptah, said to be the creator of all things. He is believed to have created the other original gods, the heavens, and the earth. Zeke loved reading the myth of Ptah, who was said to have even created himself out of the void and then created the physical universe in which to live.

Zeke was so engrossed in the Egyptian myths that he forgot about the world around him for the next few days. The myth of Ptah resonated with him the most. He could almost relate to this green man in his dream as a part of himself, a version of his own being, in another time, in another reality. And as a lightworker, he already knew there were no coincidences.

CHAPTER TWENTY-EIGHT
N. Leitner

"If something attracts us so strongly enough to draw our attention, our soul is indeed finding resonance with the frequency of it. It is pulling those experiences in and showing us the way," Zeke had once read. Just as he thought about it, another shocking truth was about to reveal itself.

A few days later, he went back to the shop. He asked Noah about the things he had seen in the dream, about the people he hugged, about his tears, and about the cat woman who had guided him. That was when Noah finally had the chance to share the recent tragic turn of events in his life with someone for the very first time.

"I recently lost my wife, my only son, my daughter-in-law, and my grandson in a freak building collapse. That's why I went back to Wisconsin. That's where I'm from, where my son lives — uh, well, used to live." He let out probably the deepest sigh of his life. "Oh, God. This is hard. It's going to take some time to talk about everyone in the past tense. My wife loved visiting my son's family, and that's why she was with them when it happened. I lost everyone I truly cared about in a single moment."

Zeke immediately froze upon hearing the news. Accidents and deaths had been a constant recurrence in his life. First, it was Nora. Then, it was Nigel Copeland. Now, it was Noah Leitner's entire family. Tears burned in his eyes. He hugged the old man tight and said, "I'm so sorry, Mr. Leitner. I promise you, you're not alone. I'll be right here. I will always be here for you. I'll be your family. I know I could never replace your son or his son, but I promise I'll do my best."

He took Noah to his favorite spot by the lake, and they spent the rest of the evening talking about everything under the sun. These were two beautiful souls from two different generations. They had very different backgrounds and upbringings, and yet, they were pleasantly surprised to discover they had much in common. They both loved books, and they both longed for meaningful company. They were both drawn to higher truths, and both were in Mackinaw City at the same time, not by coincidence but by divine guidance. They even had a strange and unique connection with the theme of facing accidental deaths in their lives.

The more time Zeke spent with Noah, the more Noah opened up to him. For the first time since the accident, Noah had someone to talk to, someone to help him grieve. He could share all his grief and cry like a child on someone's shoulder. Once Noah shared his emotional pain with Zeke, he felt much lighter. It was dark by then, and Zeke and Noah, two lonely people of unequal ages, walked home together and became the best of friends.

As the two began to spend more time together, Noah told Zeke more about the fascinating life he had lived. He told him that he had grown up, along with his four siblings, in a large farmhouse in the Wisconsin countryside. It was a beautiful, serene little homestead in New Glarus with cows, horses, goats, chickens, and just about every other animal you could think of. The children ran around the fields and explored the surrounding countryside all day.

"We didn't have a single care in the world. Life was good." he told Zeke. "I was the eldest son in my family, and I lived like those cowboys you'd see in some old western movie or TV show. I grew up riding horses with my father, milking cows, chopping wood, and building fires to keep the farmhouse warm in the winter months. Life was simple back then, Zeke, but I didn't know what actual happiness was until…"

He saw a single tear roll down Noah's cheek. "Until what?"

"Until I met my wife. We were both teenagers then. She was a beautiful young girl who came to live with her relatives in New Glarus. Her family, like mine, were Swiss farmers, so she loved farming and raising animals as much as I did. We both grew up together, and eventually, we fell in love. We had a beautiful little wedding at the local church and built a lovely house together on a little plot of land my father left me."

"What was her name?"

"Her name was Estelle, my shining star, the most beautiful girl ever." Zeke could feel the love Noah had for his wife bottled up inside. "My life was perfect there, in that little town."

"Then why'd you leave?" Zeke didn't want to ask that question, and he immediately regretted it. He could see the pain it brought to Noah's face. "I'm sorry. I didn't mean to…"

"No, no, it's okay. Eventually I had to leave New Glarus after my son was born in search of a better job. I had a family to feed, and I wanted to give them every joy under the sun. I was forced to choose the life of a wanderer, a nomad, changing jobs, cities, and even countries. As a seeker, I met so many different people, had so many wonderful experiences, and gained so much wisdom through my travels, but it was never enough."

"What do you mean?"

"No matter how much I learned, Zeke, I always wanted to know more. I kept collecting and curating antiques, books, and other spiritual bits and bobs from wherever I went, all over the world. Every time I came back to the States, I went home to Wisconsin, and every time I wanted to stay, but I always thought I'd do it the next time. The thing about next time is, kid, it never happens. I always had a sense of wanderlust that just wouldn't allow me to stop moving. I was always restless, always in search of more knowledge. Maybe it's a guy thing. I don't know."

Noah's words made Zeke realize how similar they were, for he too was often consumed by his thirst to know more. "When I finally managed to open this little store, a dream I'd cherished all my life, I thought of inviting my wife, my son, and his family to this beautiful little town called Mackinaw City where we could all live happily ever after. But I guess happily ever after just wasn't in the cards for me."

As Noah and Zeke grew closer, Zeke began to learn about life and other wonderful little secrets from him. One day, Noah shared a beautiful anecdote from his life which helped Zeke change his own understanding of life itself. It was a simple story about his wife and something she had once said to him. He loved collecting clocks and watches from around the world. He had many antique ones. Once, when his grandchild was born, he went back to visit his family in New Glarus. When he was about to leave again, he looked at his wife.

"Stellie, you know I love collecting watches, well here," and he handed her a beautiful antique watch. "I got this one especially for you. It's an antique. I want you to keep it with you. Look at it whenever you miss me. It's a token of my love."

Estelle had always known about Noah's wanderlust and never stopped him from traveling and living away from her for most of his life. Yet, with a lot of sadness in her eyes, she said, "Noah, when we got married, we promised each other that we'd grow old together. We've grown old enough now. Don't give me a watch. Give me your time!"

It was that night that Noah was so moved by her words that he realized he had lost all the precious time he could have spent with her by leaving her behind and chasing his own dreams. It was the night he finally decided to settle down and eventually call his family to live with him. He was so deeply in love with his wife, yet he took her for granted. Despite all his wisdom, he never realized that the universe doesn't operate according to whims and fancies. It has its own laws.

So, when he lost his family forever, he was not only struck by an immense sense of grief, but also an immense sense of guilt. He was gripped by the glaring realization of depriving his beloved wife of all the time and attention she deserved, and the regret of not expressing in enough words what and how he exactly felt for her. Zeke saw through his pain, and he learned from it. Noah told him everything he had been through and everything he had felt for the sole purpose of helping him evolve as a person.

Noah's story made Zeke look at his own life in a new light. He always enjoyed the little things, but now he was even more aware of them. He consciously paid attention to everything around him, and much of that credit went to Noah. He was going to play an even greater part in Zeke's life, even if they weren't aware of it just yet.

CHAPTER TWENTY-NINE

A SEED FROM THE STARS

Zeke had never thought he would share the secret of his cosmic friends Zig and Zag with anyone. Same for his love story with Zoom. Who would trust him? But Noah did. He didn't even have to try, and he believed every word Zeke said. He knew Zeke was an exceptional child. Zeke realized that the universe still had his back. At a point when he had felt abandoned by everyone around him, he found a new friend, someone he had known for quite a while, but never really noticed the influence on his life. Noah had always been by his side. He had been instrumental to Zeke's growth as a person and as a lightworker. Noah was always there for him, and now he knew why.

The realization brought in new and fresh wisdom for him. He began spending more time at Noah's shop. He even began helping occasionally with the sales. He only recognized the contribution of a certain N. Leitner and his shop, Indigo Children, once every other support was taken away from him. Their role in each other's life was mutual. Noah had to lose his whole family to recognize the significance of the child who had been visiting his shop for years.

Zeke was also pushed into thinking deeper about the supernatural powers he was gaining. Awakening as a lightworker was moving him more towards the magical metaphysical world every day. He discovered the role and the power of words and thought frequencies in changing realities for people. He learned about karma and karmic retribution and about the power of the practice of forgiveness. He learned the significance of pause, the significance of energy, and how to manage it for rejuvenation on a spiritual journey.

His energy opened up and began aligning with the universe. He learned to see and accept the guidance of his angels, spirit guides, and cosmic forces that he considered his friends. He began to understand signs and synchronicities. He found his homeland, learned about his origins, and was learning about ancient Egypt now — a place that he knew held some significance on his spiritual journey.

All of this was leading him to something he needed to know. How could he see what Mr. Leitner had seen in his dream? How could he see the same vision Gael had seen during his visualization exercise the night before he saw it? How was he able to see visions of other people's lives that were true, like Nigel Copeland? Was this a supernatural power he had acquired along his journey? He needed to know more about himself to understand this. He needed to know more about the powers of other starseeds like himself. He needed to know how starseeds were connected to ancient lands, people, and civilizations like Egypt and what their contribution was to help build the human race.

One evening, as he was lost in his thoughts, Noah smiled at him and said, "Have you finished reading the book on Egyptian myths yet? I know it's a big book, and there's a lot to read."

Zeke nodded. "Almost."

"Then I have a new one for you, kid. You'll surely need this one, too. I know you're an avid reader. Do you think you can manage reading both together?"

He nodded again, unknowingly.

Noah handed him a book entitled, "*The Starseeds*." He explained, "This is a rare book. Not a lot of copies were published. It should help you to understand some things."

That night, Zeke kept the book on Egyptian myths aside for a while and opened the new book. It vividly described the traits and signs of different starseeds that had existed on Earth. It had all the knowledge he was seeking — things no ordinary human could have known. He immediately knew that this book had been written by another starseed to guide others of their kind. He quickly ran through the index. Sifting through the pages, his eyes finally fell upon the chapter his soul was searching for: "The Lyran Starseeds."

He was excited to read about the journey of other Lyran Starseeds. They first began incarnating among the long-lost ancient human civilizations of Atlantis and Lemuria to seed the love of light and goodness among the various human races. At first, there were few — only a handful who chose to incarnate as lightworkers, but with time, their numbers grew, and eventually they were scattered everywhere. They raised the consciousness of humanity to bring it up to par with the other light beings in the galaxy. He was one of them, of course. It was a validation of something he had already known.

Wherever they are, whatever they do, Lyran Starseeds exude extremely high vibrational energy. People always notice them and feel drawn to them. As cosmic explorers, they spanned the entire cosmos acquiring a level of knowledge and experience no other beings could match, and thus, they impact people around them by teaching and guiding them. Lyrans are born leaders with a lot of lion-like traits.

They are magnetic and charismatic. If they find motivation in something, they pounce at it with all their might, but the moment the job is done, they love to sit back, relax and enjoy the fruits of their labors. Many fail to recognize that this combination of extreme dynamism and laziness is a very specific Lyran Starseed trait.

As Zeke continued, he resonated with every bit of what he read. He was among the rarest of starseeds, a special light being on a mission to awaken humanity. He was here to heal the world, to help humanity rise to its higher powers. He knew he was a wayshower, here to guide others, and wayshowers have nothing to fear. Lyrans feel a deep connection to felines like lions, tigers, and cats, as they often have subconscious memories of being feline humanoids.

As he read about this trait, he was reminded of the cat woman he had seen in his dream, the one who had guided Mr. Leitner to the underworld. "That woman could have been a Lyran, then. No wonder something about her seemed so familiar to me."

A light bulb suddenly went off in his head. "*Lyran Starseeds must have had connections with ancient Egypt,*" he concluded. After all, it was one of the most important of early human civilizations. Egypt had played its part in the evolution of the human race and in imparting its wisdom to the world. Zeke slowly started connecting the dots. If Lyran Starseeds had been incarnating in ancient Egypt, he could have been one of them, too. Was Zoom trying to remind him of that? A past life in Egypt? He wanted to run back to the book on Egyptian myths to find more — about the cat woman he had seen, about the connection between Lyran Starseeds and ancient Egypt, and possibly a clue or some insight into a past life — maybe into previous incarnations he had had there.

He read something that struck a chord in him, "Black cats are a common part of the Lyran Starseed's awakening. Many cultures consider them ominous symbols of death. People often fail to recognize death as a metaphor for new life. Black cats are highly spiritual beings who arrive not only to point towards a physical death but also when one's old unconscious self is dying while giving birth to a new consciousness."

It sent chills down his spine. He remembered the black cat that had followed him to Noah's shop. In fact, it would begin walking beside him whenever he stepped out of his house. Once he reached his destination, it would silently walk away a few minutes later. The next day, it would be right back outside his house again. He was also reminded of the discomfort he felt looking at it. Just like the barn owl that sat on the porch staring at him one night, the black cat also stared him in the eye as if reading his mind.

"If the cat is supposed to signify the death of an older self, or physical death, then is someone about to die?" he asked himself. "Or do I have to go through some kind of internal death?"

• • •

Zeke was carefully reading as much information about the starseeds as he could when his eyes fell on something. He read the lines repeatedly. He reached the segment which had the answer he was looking for. "The occult naturally draws the attention of Lyran Starseeds. As they awaken, their spiritual wisdom gives rise to their psychic powers and 'Clair' senses. Clair, meaning clear, stood for the nine supernatural senses that Zeke would eventually have to gain.

"Extrasensory Perceptions (ESPs), commonly known as the 'Sixth Sense,' increase in starseeds eventually. Clairvoyance, the psychic power to see things beyond normal human vision, lets them see the past or the future, or visuals of angels or ghosts," he read.

This was it! Clair was the reason behind his dreams and visions. He had developed the powers of a true Lyran. As he read, he recognized he could also hear messages of higher frequencies. "I'm clairaudient, too!" he exclaimed to himself. He now could see the reason behind all those strange dreams and visions, giving a connection to the lives of others and bringing valuable insights to them. He realized his psychic abilities were strong since birth and had increased multifold with each passing year. Everything up to this point was helping him know a little bit more about himself.

By then, he had reached the end of the chapter, and there it was in black and white — a quote, a line that made everything fall into place. "You can love me or hate me, but you can never ignore me." That is perfect to describe a starseed. They leave an immense subconscious influence on all they come across. They are like a constant spiral that gets burned into the memory of all who witness it. It is impossible to forget a Lyran Starseed if you meet one only once in your life.

Zeke felt a strong pull to go back to the book on Egyptian myths again, so he could know more about the Lyran connection with ancient Egypt. Books were his constant companions, and like all starseeds, he loved reading and learning. He tucked himself into bed, switched on the bed lamp, and opened the book.

CHAPTER THIRTY
HOLY AMETHYST

Zeke tried very hard to read the Egyptian Book of Myths again that night, but it felt as if somebody was forcing his eyelids shut. His eyes were too heavy, his mind had abandoned him, and before he knew it, he fell asleep. In his sleep, he felt as if he was floating in the holy waters of the Egyptian River Nile. A cool breeze blew over his face, gently touching his whole body. It had a calming effect on his mind. That night was the most undisturbed sleep he had had in ages.

The next morning, he woke up rejuvenated and felt a strange surge of happiness. He felt so fresh and so full of joy, as if a holy and positive energy was touching him the whole day. He could almost feel that something big was about to happen.

It was evening, and he planned to go for a walk with Noah. But the moment he left his house, the old, familiar black cat began following him. Zeke had slowly warmed up to its presence and didn't feel as anxious as he had been before. He always thought the black cat might begin speaking to him one day, just like Ziggy Bird, Zag, or the barn owl.

Instead, it just lazily yawned and uttered, "Mee-ooo-www." The cat stretched its meow so far that Zeke couldn't stop himself from smiling. It walked a few steps, turned around, and lifted one of its front paws as if to say something. Then, it looked straight into Zeke's eyes and called "Mee-ooo-www!" It cocked its head to one side, motioning him to follow.

Zeke didn't know what to do, but then he began to follow. The cat walked straight towards a meadow, and he kept following. The sun was about to go down when the cat walked to a certain patch of grass and lifted its front paw again. It turned around to check if Zeke was still in tow and then called him a third time, "Mee-ooo-www!" Zeke knew the cat was now asking him to come towards the patch of grass it was standing on, and so he followed. The cat stepped aside, and Zeke could see something glittering near its paw in the soft evening sunlight.

He bent down to pick it up. It was a huge, rough-edged, sparkly, violet-colored stone, big enough for him to have to use both hands to pick it up. He looked at it from every angle and tried rubbing the rough edges to clear the dirt and mud on it. The stone was so utterly mesmerizing that, for a while, he forgot about everything around him. When he finally did look away, the black cat was nowhere in sight. It had disappeared. He studied the stone for a while and then decided to take it to Mr. Leitner.

Noah loved collecting crystals and found the stone fascinating. "This is amethyst. It's a very precious crystal. Where did you get this huge piece, kid?"

Zeke explained how the black cat had led him to the meadow and how he had discovered the crystal lying in a patch of grass. He wanted to give it to Noah so he could keep it in his store, but he refused.

"Take this amethyst home with you, son. I'm sure there's a deeper meaning to it. Something big is coming your way. Crystals hold immense healing power. They're also strong energy cleansing tools."

Noah shared some very useful tips to maintain the power of the gift Zeke had received from the cosmos. "Wash and clean it properly, and then keep it in a secret place away from the reach of others. On the next full moon night, hold it under running water for about ten minutes to remove all negative energies it might have absorbed from other places or people it was around. Do this every time you wish to charge it. Then take a glass bowl, fill it with water, add some sea salt to it, and soak the crystal overnight, keeping the bowl in the open, directly under the moonlit sky. This practice will charge your crystal, bringing it back to its highest power and energy. Once your crystal is charged, you can use it to heal yourself and others."

"How do I heal myself with a crystal?" Zeke was curious.

Noah wore his signature mysterious smile on his face as he went on. "You can charge your drinking water with the charged crystal. Keep the amethyst inside or next to a jar full of fresh water, close the lid, and keep it overnight on a new moon night as it symbolizes planting new seeds. Once your water is charged, visualize being healed. Drink this magical water, and it will work. If you can't drink it, add a few drops of this magically charged water to your bath water. It's as simple as that."

"What can I heal with the amethyst?" Zeke was again curious to know.

"Amethysts heal our minds. It has the power to free us from our limited minds, which then brings us spiritual wisdom and guidance from the metaphysical realms. It can open our third eye, our higher vision, to show us our true potential and purpose in life."

"What happens then, O Wise One?" Zeke jested with a wink and a smile.

"We feel a great sense of peace and balance once our minds open to cosmic truths. We often keep running after meaningless material things because our energy is stuck. Our minds have been programmed that way for centuries. Once we consciously break free from these conditioned ways of thought, we can be in alignment with the universe. We need to chase nothing, seek nothing." He suddenly paused to ask Zeke a pertinent question nobody had ever asked him. "Have you ever thought deeply enough about what this universe *really* is?"

"The universe, um, the universe is…" he was left searching for words.

"It's nothing but the super intelligence we call God. It's made up of singular energy: the Source, and we're extensions of the same Source. We're all Source incarnates, our own God particles, little universes in ourselves, you see. When our mind opens to these magical realities, we stop standing in our own way, giving our power away to others or to our own ego, which always makes us feel insecure, and wanting to achieve something in this material world to make us feel better. Instead, we learn to stand in our power," he went on as Zeke continued to nod in agreement.

"The more we learn to do so, this Super Intelligence can connect with us more easily. It knows what we need, what our soul is here to achieve, and brings everything to us organically in a cosmic flow. We learn to let go of our worries and cares and let this Source Energy, God, this Super Intelligence, handle everything for us."

Zeke came home with the holy amethyst, thinking about the significance of what he had learned. He was reminded of a book he had read, written by the thirteenth-century Persian poet Rumi, who said, "What you seek is seeking you."

Noah had unknowingly imparted a knowledge unmatched — if we learn to master the art of letting our purpose seek us instead of us seeking our purpose, we can then become the masters of our own universe. We can all become little alchemists!

Zeke rationalized, "Sounds great in theory. Now to put it into practice!"

CHAPTER THIRTY-ONE
Akash

The Farley Street neighborhood was changing. Mr. Copeland needed constant care. Gael was dealing with bipolar mood swings. Mr. Tartal had developed a strange pattern of returning home and staying for a few days before suddenly disappearing again. His behavior made Zeke's mother extremely disillusioned with her life. The toxic cycle of him coming back and then becoming emotionally distant again made her question her relationship with him and her faith in life and in love.

Things changed even more when fourteen-year-old Leia boldly declared she likes girls instead of guys, and she wasn't going to take any flak from anyone about it, especially her father. The news sent Gael into a downward spiral, as he still had unresolved feelings for her. Mrs. Tartal was initially in shock but revealed she could work with the adjustment. And Maya, being her twin, admitted she sensed it all along and was taking a neutral stance for the time being.

Though initially surprised by the revelation, Zeke was happy to see his little sister slowly turning from an aggressive, adamant child to a resilient, responsible, and mature teenager. Maya, on the other hand and the more sensitive twin, began growing in the opposite direction, so much so it had started to concern Zeke. Originally, Kai had been around to guide her, but with him gone, she began to make more rash and immature decisions. She was staying away from home much more now, basically mirroring her father's behavior (which she abhorred), but she did it anyway. She started having crushes on older, scuzzy boys, all of whom made Zeke extremely uncomfortable because of their negative energies.

After developing his gift of Clair, Zeke began to understand the energies of the people around him. He could sense emotions and feelings, almost like reading minds. His visions also became more frequent and reoccurring. Zeke spent two weeks nurturing the amethyst, cleansing and clearing it of all negative energies by keeping it under running water, charging his crystal under the sky on a full moon night, collecting a jar full of fresh spring water, and charging it with the amethyst. The next morning, he drank his magical water and went about his day. While drinking it, a smile came across his face, instantly reminding him of his little leprechaun friend Zag, his magic potions, and his mischievous shenanigans. His consciousness was instantly raised. He was so happy and at peace with himself and everything around him that he finished his chores faster than ever.

He was reading the Egyptian Book of Myths bit by bit every night. That night, as he was reading the book, his mind was so calm that he instantly fell asleep. It wasn't a very deep sleep, though. He was only half asleep when he saw a saintly young man and a woman standing beside his bed. They both had beautiful violet halos around their heads.

"Whoa!" Zeke jumped out of his bed. "Who are you?" he inquired. "Are you from Lyra, or are you from Ancient Egypt?"

The duo had warm, disarming smiles on their faces. The woman said, "Dear child, be not alarmed. We're from the realm of Akash."

Zeke kept staring at them, trying to make sense of things, as she continued, "We have arrived because you invoked us."

"When did I invoke them… and why?" he wondered to himself.

As if reading his mind, the man instantly answered, "You invoked us by accepting the gift of the holy amethyst, child. I am Saint Germain, and this is my divine counterpart, Lady Portia, just as you have your divine counterpart in Zoom. Dear child, do not fear us for we come in peace."

"How do you know about the amethyst… and Zoom for that matter?" Zeke was less apprehensive of them now but still curious.

Lady Portia lovingly caressed his hair like his mother often did and said, "You are very special to us, Ezekiel. We know everything about you. We've been watching over you and waiting for you to invoke us so we can help you on your mission."

"It's great that I know your names, but I still don't know who you are, what you do, or what you want from me," Zeke felt emboldened enough to inquire.

"Ezekiel, you and I, we are the same. We are beings of light. I am among the many ascended masters who succeeded in transcending this physical realm to be released from the cycle of birth and death. I am the Lord of the Violet Ray, the seventh ray of light, and I promote the Flame of Freedom," St. Germain explained.

"Dear child, I'm the Goddess of Justice, one of the Lords and Ladies of Karma. I promote the Flame of Justice by maintaining the balance between mercy and judgment, heart and head. Together, we are the keepers of the mighty Violet Flame, a cleansing purifying light," Lady Portia added lovingly.

They both bowed their heads and spoke in unison. "From today onward, we are at your service, Lord Ezekiel."

"That still doesn't tell me where you come from and what you want from me."

"I told you we have come from Akash, son, and what we want is to help you," Lady Portia reiterated.

Zeke felt and looked embarrassed as he had no idea what Akash meant.

"There is a hidden realm, here on Earth, named in the ancient Indian language of Sanskrit as Akash, meaning 'sky.'"

He still had his doubts. "Why call it Akash instead of simply calling it the sky, then?"

"Trust us and come with us, dear child. You shall know everything in time," St. Germain said as he reached out his hand.

Zeke had learned to trust his visions by now, so he did not hesitate to take the saint's hand. He could see himself floating out of his body as if the saint was removing his soul from him. After a few moments, the experience became too intense, and as he was about to panic, the saint calmed him down. "Have faith, child. It is only your astral form that I have removed from its husk. You shall be fine."

As he calmed down, the three ascended to the heavens. They soon reached a palatial hall that had quite a few stairs to climb and a grand, ornate portico marking the entrance to the hall. A young man and a woman hurriedly descended the crystalline stairs as if they were waiting all along to welcome them.

"Meet the keepers of the Akashic Records, Ezekiel. As we wait for you here outside the hall, they'll show you yours," St. Germain said in a matter-of-fact way, handing him over to them.

The young man and woman gently held his hands, took him up the stairs inside the hall, and began showing him around what looked like a huge library full of books. Every book looked the same to him. They were all huge and looked like office registers. That confused him even more. He had never heard of anything like this before. He knew he was in a dream, over which he should have some control, but he didn't seem to have much control over what he saw here.

"Wha… what are Akashic Records?" He didn't know how to address them properly, but he finally mustered some courage and asked, stuttering slightly.

"The books you see on those shelves are the Akashic Records, dear child. Every soul has one dedicated to it when it chooses to incarnate as a human being. Every action from the moment of birth and the consequences of those actions are updated and maintained in these records for all the lifetimes spent on Earth. The Akashic Records hold the key to the past, present, and future. They show you the accounts of your good and bad deeds."

Zeke felt extremely overwhelmed by all that he saw. He dropped to the floor of the library, just sitting there and looking all around in utter amazement. He now understood why St. Germain and Lady Portia had introduced him to the ancient Indian word 'Akash.' He looked at them, wanting to ask something again, but the man had already read his mind.

"Yes, the knowledge of the Akashic Records was first revealed to the philosophers of Hinduism, the ancient Indian religion, but every part of the world will eventually become aware of it through lightworkers like you. Once people know there's a library up in the sky, which maintains a book of records for every human action, they'll learn to become more cautious with, accountable for, and responsible towards their actions, words, and deeds," Saint Germain explained to him.

Zeke still felt overwhelmed by what he saw. It was an infinite library, full of an infinite number of books of record, so neatly kept in such an organized manner. "Who maintains all of this, and how? The life of every human is recorded with such precision and perfection. How can that be?"

"We maintain everything," the woman declared. "We are the keepers of human fate. We record every deep thought, every action, every fraction of a second, and at one time, so did you. You have had many, many lives, Ezekiel."

They brought him a massive book of records, and it was far larger than any other book in the hall. It had pages of gold leaf and his name, Zeke Tartal, printed on it in bold. Zeke felt uneasy about this whole thing and was terrified of what he might find if he opened and read the book, so he asked them, "So, this holds the deeds for all the lives I've lived? Is there any way I can reduce the effects of my bad deeds from other lifetimes, heal myself in this lifetime, and become free of the burden I carry?"

The keepers of the Akashic Records looked at each other and smiled. "You'll receive your answer soon. Come with us."

They took him to another part of the library where Zeke saw the shimmering silhouette of a woman sitting in the lotus position on the floor between two rows of bookshelves. Seven different colored lights radiated from seven different parts of her body. The lights, as bright and powerful as sunlight, almost encapsulated her entire being. Unable to look directly at the dazzling lights, he instinctively covered his eyes.

"We know your book of records scared you. It looked huge, heavy, and daunting to read," the young woman said with affection. "The Book of Records is not meant to be read like physical books, my child. It is read through higher wisdom, through the mind, like you see this woman reading her Akashic records here."

The young male guide intervened. "Look at her again and carefully look this time. You'll see how she is letting the knowledge seep into her."

It took Zeke a couple minutes to acclimate his eyes to the dazzling effect of the lights. When his eyes finally did settle on her, he was left in absolute awe of what he saw in front of him. Sparkly white bits of letters and words flowed from the shelf, gathering in a circular motion above her head, forming a crown of snowflakes. They settled for a brief moment, then entered her brain one by one.

"What is this? Is this like the abilities I read about?" He was left spellbound, and he wanted to know more about the magic he was witnessing right before his eyes.

"It is far more than that, child. It's a direct descent of information from Source when your mind is in perfect harmony and attuned to the wisdom of your highest self." The woman smiled at him reassuringly, observing the bewilderment in his eyes.

"That is amazing! Will I ever be able to learn this and attain this state of perfect bliss and harmony? Can I connect with Source like her?" he inquired innocently.

"Of course, son. That is why you are here. You can connect with Source Energy from anywhere on Earth, even from a corner of your little house on Farley Street. This is just a practice of expanding your consciousness beyond the physical plane and touching your multi-dimensional, non-physical, and metaphysical aspects. This woman is in a state of oneness with the universe, which you humans term the bliss of meditation. Every human being can eventually attain this state with a little practice and dedication. Anybody can become an ascended master if they learn to shed the density blocking their energy field. You lightworkers have an advantage of reaching this state faster as you are old souls who have achieved so much already."

"How can humans shed their dense energies?" He was immediately reminded of the childlike joy he saw in St. Germain and Lady Portia, as opposed to the dense, toxic energies carried by his father and the boys Maya hung out with.

"By shedding the darkness inside of them," they answered as they walked out of the Akashic Library and brought him to St.

Germain and Lady Portia. After what seemed like quite a few miles to him, they reached a temple-like structure further up in the sky.

"This was once an ancient Hindu temple that no longer exists on Earth," said St. Germain. The Akashic Library and the temple were both roofless, with countless stars twinkling above them. He had seen many ancient Egyptian temples and the underworld in the book of myths. All of them had statues of different deities in them, but inside this Indian temple, he could see no statues of deities.

Instead, he saw a heavy old man sitting under a banyan tree rooted within the temple's inner sanctum. The man held a string of beads in his hands, which reminded Zeke of the hundred-year-old Hawaiian healer who left him a string of very similar-looking beads. The man was sitting in the lotus position with his eyes half closed, in a state of trance. His body was draped in a long and unstitched piece of a saffron-colored robe. He had a head full of shiny long white hair and an equally long white beard. A few strings of beads adorned his neck, too.

As Zeke and the two saints walked towards the temple, the old man opened his eyes for a moment, looked at them and smiled, and then went back to a state of meditative trance again. Then, Zeke stopped dead in his tracks, watching the transformation of the man right in front of his eyes. The old man began chanting a mantra, unlike anything Zeke had heard before. It consisted of seven distinct sounds.

"Lam-Vam-Ram-Yam-Ham-Om-Aum."

With each different sound, a different part of the man's body lit up, from his forehead to the base of his spine, areas Zeke knew to be the centers of the seven chakras. He looked on as the man's physical body slowly turned into a shimmery silhouette of light, with all the dazzling-colored lights spinning from different centers gradually covering his entire body, just like the woman in the library.

"I saw a similar person at the Akashic Library. Why are these different colors emanating from these people? Why do their bodies turn into silhouettes of light?" he asked.

"It's because you see their real bodies. The woman at the library and the man you see here are from two very different times in human history. The woman at the library is a modern-day woman, alive and living currently on Earth, while the man you see in front of you now is an ancient Hindu sage who has left his physical body. As they have both attained their light forms, you can see both equally well. The light forms of humans don't get destroyed like their physical bodies. They simply lie dormant, waiting for their physical selves to activate them." The saints' words almost gave Zeke a headache because he was processing so much information so quickly, but he continued to listen.

"Whenever a soul reincarnates on Earth, the light form reattaches itself to its new physical body and continues its journey of evolution. This is why many people have memories from their past lives once their light is activated. Because of that light, their knowledge integrates into their cellular memories."

"So that's why I remember my life on Lyra! Zoom touched my light form, and I gained memories from my life as Ezekiel." His mind flashed like snapshots as the saint went on.

"A triad of light, spirit, and body creates a vehicle of light called Merkaba around your physical body, waiting to merge with it. The more you shed your darker energies, the more this Merkaba integrates into your physical body and activates your light form, opening your mind to cosmic wisdom."

"But how can humans achieve this higher state when most of us aren't even aware of its existence?" Zeke still had many questions to ask.

"That is your mission," roared a great voice from inside the temple. "To spread the word on Earth, so people become aware of the limitations they create in and around them. It is your mission to learn how to unload this burden humanity has put upon itself and make them aware of it so they can heal themselves and become eternal beings."

As the voice came closer, a pure, luminescent form magically appeared. Zeke rubbed his eyes in disbelief as an angel with marvelous wings and a flaming sword in his hand stood before him. He immediately recognized this to be the archangel Michael from his dream and the crystal statue he purchased at Noah Leitner's shop. "Dear child, now that we have finally met, allow me to explain it all. All lightworkers currently on Earth correspond with a ray of divine light, and each light has an archangel guiding and protecting it. I, Archangel Michael, am the guardian of blue light. I protect Blue Ray beings, such as yourself."

"Protect us? From what?"

"From darkness. From evil, my child. We angels, as multidimensional beings of light, we can be everywhere at once. We watch over the human race, yet we cannot meddle in their affairs unless we are invoked."

"So, you can help anyone once they invoke you? And how do you do that?"

"I can be called upon by any lightworker of the Blue Ray. They can summon me once they learn to cleanse their mind of all negative thoughts. Even you can call upon me. With my flaming sword, I can cut through all evil and all that may seek to harm you or your loved ones. But my power must be earned. To have the power to summon me, you will have to face my trial, just as you must face the trials of the others."

A lot of what Archangel Michael said confused him, but nothing more so than what he said at the end.

"Others? What others?"

Then, the six remaining archangels came out from six corners of the temple to meet Zeke. Archangel Zadkiel came ahead of the others.

"Dear son, I am the guardian of the Violet Ray, the champion of change and transformation. I guide and protect all those who wish to change and evolve. I represent the light of the Holy Amethyst, and I stand for the cleansing of all darkness from the hearts of men."

Zeke stared in awe at Zadkiel as his divine counterpart, Holy Amethyst herself, emerged from the shadows. "We were sending you constant signs to let us help you. Finally, you brought my power home, nurtured it, and invoked us," she revealed.

Zeke listened carefully, trying to decipher the role of the archangels and the significance of their presence in human lives. Once again, his mind was read, and this time it was Archangel Raphael who spoke. "I sense the questions that invade your mind, Ezekiel, and the answers are simpler than you think. You, a child from a city in America, stand in an ancient Hindu temple, surrounded by European saints and archangels recognized by all the Abrahamic religions of the world. Look around. All of this, all of us, are connected by faith.

"Humans can attain their true light form simply by having faith. There's nothing more to it. Break the walls of your mind. You have more to grasp, Ezekiel. You had a Portuguese nanny in Michigan, a Lyran lover on Earth, a mythical Irish leprechaun living in your shoe, a cosmic hummingbird reciting rhymes on Farley Street, a hundred-year-old Hawaiian sage teaching you how to heal, an old American man leading you to a book on ancient Egypt, a black cat helping you find a magic crystal, and even a night owl chanting pearls of wisdom into your ears. Do you still not see?"

Zeke stared at him blankly as he failed to understand where this was all heading. Archangel Michael smiled warmly as he answered the question asked by Raphael.

"We are all one — you humans and all of us here in the etheric realms. Everything is one, dear son. We do not have separation in the higher realms. There are no constraints of time and space, no past, no present, and no future. Everything is happening here and now. There's no death or suffering, no religions, races, sects, or fragmented societies here, either," he reiterated.

Archangel Gabriel added, "Those are human-created concepts that have shackled their feet. The metaphysical world is the world of non-duality, oneness, and freedom. This is the realm of truth and eternity. Whenever cosmic beings have tried connecting with humans to help them understand this, they've been able to grasp only a small bit of the entire truth and began propagating it as the ultimate knowledge. They've fought with each other and created so much separation, divided humans into tiny little segments and groups, created religions and belief systems around these little fragmented truths they received upon contact with us, ignoring the bigger picture and the magnitude of it."

"All of this, it makes me want to learn more, but I still do not understand what you meant by 'trials.'"

Now, it was the Archangel Uriel who spoke. "We will cleanse your chakras, Ezekiel, but to gain our guidance, you must be tested and purged of all that would make you impure. We will test your faith, your knowledge, your connection to the universe, and your resolve to see it all through. But first, we must heal you."

The archangels had him lie on a bed of granite inside the temple sanctum. Archangel Raphael came ahead and touched Zeke's chest, pouring out a beautiful and warm green light that swirled around his little heart and began healing it. One after the other, they came forward and touched the corresponding chakra center in his body, sending healing lights to each of his chakras.

"Human beings have hurt and wounded each other's divine and holy hearts for far too long, and their wounded hearts need healing," he said. As the angels were busy healing him, St. Germain and Lady Portia slowly began walking away from the temple.

"Will you not stay and help me heal?" Zeke asked them.

"Our work today is done, child." they both said in unison. "Now, your trial begins."

CHAPTER THIRTY-TWO

ZEKE MEETS HIS SHADOW

Zeke woke up to a sudden, loud ruckus outside his room. Before doing anything else, he frantically looked around, searching for the archangels who had been around him, but he was alone. He scratched his head, wondering what the saints had meant by "your trial has begun." That morning Maya fought with Leia, ignoring her sister's advice about her immature and impractical attitude. Instead of listening to reason, Maya ran out of the house in a fit, leaving her already sick mother heartbroken. She was still a teenager, and nobody thought she would become as headstrong as she did. She didn't want to accept life as it was, so she acted out. She began cutting herself with razor blades. Sometimes Leia would walk into the bedroom or the bathroom they shared to find Maya cutting her wrist, her forearm, or the topside of her hand. One day it was just too much for her to take and she exploded.

"What the hell are you doing??? Are you crazy or something?"

"I just like the sight of my own blood," Maya countered. "I like the color and I like to watch it flow down my arm."

"This is just sick. You really hate yourself, don't you?"

"I haven't decided yet."

"One of these days I'm going to walk in and find you dead on the floor."

"I guess time will tell."

"This family is nuts."

"Ya think???"

Leia let out a sigh of disgust and stormed out of the room shaking her head. Then she went down to the basement and cried her eyes out. She knew her family was falling apart, and she was just too young to know how to deal with it. It would eventually fall to Zeke. He would have to guide his sisters and make them understand how life worked. Once again, it was Zeke who had to be the guide. He loved his sisters dearly, and he did his best to help heal their wounds, especially Maya's.

Zeke continued on his spiritual path. He decided to hold on to his light and keep it shining against all odds. He carried on with all his spiritual practices, from Ho'oponopono to having crystal-charged water now and again and chanting seed mantras he learned from the Hindu sage. He also invoked the archangels during his chakra-clearing practice and whenever he needed help in general. Of them, Michael always answered his call, for by staying true to himself and his knowledge, Zeke had proved his faith. He didn't know where his life was heading, but he had faith in his divine light and the universe, and he knew the secret of non-duality, so he continued helping others around him and waited patiently for his next trials.

He honored his friendships, too. He religiously visited Noah and continued to learn from him. He learned every chakra had a corresponding crystal, and keeping the crystal around that chakra center after charging it would increase the power of that chakra, thus clearing his blocks faster. Through these constant practices, he felt extremely healthy in mind, body, and spirit. Every night he called upon Archangel Michael to shield and protect him and his family. The blue shield of protection was always around him, making him fearless and empowering him.

• • •

As it always does, time continued to fly by, and eventually a whole year had passed. Zeke was almost eighteen now, an adult ready to take on the world, but he started to have his doubts. The trials he waited for never came. He was still busy with high school and had read the book of Egyptian myths many times over. It was a very detailed book, and he had to keep at it, learning something new every time he read it. He also read other books on chakras, karma, and crystals and even managed to find some information on the Akashic Records. What interested him most among the Egyptian myths was the story of Imhotep – a vizier, a sage, an astrologer, an architect, and a medicine man all rolled into one. He is thought to be the son of the creator god, Ptah. Zeke was fascinated by what he read about this man. After reading thoroughly about Imhotep, Zeke met Noah as usual.

"What have you been reading all this while, kid?" Noah was always interested in helping him make sense of all he had learned. This was a regular routine they followed. Every evening Zeke would share with him the details of what he had read.

"The story of the Egyptian architect Imhotep," he excitedly told him.

"Oh…" Noah had a curious look on his face. "Zeke, would you like to join me for dinner tonight?" Noah gave no reaction whatsoever to the story, but his eyes twinkled mischievously, and a smile played on his lips.

Zeke thought of the old man as family and had always been there for him, so he happily obliged. Noah lovingly made dinner that evening, which consisted of leek soup, pasties, and fresh fruit for dessert. Then he made another gentle request, inviting Zeke to stay over for a movie. Zeke wanted to go back home to check on his mother, but he trusted Leia at this point, so he decided to stay back with Noah instead. He called Leia and asked her to keep an eye on his mother and she agreed.

Noah guided Zeke to a small movie room he had in his house. It was a dark room with an old projector, a screen, and a couple of easy chairs, making it look like a mini movie theater. He had a collection of old classic movies that he was quite proud of. He and Zeke sat together in this dimly lit room, ate buttered popcorn, and watched an old 1932 American horror movie – *The Mummy*. A little into the film, Zeke realized he was watching the story of none other than the man he was reading about! It was only then that he understood the real reason behind Noah's weird silence after hearing the story of Imhotep. It was all for this little surprise.

A centuries-old myth had given rise to the idea that opening a mummy's tomb would unleash a terrible curse. The movie's script was based on a similar concept woven around the resurrection of the cursed mummy of Imhotep. In the movie, an archaeologist and his team discover and resurrect the body of the ancient Egyptian high priest Imhotep by mistake. As a result of a curse, Imhotep comes back to life and brings destruction to the modern world in place of the ten plagues he brought to Egypt in the original myth. Noah had a lot of fun scaring Zeke that night, like a little child successfully pulling a prank on a friend. Zeke had been extra sensitive to energies since childhood, and the one thing that could scare him to pieces was the perpetuation of darkness around something, and there was no dearth of it in this frightening movie.

That night, Zeke had a very peculiar dream. In his dream, he found himself in a small Victorian-style dressing room. He was looking into a large, standing mirror in the corner when he suddenly saw the figure of a man standing right behind him. He turned around immediately, feeling threatened by the menacing presence of this figure. But there was nothing there, so he turned back to the mirror, only to find that the creature was still behind him. Zeke looked behind himself many times, but the figure only existed in the reflection.

"Oh God, this is just like *Phantom of the Opera,*" he said out loud.

The figure was around the same height as him, with a strange cloth wrapped all around it. Through the cloth, he could only see its menacingly calm eyes. It wasn't a welcoming presence by any means. Zeke was petrified at the sight, as he had never experienced anything like this before. He was so scared of the presence of this creature that he thought he must have resurrected some ancient mummy by mistake. It had a bone-chilling dark aura around it, and it made him fear for his life.

"Who are you, and what do you want from me?" he managed to say, with immense fear and anxiety in his voice. He received no answer. The figure didn't move or say anything. It simply continued to stare at him, so Zeke repeated it again, only this time louder, clearer, and bolder.

"WHO **ARE** YOU?"

Yet again, there was no response from the other end. He was quite anxious due to its daunting and silent presence and hence started to get angry. Just as he felt a tinge of anger, the atmosphere of the room changed. He could feel the creature standing behind him now. He immediately turned around. His reflexes had become extremely sharp over the years, and feeling a surge of aggression and hostility, he went in for the kill. As he did, he realized for the first time how strong he had physically become. He sprung off the floor like a boxer and took a swing at the creature, only for his fist to pass right through it like a ghost. The creature was an apparition, untouchable.

"It can't be a mummy, then," he thought.

Zeke took another swing at it, and again, he hit nothing. One would think the figure would have laughed at this comical dance, but it remained unfazed by the whole scene. He could see he was getting nowhere with it and thus contemplated his next move. He was growing impatient now.

"Who or what in the devil's name are you?" he asked one last time.

This time he finally got a reaction out of it. The creature lifted its arms and removed the bandages covering its face. Underneath, it revealed a terrifying sight. It was a man with the same curly brown hair and the same green eyes as Zeke, and there was a curious smirk on his face. It looked into his eyes and spoke in a very familiar voice.

"I see you."

Hearing his own voice and seeing his own face sent chills down his spine as he tried to understand what this apparition meant. In the center of the room was a plush armchair with a tall back. The figure immediately went over, sat in the armchair, and crossed its right leg over its left thigh. It clearly gave the indication that it wasn't going anywhere for a while.

"Oh great," Zeke said to himself. "Now what am I supposed to do?"

He desperately wished for some cosmic support to come and save him from whatever this thing was. He called for help from Zig, Zag, and Zoom and desperately called for help from his angels, too. Yet no divine aid came. He was left to fend for himself. Since the figure didn't respond in any way, he started to feel that its aura wasn't as ominous as he had originally thought. He understood it didn't necessarily intend to do him any harm. If it felt more like a reflection — or a shadow. He simply couldn't wrap his head around why this copy of him was there. So, he chose to circle the figure again, only this time he had no intention to attack, but rather tried to assess who he was and what he was doing in his life, let alone his room.

"What does this guy possibly want from me?"

He circled it a few more times, trying to look hard at it before finally stopping. Now it was the transparent, shadowy figure's turn to make a move. Oddly enough, Zeke didn't retreat in fear this time but decided to face it head-on. The shadow came closer to him and stood directly in front of him.

"Who am **I**? Who are **YOU**?" the shadow asked him.

His eyes shifted back and forth. "I… I am Zeke Tartal." That was the only answer he could think of.

The shadow repeated his question. "Who **ARE** you?" Only this time, there was a strength behind his words that carried much more power — an energy that made Zeke instantly feel something.

Zeke had no answer, but that was when he realized what this apparition was. This was no ordinary shadow. This was *his* shadow, a reflection of himself, of his being, of everything he was, wanted to be, and didn't want to be. That was when he said, "I am… YOU!"

The shadow heard Zeke's words and smiled. "… and I am you," he said as well. "We are one. We are the light. We are Ezekiel."

Then, the shadow embraced him, and it was the most benevolent feeling Zeke had ever experienced. For the first time in his life, he felt complete. He felt whole. He had never felt such love before. His eyes were filled with tears of pure joy. He hugged the shadow figure and cried to his heart's content.

• • •

The next morning, he rushed to Noah and told him the story. "I still don't understand what that dream was about. Do you have any idea, Mr. Leitner?" he innocently asked him.

Noah was left speechless for a while. Then he said in a deep and profound voice that Zeke had never heard before, as if he were channeling information from a higher source, "What you went through was a spiritual experience, my son. It's quite possible that this was some kind of test." Zeke already knew he was awakening, and this was nothing new to him, but then Noah whispered, "You are gearing for a much deeper and more intense awakening than you could have ever imagined."

Zeke felt a bit nervous and uncomfortable hearing this. Was he about to hear something he wouldn't like or be fully prepared for? He was reminded of what the barn owl had said to him one night. It said he was awakening from thousands of years of slumber. It was sure to be a slower process than he had originally thought. He was also reminded of the black cat that still loitered around his house, indicating there was something more to come. He knew there was no escaping the spiritual awakening process once it began.

Instead of trying to run from the instant discomfort he felt, he thus chose to delve deeper. "What was I being shown through this dream? Nobody came for my help when I called them," he declared.

"You met your own shadow, son. The process probably began with you choosing to read the story of Imhotep. Your true self was guiding you. I unconsciously became a catalyst, too, as I made you watch the movie. Spiritual experiences aren't always about rainbows, roses, or unicorns; they aren't always about love and light. There are challenges you need to face and transcend — all parts of the darkness that need to come to light."

Zeke nodded as he followed.

"There are fears you need to let go of. We're often so scared to face our own shadows that we keep running from them. Once the spiritual experience begins, we become connected to our light and the universe. The light shines upon the darkness and brings the shadows in us up to the surface. We can't hide from them. We can't escape the light, and we can't escape the darkness within us, either. The more we awaken, the more we're forced to look deeper into those hidden areas within ourselves."

"You know, I was more aggressive towards my shadow than it was towards me! I was thinking of it as a monster. I even thought it had risen to destroy me. So, as an 'offense is the best defense' policy, I attacked it instead. I have never been that aggressive in my life! Why did I do that?"

"You were aggressive because you were triggered by it. You were seeing your true self for the first time — the other half of the whole. Your own being made you furious because you were unwilling to accept yourself, but by embracing it, you came to terms with your own truth. You accepted your light *and* your shadow." Right then, Noah remembered something. "Zeke! Do you remember one of your trials was to prove your connection to the universe? I think this was it. You passed, my boy. You accepted it all!"

CHAPTER THIRTY-THREE
LION'S GATE

About two weeks after the shadow incident, Zeke started reading the book of Egyptian myths again. He revisited the story of Nefertem, another son of the creator god, Ptah. Nefertem was depicted as a handsome young man wearing blue waterlily flowers around his head. Egyptians referred to him as "he who is beautiful" and "waterlily of the sun." Zeke had always felt a connection with Nefertem, as he, too, was a true romantic. That night, in his sleep, Zeke had the vision of floating in the flooding waters of the River Nile again. This time, he saw himself rising from the primal waters as a blue waterlily in the first sunlight. The story of Nefertem felt so soft, pleasant, and poetic to his senses. Even in his dreams, Zeke could feel the waters of the Nile and the smells of the flowers all around.

The following day, he woke up early, feeling fresh, with a beautiful fragrance surrounding him and the first rays of the soft morning sun shining on his face. He developed a habit of clearing his house of all negative energies every morning by burning sage or Palo Santo that he picked up at Indigo Children. That particular morning, he took a long, steamy shower and burned white sage, spreading the thick smoke in every corner of his room and all around the house. The sweet fragrance lingered around the house for the rest of the day, and he could smell it wherever he went.

Noah had given him a vintage record player that he kept by his bedside. He felt refreshed, energized, and happy every time he played an old record in the morning. Today he chose to play one of his favorite songs, the original 1961 version of "Can't Help Falling in Love." The record was also a gift from Noah who knew Zeke, like himself, was an old soul, and he loved everything classic — old music, old singers, old gifts, old books, and basically anything before his own time. Zeke also loved the name of the album, *Blue Hawaii,* as much as he loved the song and the singer, Elvis Presley. He kept humming the song as the music kept flowing through his ears all day.

Everything from the album resonated with his life. The title mentioned the color blue which held meaning to him, especially after meeting Archangel Michael, who oversaw the Blue Ray beings. Nefertem was also called "the Blue Lily." It also had the word "Hawaii" in it, which was equally significant after the Hawaiian healer had left him a treasure trove of ancient wisdom.

Elvis Presley was known as "the King," and the title reminded him of ancient Egyptian kings and pharaohs. The lyrics mentioned the river flowing to the sea, reminding him of the floods of the River Nile again. He knew the record had been sent to him through Noah for a reason. Everything was synchronistic for him; everything was always pointing to something. There were no coincidences in his life.

He remembered the truth about non-duality, and everything being connected. But as he walked around that day, he felt as if it was his heart crying and singing the song, longing for his beloved. He suddenly began losing all hope and faith. It was nearly two years now, and he had not seen his beloved Zoom nor his cosmic friends, Zig and Zag. Would he ever be able to see them again, or will they remain in his heart forever as figments of his imagination? Was he insane? Had he imagined them his whole life? Were they just hallucinations? All these questions took over his mind.

That evening, he carried along with him his desperate thoughts, a nagging headache, and a strange pain in his chest. It was the pain of separation that had suddenly become unable to bear. He was walking past the woods at the time when he saw this glittery little thing on the ground. He was instantly reminded of the holy amethyst, the beautiful violet crystal he had found once in the meadow. He bent down to pick it up. It was a little golden pyramid made of pyrite. Zeke had learned enough about crystals, gemstones, and minerals through different books he had read to know what it was. Pyrite, a brass-yellow mineral with a bright metallic luster, is said to reflect the energy of gold. People often call it "Fool's Gold," and he loved the name.

The moment he touched the little pyramid, it began giving off heat. He felt a huge jolt of electricity pass through his body. The pyrite jumped out of his hands, and it fell to the ground beside him. He looked at the tiny pyramid glowing under the soft evening sun.

"Since it's a pyramid-shaped pyrite, could it have a connection with ancient Egypt? Oh, of course! It traditionally symbolizes the color of kings, riches, and the sun. How could I forget that?" A chill ran down his spine as he kept looking at it.

Suddenly, the pyramid started to grow. It got bigger and bigger, right in front of his eyes, leaving him completely baffled. What Zeke didn't know was that this was no ordinary day, nor had he found just an ordinary stone. Every action he had taken that day and every emotion he felt had all been part of a higher plan, pushing him to this one moment.

As the pyramid continued to grow, Zeke himself felt a growing attraction to it. The sun had just set by then. The sky looked like a rose petal as the last hue of the setting sun painted it pink and red while the moon was already slowly rising. The glowing pyramid was inviting him from the woods, and he had no power within him to resist it. He touched its surface once again with his hands, and once again, he felt a shock wave pass through his body. Only this time, it was much stronger and lasted much longer than the first.

Something strange seemed to have happened to his body. He had no idea what it was. It felt as if he were drowning, like something was wrapping itself around him and choking him to death. He almost felt paralyzed as lights flashed in front of his eyes. He couldn't even breathe. All he could see were colors flashing, floating, and swinging as all his senses went numb.

Then, after what seemed like an eternity to him, he felt as if he was back from the dead, as if he had been suddenly released from something that had his soul in a grip. Once he regained his sight, he was completely amazed by what he saw. He wasn't in the woods of Mackinaw anymore. He was standing in a desert with cold sand under his feet. A cluster of three real, giant pyramids stood before him, and a full moon peeked from the sky behind them as an ancient city rested in their shadow.

Zeke knew exactly where he was. He had read about them and had seen their pictures in the book of Egyptian myths. They were the Great Pyramids of Giza! Left absolutely awestruck, he stood there staring blankly at the pyramids for a very long time.

"What on earth is happening to me right now? Am I really in Egypt? But how?"

His mind was fogged with questions, making him unable to think clearly. He saw a few camels sauntering in the distance and thought of calling out to their riders so he could confirm his assumptions, but his voice choked. He couldn't speak, couldn't utter a word, couldn't call them. So instead, he walked towards the pyramids in a state of trance. Nothing distracted him, and all he could think of was reaching those pyramids. Just as he had touched the pyrite pyramid earlier, he now went ahead and touched the walls of the real Pyramid of Khufu.

The moment he did, something strange happened. The sky above him was instantly filled with dazzling lights. They became so bright that Zeke found it difficult to see and was forced to shut his eyes. Once he opened them again, he saw two lion-like formations right above the pyramids. At first, he thought clusters of bright blue lights and stars must have created those lion figures. Slowly, though, they began changing colors and turned into a transcendent luminescence of every imaginable color. He eventually realized the two lions were the gatekeepers who had opened a floodgate of light from the heavens. It was a cosmic portal through which an immensely powerful light was being sent towards the Earth.

The light poured straight over the pyramids. He was reminded of his homeland, the Lyran Empire, and the palace with the lion-headed gatekeepers he visited with his beloved Zoom. He wanted to rush back to the sky and be reunited with his people, his Lyran mother, his friends, and the head of the High Council, but he couldn't move an inch. He stood there as his feet were anchored firmly to the desert sand.

Zeke couldn't believe what had just transpired before his eyes. Slowly, the lights softened, and he could clearly see two pairs of beings – a pair of humans and another pair of angel-like figures with wings coming down the portal of light towards him. Once they came closer, he recognized St. Germain, Lady Portia, Archangel Zadkiel, and Holy Amethyst floating right above him.

"Welcome to the land of the pyramids on this holy day, dear child!" they pronounced.

"How did you know I'd be here today? Are you the ones who brought me here?" Zeke was utterly surprised by their presence.

"Oh yes, son," St. Germain exclaimed with a wink and a chuckle in the childlike exuberance he always exhibited. "Do you not remember what I said to you? I told you, 'We'll meet another time and in another place — again.' Well, today is the ancient Egyptian New Year, the time of the year when the Nile floods and brings in fertile soil and water to the crops, nourishing an entire civilization in the middle of this dry desert. This is the place, my child, so we brought you here — today of all days."

"On this day every year, a portal known as the 'Lion's Gate' opens for the Earth," Lady Portia added and caught Zeke's attention immediately. The term "Lion's Gate" reminded him of his lion-like Lyran people. Thus, it piqued his interest.

"*What's the Lion's Gate? I've never heard that term before,*" the thought passing through his mind.

Angels don't hear words; they read thoughts, and Archangel Zadkiel was quick to respond. "It is a magnificent celestial alignment, child. It appears on the eighth day of the eighth month, and eight is the number of renewals. This alignment occurs as the Sirius Stargate opens in the constellation of Leo the Lion. What better name than the Lion's Gate, then? For centuries, when the star Sirius stood perpendicular to the Great Pyramids of Giza, the Earth's stored energy was released, giving all of humanity a chance to embody its purest self. This chance comes every year, and every year it is ignored."

"Then there must be a purpose for our meeting here at this time. Why are we all here today?" Zeke's wisdom guided him to ask.

"We come here every year on this portal date to rid the Earth of universal karmic debts, to cleanse and purify its energy, but today we have come here also to welcome you to this ancient land of wisdom and to give you a special gift. We are the keepers of the Violet Flame, the Flame of God. It is a multidimensional tool that has the power to burn the evil and darkness that lies within the hearts of men, allowing them to connect to a higher world. It also holds the power to transmute all external dark and dense energies from around you.

"You can use this magical gift all your life when you invoke us, dear child. You are here in Egypt today because you wished to be here, and the universe has granted your wish. Now, as we pour the magical Violet Flame upon you, it will cleanse and clear you before you step out to experience this new chapter in your life," Holy Amethyst happily proclaimed. "May you use the power of the flame wisely. As its keeper, you will have a great responsibility. You will carry the power of divine goodness."

Together they held a beautiful giant golden pot in their hands and began pouring the mighty Violet Flame upon Zeke from above. He was encapsulated by the fire, but it didn't burn him. Instead, it burned away all hidden patterns of human darkness from every cell of his body, from every molecule, and from his very DNA. It freed him from all the deeds of his past, present, and future, making him free of all burdens of karma and guilt. He stood in this holy fire feeling lighter than the lightest of feathers. Once his energy was fully purified, the Violet Flame slowly receded and went back into the sky. He felt incredibly light and fresh as if a lifetime of emotional garbage was cast out of him.

"I feel like a brand-new person, he happily exclaimed. "That alone was worth the trip!"

CHAPTER THIRTY-FOUR
THE MYSTERY WOMAN

It was a beautiful moonlit night. Zeke came out of the holy fire feeling a fresh surge of energy run through his body. He was finally "in the land where the river floods and the floodgates are opened, where the body never dies, the dead can walk, and where the sun travels towards the timeless." Zoom's words echoed in his ears, and his heart skipped a beat. He was anxious and apprehensive about what was to come. Would he finally be able to see her again? A little further from the pyramids, he could see a few people in a festive mood, singing and dancing around a bonfire. They looked like a group of travelers to his eyes.

"Looks like these people are here for some kind of festival. What are they celebrating tonight? Even the camels look like they're having fun!"

Zeke's head was full of endless thoughts as he hurriedly walked towards them. He inquired where they had come from and where they were heading. None of them could speak English well. Using a few broken words and gestures, they explained to him they were Bedouins, a group of ethnic Arab nomads traveling across the Sahara Desert. They had chosen this place near the Pyramids of Giza for their night halt, so they could celebrate the annual festival known as Wepet Renpet to mark the beginning of the Egyptian new year. The next morning, though, they would move ahead. He tried hard to learn more from them but was unable to grasp most of what they said beyond that.

The travelers were drinking a form of wine mixed with a special Egyptian extract from small pots made of dried mud which looked like clay cups to him. They offered him a pot, asking him to drink the special wine as a sign of respect and celebration. They also offered him some dried fruits and other snacks. He sat there, watching the nomads dance and drink. As a few pots of wine went down his throat, he began enjoying their company, celebrating and dancing along with them.

"Young Mister Tartal, you don't care for me at all! Enjoying such mouthwatering potions and not thinking once of me? Oh, poor, pitiful me."

Zeke was startled to see little Zag dancing along with him around a bonfire in Egypt next to the Pyramids of Giza after two long years of absence. He ran and picked Zag up in his arms like a father meeting a long-lost child and spun him around.

"See, Mister Tartal, just see how biased you can be! You see him, but you don't see me. You miss him, and you don't miss me?"

Zeke looked up above him and spotted Ziggy Bird hovering over his head. He was overjoyed to have been reunited with his two ever-nagging, ever-quarreling, and ever-restless cosmic friends. The whole world seemed to be swirling around him as he danced and danced until he finally fell to the ground.

His face was touching the soft sand of the Sahara Desert on that cold August night when his eyes suddenly fell on a tall, lean woman walking towards him from a distance. She seemed to have risen out of the seemingly endless blanket of sand. She had an extremely sensuous body and walked with a grace and élan very few could match.

Her face was covered with a thin, red veil. All he could see was a pair of dazzling, hypnotic, cat-like eyes looking intensely at him. As she came closer, a cold breeze suddenly blew over his face, and the scent of her body filled his senses. It was a beautiful fragrance, and yet it sent chills down his spine. Then, just like that, she vanished.

"Who is she? Who is this woman? I know her, sure I know her, but how's that even possible? She must be an Egyptian or an Arab woman."

Just then, he heard someone whisper, "Sekhmet. They're celebrating the lioness. Have you heard of her, young man?" It was the husky voice of a woman — and a very familiar one. She stood next to him and spoke in clear English with a beautiful Arabic accent. He was drowsy, and his eyelids were heavy as he barely managed to move his head from side to side, indicating he hadn't.

"Let me tell you a story then," she whispered. Her words sounded like a lullaby to his sleepy ears. "Mankind once plotted against their ruler, the sun god Ra, wanting to overthrow him. Their disrespect hurt and angered him so much that he sent Sekhmet, created by the fire in his eye, to teach the rebels a lesson."

As Zeke lay motionless, the mystery woman continued. "Sekhmet was the embodiment of Ra's rage. Her fury was unquenchable. Even after she had punished those who had risen up against her father, she still wished for more carnage. Fearing that her rage would destroy the human race forever, Ra finally resorted to a trick to stop her. He poured thousands of jars of a beer-like liquid dyed with red ochre on the ground in front of her. Mistaking it for a pool of blood, Sekhmet swooped down and lapped it all up, becoming so drunk that she forgot her killing spree. Giving up the slaughter of men, she returned peacefully to her father. Humanity was thus saved, and the gods and humans became allies once again."

Zeke dreamily looked at her, half asleep and half awake. She suddenly burst into a giggle as she spoke. Then she began laughing insanely, so loud that the sound of her laughter spread across the entire sky and echoed all around the silent and cold desert.

"Sekhmet breathes fire as they dance and play music to soothe her wild nature and drink wine to imitate the extreme drunkenness that calmed her fury. Can you imagine what fun it is — Egyptians celebrating a festival of intoxication to honor the 'Lady of Drunkenness'?" a voice came out of nowhere.

She picked up a little mud pot from the sand and held it in her hands. One after the other, she drank all the red wine from the little pots lying around her. She drank and drank until she could drink no more. Fully intoxicated, she stood up and began clapping her hands in joy, laughing and dancing around the bonfire. Lying on the desert sand in front of her, Zeke silently watched her move. She danced until she could barely drag her feet. Slowly, she walked away from the crowd, turning her head one last time to bid him farewell.

She then removed the long veil covering her face and hair and mischievously smiled at him, unleashing a whole new world of mysteries in front of his eyes. A breathtakingly beautiful young woman was now standing in front of him in a flowy red linen gown with her yellow, catlike eyes and long, wavy auburn hair.

He was too groggy to be able to stand up and walk towards her, so he stayed under the stars, quietly watching her. Even in this extreme state, he didn't miss her features – her sharp feline face, her grace, her boldness almost matching that of a fierce lioness, and the glowing red sun disk on her head. She disappeared into the wilderness as he continued lying under the twinkling night sky, the moon smiling at him.

His eyes felt heavier. A soothing breeze blew over him again as if someone had lovingly put him to bed. His heart recognized her immediately. It knew who she was – the warrior goddess, the divine

'Eye of Ra,' a fierce lioness indeed, but she was also the one he had come to search for in this distant and dry desert land.

• • •

Zeke opened his eyes with a heavy head. *"I shouldn't have had so much to drink last night. I am so hungover,"* he thought as he tried hard to pull his head up. It was almost noon, and he was still lying on the desert sand. He felt the scorching heat of the sun on his skin, his back burned from the heat of the sand below as if it were on fire. He could see nothing but the blinding sun and feel nothing but the hot desert wind blowing over him.

"The travelers must have left already. I need to get going, too."

Feeling almost dead as he lay there, he tried to force himself to stand up and drag his feet at least. What he now saw was enough to startle and outright shock him. There were no pyramids, no humans, and no sign of life anywhere around him. For miles and miles, all he could see was the desert sand and sand dunes. He realized he was in the middle of nowhere.

"How did I end up here? The last thing I remember was watching the sky lying on the sand next to the pyramids." His mind raced as he anxiously called out, "ZIG! ZAG! ANYONE???"

He desperately tried looking around to find them, but they were nowhere near. He was reminded of the bonfire and the mud pots, too, but there were no traces of those, either. Tired and disillusioned, he silently lay there, feeling hopeless.

"Is this how I die?" He began missing his family, his friends, Mr. Leitner, and his dog, Coconut. He even began missing the black cat around his house and the entire Farley Street neighborhood.

"Will I ever be able to go back home? Will I ever be able to see my friends and family again? If I die out here, the sands will cover my body,

and nobody will ever even know about it. They'll never be able to find me!"

Just then, her name popped into his mind. He called out, "Zoom, oh Zoom! Where are you? I came all this way to see you! How long will you still stay away from me?" Tears of despair began rolling down his cheeks.

He had no idea how long he had been lying there on the sand, woozy and exhausted. It felt like forever. Then, suddenly the hot desert wind began to blow again. In front of his eyes, a twister of sand rose from the dunes off in the distance. From the rising sands emerged a beautiful feminine figure that slowly began walking towards him. The desert heat, the sand, and the sun had almost turned red by then. As she came closer, he saw a woman draped in red linen, with the head of a lioness wearing a red sun disk like a royal crown, the sun shining brightly behind her. Zeke instantly recognized her as Sekhmet from the night before.

"You fell asleep last night before hearing the entire story," she said with a smile.

It was difficult for him to even move his face, but he managed to smile back at her. His heart was thumping hard.

"Can I share the rest of the story with you now?" she asked.

"Where am I? This isn't where I was last night." He couldn't move or speak, but he had already learned to communicate using his energy. Whenever he traveled out of the physical dimension, he experienced and realized how immaterial and redundant the use of words was. He knew higher beings could communicate through their thoughts and feelings.

"You're amid the great cosmic nothingness. You've reached the beginning of time. Nothing's been created yet. You still don't remember who you are, do you?" She held his head as he lay on her lap, gently caressing his hair.

"You're the one who dreamed the creation of the universe long before you were Ezekiel. You deemed the entire world, bringing it all into existence! It's okay. I shall remind you of everything again," she said with all the love in her eyes as he silently rested his head on her lap. She continued with her story.

"Once Sekhmet returned to her father, Ra, she slept in peace for a long time. Then, when she finally woke up, she saw Ptah, the god of creation. The two, lost in each other's eyes, fell in love in an instant." She looked deep into Zeke's eyes as she reminded him of the love story of Ptah and Sekhmet, and he instantly fell in love with her — all over again.

"Remember the divine marriage, Zeke?" She uttered his name for the first time since they met, and he felt a rush of energy flowing through his body. His body was desperate to come back to life as she continued her whispering tale of love. "Sekhmet and Ptah were and will always be eternal lovers. Their union is the celebration of the two eternal halves of the same cosmic force. Their union restored and reestablished the cosmic order and brought healing to life in the form of their son, Nefertem, 'water-lily of the sun.' Do you remember him? He took on your qualities at times and mine at others." She laughed like a child as she narrated the story of their son.

Tears of joy began rolling down his cheeks as he remembered everything. Her words were so soothing they calmed down his burning body. He recognized himself, his beloved, and the son they had once had.

"Don't you remember us, Zeke, even now? Don't you remember me? I'm the protector of the cosmic order of Ma'at — the one who loves Ma'at and detests evil," she proclaimed.

Tears continued to flow as he silently rested on the desert sand with his head still on her lap. He had finally recognized the one who had lovingly written the letter to her husband while leaving for war, the papyrus which came flying towards him that one evening in the city of Mackinaw.

"I do! See, I found you! I followed your letter, I followed your clues, I followed my heart, and it brought me here… to you. I recognize you, Zoom, my beloved Ezra, my Sekhmet, my eternal half." His eyes spoke a thousand words and brought a glowing smile to her face.

"Yes! Love knows no boundary, my darling. The fragrance of love has the power to transcend all barriers of time and space. See, you finally found your way back to me."

At last, he found all the answers to all the questions running through his mind. He now understood the reason behind his being transported to the ancient land of Egypt on the day of the Lion's Gate. He had lived more lives than stars in the sky, he had existed since the beginning of time, and he had once been Ptah, the god of creation.

He smiled at her one last time, reassuring her of his undying love, and then closed his eyes and fell asleep. It was a deep slumber, a sleep of peace, joy, and abundant love. He began dreaming. In his dreams, he created the cosmic order. The stars, the planets, and the galaxies all came into form one by one. Finally, he created the Earth and human life. Structures were raised and civilizations were born. They built temples and pyramids, grew crops and trees, and developed languages to communicate. Lying there in eternal peace, the creator god watched everything come to life from the great nothingness. Once creation was complete, he opened his eyes.

He saw himself lying under the twinkling night sky near the Great Pyramids of Giza once again. He could hear the sound of splashing waves as the high tides washed the shores of the Nile on that cold, breezy winter night. Only this time, he wasn't Zeke Tartal anymore. He wasn't the timid little boy from Farley Street, trying to cope with a difficult family life in a modern world, learning the spiritual ropes, or waiting to finish high school. He was another being, alive in another space and another reality. He was the ancient divine blacksmith who dreamed the universe into existence.

His body had come back to life again. Standing in front of his eyes was his divine counterpart, not in the form of an alien lover but as the fierce warrior goddess Sekhmet, wearing a red linen gown and smiling at him mischievously. He looked deep into her eyes, and she reached out her hands to him. He took them as he rose from the bed of sand, and they began walking towards the lofty pyramids. They married each other again under an iridescent moon, reenacting their cosmic union. Zeke Tartal learned what he had once been: he was more than Ezekiel, and he was even more than Ptah.

As Ptah and Sekhmet, the union of the divine lovers was a union of creation and destruction. Zoom wanted Zeke to experience this great cosmic union, a game they had played over and over again. It wasn't new to them. They'd had many incarnations on many planets and in many gender combinations. Besides, they had helped civilizations evolve even before they had existed on Lyra. They were two halves of something much older, far more primal, and unfathomable — and Zeke was very much a part of that something. He was there at the inception — the inception of the Christ light.

CHAPTER THIRTY-FIVE
THE MISSING WEEK

Zeke woke up to the sound of a heated argument. He jumped off the bed and ran out of his room. Leia was having an argument with their father over her sexuality, and it was an argument Zeke had heard many times before.

"Mom doesn't have a problem with it. Why should you?" Leia protested.

"Look. I've had enough of all the crap in this house. My own wife won't even look at me, my son thinks he's a space warrior, I have one daughter who's into chicks, and another who digs the sight of her own blood... and people wonder why I drink. I just can't take it anymore. I'm going to sell the house and move to London. I'm sick of my life not heading anywhere and my family going to hell in a handbasket. I'm going to start all over — a new life, in a new city, in a new country."

Just then, Maya walks in after a few days away. "And YOU! Where in hell have you been? After a brief pause, "Well???"

Maya just stood there silent.

"That does it. Call me selfish, but I'm washing my hands of all of you. Goodbye and good luck!"

Zeke was startled to hear his father lash out like this. He still hadn't finished high school and couldn't hope to afford a roof over his head, much less care for his sick mother if Ben went through with something that far-fetched. Zeke had always been at odds with him, but he never thought Ben could be as selfish and vicious as he sounded. Leia was furious, too. She was still in school and had been handling a lot already. Maya was barely ever home, and their mother was still bedridden. The Tartal siblings couldn't simply let the house be sold because of their narcissistic father. Regardless of their family issues, it was still their home.

Zeke tried to remain calm and think of a solution. It didn't take long before a thought struck him and made him smile. Tartal House wasn't in his father's name in the first place. The legal and rightful owner was Audrey through her parents, not Ben. An instant knee-jerk reaction wanting to stop his mother from giving in to any pressures or emotional blackmail made him rush to her room, but he paused immediately upon entering, extremely pained by what he saw. She was wide awake and lying silently in her bed, tears rolling down her cheeks. Ben had broken the news of his leaving to her, and the reality of a terminal illness, a failed marriage and a broken family staring her in the face was just too much for her. She couldn't fight back and she had nothing left to give. It was a tragic ending to a dream and goal she worked so hard to achieve: a complete and loving family.

The Tartal children had never really been fond of their father. Their immediate survival instinct had thus made them forget the emotional impact of his decision on the family. Whether they liked him or not, whether they loved him or not, their family would still break forever if this man left. Tartal House wasn't just a place; it was the cradle of a family, no matter how broken it was. This place, this family, was the only thing that mattered to Audrey Tartal.

Zeke was immediately reminded of his responsibilities as a lightworker; his job was to guide and protect. Charity always begins at home, he realized. That was when he decided to speak with his father, mother, and sister individually to try and sort out the problems that had divided his family. It wasn't possible for him to speak with Leia and his father together, as they both stood at opposite ends of the argument, so Zeke's words would mean nothing. Instead, he chose to give them some time and went to his mother first. She was the most rational of anyone in the family anyway. He sat beside his mother's bed and lovingly stroked her unkempt hair. He simply sat there for a while, and then she broke the silence.

"Don't worry about me, dear. I'll get through this," she smiled at him and spoke. Zeke and his mother always understood each other without words.

"I know you're very hurt, Mom, and I know what you've been thinking. I am so sorry to have taken this long. All this time, I just overlooked your pain. Well, it ends now. I'll try my best to stop him. I'll do everything in my power to keep us all together," he said as he held his mother's hands.

Audrey was amazed at the conviction she saw in her son's eyes. At that moment, she realized her little boy had grown up. Although she could never publicly admit it, Zeke had always been her favorite. He was her one achievement, her greatest source of pride, and now, looking into this young man's eyes, she felt prouder than ever.

"Just promise me you won't sign the papers. Give me just a little bit of time, please," he pleaded. At this, she turned her eyes away. She couldn't face him, as she didn't have a clear answer to his plea. Not yet.

Zeke came out of his mother's room, lost in thoughts. He chose to ignore the argument between Leia and their father. It was still ongoing. He finally decided to play his part in resolving the brewing tension before the situation got out of control. He knew his sister trusted his decisions and would listen to him more than his father.

"Leia, stop arguing with him. Everything will be okay. It's not your fault. Remember, he's just a selfish drunk, and he's acting out. Tartal House belongs to Mom anyway. He can't sell it, and besides, she won't let him."

"I suppose not, but this is serious — unless it's just a threat. What if he actually sells the house, though? What are we going to do?"

"Don't worry about that. I'll take care of it. Everything will be as it should."

"Oh, boy…" she muttered as she turned away, shaking her head in confusion.

• • •

Zeke finally got back to his room. He didn't have the chance to pay attention to anything because of the fight. Lying down on the bed, he closed his eyes and tried to relive the experience of being with Sekhmet, but it wasn't easy. He opened his eyes, sat up, and looked at the calendar on his study table. It was August 15th. Zeke was left spellbound for a moment, and it took him a while to understand what he saw.

"*The Lions' Gate was on the eighth. How can that be a week ago? Where have I been?*" He went straight to Leia's room to find out where he had been all week. She was both intrigued and amused by his question.

"Oh, God. Here we go again. Don't you remember where you were last week? I thought you stayed over at Mr. Leitner's place since you went for a walk that evening and never returned."

"Evening? Which evening are you talking about? Do you remember the date?" He wanted some confirmation.

"Umm, last week. It was, it was… oh yeah, now I remember. It was the eighth. I waited for you, so you could take care of Mom for a while. When you didn't show up, I thought maybe you'd call, but then finally, I thought you must have stayed over at Mr. Leitner's house."

"What happened after that night? How could you be so sure I was at his place? Did you check, or did I call to let you know I'd be staying over?"

"No, you didn't. You didn't bother to call back for the whole week. I was somewhat concerned, but then I figured Maya and Dad stay away for days at a time, so why not you? I waited for you to come home on your own and chose not to bother you. I didn't want Mom to worry either, so I told her Mr. Leitner was sick and that you were staying with him for a while to help out."

"When did I come back home?"

"I saw you this morning when I was fighting with Dad, but hey, wait… what's wrong with you, Zeke? Can't you remember where you were all week? Are you sure you're okay?" Leia was really looking worried now.

Zeke understood the gravity of the situation and immediately decided to change the subject to ease the tension. "Of course I re-member where I was! I was at Noah's house, and you're right. He really was sick, so I was helping him get better. I just wanted to check how grown up and responsible you've become. If someone suddenly goes missing for a week, you should dig a little deeper into the matter than you did. I was just trying to make sure you knew what you're supposed to do, my dear little sister." He was wise enough to laugh it off and calm her down.

"You always do this, Zeke. You behave in ways I can't under-stand. I only have a common human brain, you see — not a cosmic one like yours." She was a bit upset with her brother's strange questions. He was the eternal outsider, but ever since Maya started acting out, the bond between Zeke and Leia had only grown stronger. She knew her brother would always be by her side and would never let her down. She secretly wished Maya understood that because Maya was a beautiful, fragile soul, and the very thought of her coping with emotional hurt pained both her siblings. But Zeke's wisdom also told him this was a choice Maya had made way before she was born. She needed to walk her path, learn her lessons, and evolve as per the plan that Source had made for her.

• • •

Zeke was reminded of Noah once he discussed the missing week with Leia. The next morning, he decided to visit his friend. It was quite early, and the weather was cool. As Zeke stepped outside of his house, he noticed something unusual. His eyes were used to seeing the black cat roaming around his house whenever he stepped out. This time, it wasn't there. Yes, the same jet-black cat with the glowing yellow eyes that initially made him feel uncomfortable, and eventually began to make him feel protected, was gone.

"It must be somewhere around. I'm sure it'll start following me once I get to the street," he tried to console himself. "Is it gone because of the week I missed? It must have waited for me and finally left after not seeing me."

He was trying to rationalize things. He kept turning around, looking around every corner, under every bench, and under every car, but the cat was gone. Zeke had lost yet another friend.

When he reached Indigo Children, he found it closed, so he went to Noah's house, which was locked. Not being able to find Noah made him anxious. He dreaded the possibilities of what might have happened during the week he had missed. He went around the neighborhood and asked if anybody knew anything about the old man. The neighbors informed him that he had a sudden cardiac arrest and needed to be hospitalized. They also told him there wasn't much to worry about, as it was a mild attack, that he was feeling better, and that he would be returning that afternoon.

It still took him some time to come to terms with all the things that had taken place in Mackinaw during his absence, in what he would soon come to call "the missing week." He waited at Noah's house until he arrived with a neighbor who drove him home from the hospital, and he was very happy to see Zeke again.

"Hey, lad. How have you been? I was so worried I wouldn't be able to see you again!"

"Noah! I am so sorry. If I had known you were…"

"It's okay, son," he interrupted. "In fact, it's better you didn't know. You would have gotten all worked up. I thought you were busy at home, so I didn't bother you."

"When were you admitted to the hospital? How long were you there?" Zeke posed these questions as he wanted to make sure Egypt wasn't just a figment of his imagination.

Noah thought about it for a moment, trying to recall. "Oh, yes. How could I forget? It was the eighth."

"The Lion's Gate. Oh my God." The reality of it hit him like a ton of bricks. Zoom instantly appeared in his mind. *"I really crossed time and space to be with you, Zoom!"* he silently exclaimed as a surge of happiness filled his mind, body, and heart.

Just then, a feminine voice whispered to his ears, "Yes, my dear, and now you have the proof!"

After Noah's discharge from the hospital, Zeke stayed with him, helping him get healthier and stronger so he could go back to work, happy and full of energy. The secret of the missing week remained hidden in his heart forever, reminding him of the miraculous journey he had been on – a journey where he could break free from all human limitations, a journey through time and space itself.

CHAPTER THIRTY-SIX

THE GREAT RETURN

Back at home, Zeke finally decided to face his father. He knew he had already touched a lot of lives – Mr. Leitner, Gael, the Copelands, and his little sister Leia. They had all seen profound changes in their lives because of him. They had all unknowingly turned into little beacons of light themselves because Zeke had been gradually empowering them, helping them to grow and shine.

He had finally decided to fulfill his duty to his own father and help him out of the darkness. Zeke knew he had been shying away from the responsibility of clearing his father's negativity, allowing it to pile up for far too long. His instinct told him it was time to purge it all. He wanted to cleanse his home of the evil and poisonous toxicity that had silently crept in and contributed to his mother's ill health as well as Maya's fractured state of mind.

He needed to fix things. He needed to heal his father. He chose to tempt fate and finally began speaking with him after many years of cold silence between them, and as he did, he realized how lonely Ben had been all his life. He was surprised to see how receptive his father was towards his advice. The man was growing older and needed help overcoming his issues and blocks. He was a victim of societal conditioning. All Zeke had to do was shine his light upon him.

He put his hand on his father's shoulder. "What?" Ben was startled. "What do you want?" His tone was extremely frustrated and almost hateful, but Zeke's positive energy had already started working on him.

"I want to listen to you, Dad, for the first time ever."

"Listen… to what?" Ben could feel something he never had before. It was pure love from his own son and his power as a lightworker.

"To everything, Dad, to anything you want to say. I'm all ears."

"What in hell are you going on about? If this is something from one of your space odysseys, just stop it right now."

Zeke felt a surge of negative energy boiling out of his father's body. But his own light was far more powerful than all of Ben's pent-up rage and negativity. As Zeke tried to move in closer, Ben reacted more negatively. He grabbed Zeke's collar.

"Look here, kid, I don't know what kind of game you're playing here, but I'm not falling for it. After all these years, you expect me to believe that now? NOW? You want to listen to ME? No one here wants to listen to me. None of you care, you never have."

Zeke almost wanted to cry once he saw how much sadness he had let his own father go through. Ben Tartal was painfully alone, and Zeke had to help him. He put his own hand on his father's. "I do, Dad. I want to listen. Please, just give it to me straight. Let it all out now, while you still can."

Zeke poured every ounce of his power into an appeal that his father could not look past, and that was when Ben let it all out — everything that had been eating him alive all his life. He wanted to hold his tongue, but his words betrayed him, and tears flowed from his eyes. He divulged all his pain, something he thought in a million years he would ever do.

Ben Tartal had always blamed his family for not being perfect, for his dreams being shattered, for all his unhealthy addictions, and for all that didn't match the vision of a perfect life. Yet, the fact of the matter was that he secretly craved to be with his family and wished he could feel like one of them. He was lost and just didn't know his way back. His entire life, he had been an outcast. His own parents never understood him, so why should his children? The more he was shunned, the more isolated he became. He turned to alcohol and gambling to fill the void felt by what he saw as abandonment. All his angst and his anger had come from his own insecurities and his fear of being left alone.

Zeke had turned into a true healer and a guide. He understood his father's position better than anyone could, and he helped him along. He continued having conversations with Ben after that. At first, they were about mundane things — about sports, about cars, and even the weather, but eventually he helped his father see the bigger picture.

"Don't you ever feel like you want to change, Dad?' he asked him one day. "Don't you feel like there's more to life than whiskey and betting?"

"I… I do, Zeke. It's very hard for me to admit, but I don't like living like this. I want a normal life like everyone else. I want to live with my family, and I want my kids to look up to me, but how could you? Now I'm nothing but a drunken fool."

At that moment, Zeke knew exactly what he needed to do. He again put his hand on his father's shoulder and said, "Dad, there's always time — time to heal and grow, and I'm sorry, sorry for making you feel this lonely. I am sorry for never opening up. I love you, Dad." As he used the magic of Hawaiian healing on his father, he let the power of the divine of the Violet Flame flow into his father and purge him of all negativities.

Then Zeke convinced Ben to go into rehab, to which he reluctantly agreed. That was the first time he realized how powerful he had become. His gained power and skills had now turned him into a completely realized lightworker. Life was smooth for Zeke, Leia, and Mrs. Tartal for a while after that. Zeke had consistently performed well in his studies and was sure to finish high school with flying colors.

Mr. Leitner was also a lot happier in his life, too. Seeing Indigo Children gain a sudden popularity among young boys and girls made him feel happy and useful. The store had become the right tool for guiding young, impressionable minds who held the keys to the future. The young folk could learn more about the spiritual and metaphysical worlds through the various books, crystals, and other articles the store provided for them.

What they loved most, however, was speaking with old Mr. Leitner, who became a walking spiritual encyclopedia for them. They would sit on the floor gazing at him with eyes wide open, hanging on to every word, as if he were telling ghost stories to his own grandchildren. Zeke was happy to see Indigo Children flourish so much in such a short time as well. It was satisfying for him to see Noah make new friends and not feel as lonely anymore. The responsibility Zeke had taken upon himself to keep this old man happy was now being shouldered by many others his age.

• • •

Once Ben came home from rehab, he was a completely changed man. He had discovered his softer, nurturing side. He started to love being at home with his wife and children. He began cooking for Audrey and the kids and discovered that he had a skill for the culinary arts. He even started writing poetry. His ego was finally gone, giving way to an open and accepting man. He would often laughingly proclaim that he could have easily become a renowned chef had he started cooking a little earlier in life.

Ben and his wife had been living through an unsatisfying, unhappy, and cold relationship for years, and Ben took every chance he could to make up for that. He helped her, cared for her, and ensured she had everything she needed. All the manipulation and selfishness were gone, and Ben did everything in his power to make his wife feel loved. They had finally developed pure, selfless love and respect for each other. They both shared a love of food and cooking brought them closer. They nurtured their little garden together and took care of Coconut. Their sweet and loyal dog had grown old, and looking after him was a good way for them to heal. They loved being with their children as they saw their little kids grow into beautiful, talented, and promising young adults.

The most miraculous transformation, however, was in the relationship between Leia and her father. He had begun focusing on his daughter and truly paying attention to her needs and desires. The father-daughter duo was slowly becoming the best of friends because of their passion for automobiles. He began taking her to his garage again to teach her the nuances of cars and the tricks of his trade. Leia was on top of the world as, for the first time, she finally had a father in her life. His guidance helped prepare her for a successful career in the auto industry as well as a capable heir to his company. It was nothing short of a dream come true for her. It brought a gleam to her eyes, and Zeke could clearly see the glow of joy on her face every day.

Ben still had work to do on himself, however. His relationship with Maya was still strained and in dire need of repair. Audrey and Leia decided to throw Zeke a birthday breakfast party on Christmas morning, and as they celebrated his eighteenth birthday, fate brought them the best gift of all. Maya turned up after being gone for almost five days, and this time she had come to stay.

"Well, well. Look who's back… the 'prodigal daughter,'" Ben playfully teased, but was concerned nonetheless.

"Ben, please don't start. It's Christmas," Audrey pleaded.

"Where have you been… *darling?*" he mockingly asked.

"With friends."

"What friends? Who are they? Where do they live? Have I ever met them?"

No response.

"Ben, let's save this for later," Audrey firmly stated.

"Fine, fine. Let's just sweep this under the rug, too. I'm going to need to build an addition on to this house to accommodate all that's hidden under this 'rug'."

"Maya, we've missed you so much," a joyful Audrey exclaimed, embracing her warmly.

"Yes, we have," Ben concurred. "It's good to have you home. You are here to stay, right?"

"I'm pretty sure." Maya heaved a sigh of relief. She had been staying away from home off and on for the last year and hanging around boys older than her. Her attachment issues and her need to be loved led her to cling to a boy who was narcissistic and toxic. She stopped showing up at school, she almost never talked to her family, and she had spent many a night sleeping at friends' houses and occasionally in random corners of town just to avoid going home. Everything she had gone through changed her from a little girl living in a fantasy world into a cynical teenager.

All those tormenting days she spent away from her family made her realize how much she needed them, and they needed her. She had distanced herself from them for so long, she didn't know if they would accept her back. She chose Christmas to make amends. She knew it was Zeke's birthday, and she learned from Leia that her father was trying hard to change. Seeing them potentially heal as a family made her feel like she, too, could finally be loved for who she was. She chose this day to ask for their forgiveness and finally be the daughter and sister she was meant to be.

That Christmas made the Tartals realize how much they loved and missed each other and how incomplete their family had been with Maya gone. It was a day of unmatched joy for her, too, as she felt the unconditional love of family for the first time in her life, something she feared she would never be able to feel.

Leia was the happiest of them all. For her, it was as if her child-hood had returned: cuddling up under blankets on cold winter nights, listening to bedtime stories as Mother read them aloud, sharing dreams, goals, and clothes with Maya — even indulging in those friendly fights. As identical twins, they were like two halves of each other, two sides of the same coin. Whether they hated each other or loved each other, one was always incomplete without the other. Leia always felt like a part of her was missing and now she had that back. With Maya permanently home, the Tartal sisters started helping their father with the garage and learning the trade together. With Leia's knowledge of cars and Maya's understanding of sales, they had an unbeatable combination.

Zeke knew that all these little miracles were linked to the one missing week in his life. All this change was triggered by his journey to Egypt and all that he had learned about his past life as Ptah. He was a Lyran lightworker and keeper of the Violet Flame. The idea of having been a creator god sent chills down his spine. He still could not comprehend all that he had been and all that he had the potential to be. As a lightworker and one of the oldest souls in all of creation, he had the power to erase every thought of evil at will, but he was still a young man, and he had far more to learn.

CHAPTER THIRTY-SEVEN
PREMONITION

It was the best Christmas ever for the Tartals. Everyone who carried the Tartal name was now under the same roof, united as a family for the first time in a long time. Since Ben had distanced himself from the family, the Tartals had not gone to mass in ages, but that Christmas morning, the Tartals went to church as a family. Once they came home, Ben made a wonderful meal for lunch, and Audrey was busy wrapping last-minute gifts. She baked a special birthday cake for Zeke. The comforting aroma of butter and cinnamon filling the house brought back many memories of Mrs. Braganza and the days of his carefree childhood when he played with Coconut all the time. Coco was very old now and barely left his little doghouse that Ben had brought inside for the winter.

"The family could have been complete if only Mrs. Braganza was here like before," he thought.

He also wished that poetic Zig and naughty Zag could be there as they often had been in the old days when he was just a kid. But Zeke knew that not all wishes were meant to be fulfilled, and he was okay with it.

The new year brought a lot of peace and tranquility to Zeke's life. He could feel the harmony and prosperity all around him. Maya was attending school regularly again, and she excelled as a sales trainee at Tartal's Garage. Everything in Zeke's life was looking up except for the fact that he still missed his cosmic friends. Zeke and Gael finally graduated high school that June with good grades and immediately started looking into colleges. Zeke was passionate about art, literature, and history, while Gael had an interest in management studies, wanting to be an entrepreneur and establishing a lawn care business of his own after all he had learned in yard work and landscaping.

• • •

Everything in Zeke's life was perfect, and he had nothing to worry about. He had his family and friends around him, yet one morning late in June, he woke up feeling restless. The state of perpetual bliss, harmony, and happiness that Zeke had attained had suddenly turned into a deep sinking feeling he couldn't quite explain even if he wanted to. This restlessness continued for days. It began bothering him so much that he stopped reading books and even stopped listening to his favorite music, which had always lifted his spirits.

Days turned to months, but the feeling of hopelessness never went away. Moonlit nights would come and go, and the magical amethyst would lie in one corner of his drawer, uncharged, unused, and almost unwanted. All of his crystals would lie unattended as well. He felt no motivation to clear his chakras or to meditate. He even stopped doing the Ho'oponopono practice. He could no longer feel his connection with his spiritual guides and angels. This feeling of loneliness and a divide with everything around him wasn't an uncommon feeling for him, but the unease he felt this time was unmatched, different from anything he had felt before. Even though everything around him was perfectly fine on an apparent level, something inside him was wrong — seriously wrong.

Then one morning, all his negative thoughts, all his internal emptiness, started to manifest as he woke up, and a shocking bit of news awaited him. Coconut was missing. Zeke started feeling dizzy almost immediately after hearing the news, and he felt like he would faint. It was a feeling that lasted for quite a while. Maya had fed Coconut and put him to bed the night before, but when Leia checked on him in the morning, he wasn't there.

Coco was really old and frail, and he had lived far longer than anyone could have hoped for, but they were sure he wouldn't be able to walk too far on his own. They searched for him everywhere — in and around the house and throughout the neighborhood, but he was nowhere to be found. They looked for days but could find no trace of him. Coconut, their dog, a member of their family and Zeke's constant companion since childhood, was gone and presumed dead.

Zeke had been through a lot of emotional challenges in his life. His journey towards a spiritual awakening hadn't always been easy, but this trepidation was very different from anything he had ever faced. A strong premonition of an imminent change slowly surfacing from his core was getting the better of him. Was everything about to fall apart? Was he heading toward some sort of darkness? This sudden change in his thoughts left him terrified, far more so than anything he had ever faced in his physical life. But what he felt had very little to do with Coconut's disappearance. His despair had been caused by a much darker and more malicious energy. Zeke felt the menacing presence of an old acquaintance — a being of pure evil, a being so unbelievably corrupt, it penetrated Zeke's pure aura and sent him into a deep, downward spiral.

Everybody hoped and prayed that Coconut would come back home somehow. At that point, however, it would have been nothing short of a miracle. Nonetheless, something that concerned them more than that was the strangeness they observed in Zeke's behavior. He had been a loner for most of his life, and his family and friends had learned to leave him alone when he wasn't in the mood to communicate. Nobody really noticed the changes he was going through because no one could ever understand how deep they were. He felt the presence of true darkness for the first time in his life, and Coconut's disappearance had taken this feeling of dread to a much deeper level.

"Holy Tony, look around. Coco's lost and must be found!" he prayed earnestly night after night.

Coco unfortunately didn't return, and Zeke's sense of foreboding didn't leave him. It stayed with him for months and eventually grew stronger, keeping him awake in bed and making him question the nature of good and evil as well as everything around him. Some days, the presence of dread he felt was so strong that he could feel it like a knife in his stomach.

The fear of death that he once held had now returned, and it grew larger, deeper, and darker with each passing day. He often felt as if the walls of his house had suddenly come alive and came closer and closer to choking him to death. It made him feel like he was losing his mind. He didn't even wish to meet Zig, Zag, or Zoom anymore. He had applied to many colleges before graduation, but now he couldn't even bring himself to open the response letters. He decided he wasn't ready for his first year of college and the pressure that went along with it. Higher education would come in time, and he promised his father he would read tons of books in the meantime to keep his mind active.

"Good, because I didn't want to fund your college education anyway," Ben admitted openly. "Nevertheless, you will have to get a job."

"I'm making money online, Dad. I have a small business, but I'm not going to tell you what it is. I *will* tell you that I'm developing a video game about space warriors, though."

"Naturally," Ben replied. "Where else would your mind live?"

Zeke just chuckled and said to himself, "If you only knew…"

CHAPTER THIRTY-EIGHT
THE DARKEST NIGHT

"Caw-caw-caw."

Zeke woke up to the loud calls of a black raven sitting on his windowsill. Ravens were a rare sight around his house, let alone inside his room. The sun hadn't fully risen yet, which made the horizon look like it was on fire. The half-open window was right next to Zeke's bed, and he was taken aback by the sight of a raven looking him right in the eye. Once he managed to roll the remnants of sleep out of his eyes, he sat straight up in his bed and stretched his arms. The raven gave him one final look like it was trying to ask him something and then flew away.

He looked at the calendar above his study table, and his heart skipped a beat. It was August 8th, 2018. Just a year ago, he had been in Egypt. He had traveled to the beginning of time, and before he knew it, a year had passed. He sat on his bed, still as could be for a while. A few moments later, a pair of black ravens flew close to his window. "Caw-caw-caw," they called as if they were warning him, signaling the approach of some predator, as birds often do in the wild.

"This is… well, unusual. What's wrong with these birds? They're really making a ruckus now," Zeke said in his head.

As he poked his head out of the window to send the birds away, he was struck by a sudden gut-wrenching feeling as he heard a very familiar sound. "Meeeoooww!"

As he looked down, he saw the black cat sitting right there on the steps of the back porch. Zeke immediately ran out of his room and headed straight to the porch. The black cat was back, wiggling its long and furry tail. This time it was accompanied by a raven that sat quietly by its side. The bird and the cat sitting together made for a strange sight indeed.

"Meeeooowww. Meeeooowww," it called again, immediately followed by a series of loud and shrill, "caw caw caws."

Zeke should have been happy to see his old friend after a whole long year, but he wasn't. He instinctively knew that it had returned as a messenger. Zeke had no idea how right he was or what that would mean for him and his family, but he would soon find out, for not long after, a horrific reality was revealed.

It was a heart-wrenching truth nobody in the family had been prepared for. When everybody was at the breakfast table, and their mother hadn't turned up yet, he went to call her. She was still lying in bed, just as he had left her earlier the night before in a deep and peaceful slumber, the smile still lingering on her face. He lovingly stroked her hair and tried to wake her up. It was only after he tried to wake her a second time, he touched her hands and found them ice-cold. He then realized his mother had left him and the family forever.

Audrey Tartal had finally found happiness in her life after years of enduring pain, loneliness, and a debilitating disease. Her weak, little heart had suffered through years of pain and sadness, but that final year's worth of fulfillment and love was all it could handle.

Death had struck Farley Street once again, and this time it claimed the most loving person in the Tartal home. She had suffered so much, only to see her family achieve true happiness just before she had to pass. She was only forty-six years of age.

As a lightworker, Zeke consciously tried hard to find at least some source of light, but this time he could find none. There was nothing but all-encompassing darkness. One night, he woke up in his bed and his eyes were pools of tears that simply refused to leave. He suddenly felt someone else crying along with him. He immediately froze, wanting to run away, scared, thinking it might be supernatural. He wasn't prepared to deal with a ghost or a vision today. He finally realized it was no ghost but his own soul crying along with him, very clearly as a separate entity. He was drained. His body was giving in. His head was so heavy he couldn't lift it. He wanted so desperately to stop crying, but he couldn't. He finally fell asleep on a tear-stained pillow.

Zeke had read all about people's spiritual experiences, even those of starseeds and lightworkers like himself. He also read about what many call the "Dark Night of the Soul" experience, but reading about such matters did him no good when it came to actually experiencing them. He wanted to go back to the comfort of his mother's lap. He wished to be in Zoom's arms. He wished to navigate this with all the wisdom he had gained or using the guidance of his cosmic friends, but he had no respite.

He had to finish this journey alone, without any light to guide him or show him the way. It was now that his mettle was to be tested. An unseen force had thrown him into an ice-cold ocean with waves pushing him down and choking him, and he didn't know how to swim.

"This can't be something spiritual," he angrily thought one day. *"Spiritual experiences are made of love and light. They can't be full*

of muck and filth. I might not even be a lightworker, for all I know. Otherwise, why would I have been subjected to such intense pain and grief? God would spare me such pain if I were one of his soldiers, would he not? There would at least be some light somewhere to show me the way. Oh, God, I don't want to live here anymore. I just want to die and go home now," he cried as he begged to be taken from his mortal cage.

"She was too young to have left this world. Everything was so beautiful. Everything was falling into place. Why did you have to take her away now? I could probably handle it better if I were older, but I still need her. I'm not yet ready to live without her." He was justifiably angry with God and even cursed his angels. *"I listened to you, I followed your guidance, I lived by your rules. I did everything in my power to do my duty as a lightworker... and this is what I get in return? Sounds like a bum deal to me!"*

Losing his mother changed him, and now it was forcing him to question God, to question all his beliefs, and to delve deep within the trenches of his heart and mind, bringing out all that was unhealed in him.

"Why should I pay any attention to you then if you don't listen to my prayers? Shouldn't love, respect and loyalty be mutual? I am suffering, and you're sitting up there watching me suffer? Where are you now? Why can't you hold my hand and bring me out of this darkness? No, God, no. I could forgive you for anything, but I cannot forgive you for taking my mother from me. Not this soon."

His head was being bombarded with a myriad of unanswered questions, and the more he thought, the more they grew, and the more they grew, the angrier he became. The spiral that followed Audrey's death took Zeke to a dark place in life, but that was not meant to be for much longer because, like a phoenix, he would rise again.

CHAPTER THIRTY-NINE
SUNSHINE

One afternoon Zeke visited his mother's grave. Not wanting to leave, he stayed there until the sun went down and evening rolled around. It was nearly dark when a little girl came and sat next to a fairly new grave close to his mother's. The girl was around ten years old and holding a little doll in her arms. She lovingly set some flowers by the grave and sat there, talking to whomever was buried there. Zeke was curious as to why she was there alone, so he said, "Hello," asked her name and whom she was visiting.

"I'm Angela. Mommy used to call me her angel. That's her right here," the little girl replied as she pointed to the grave. "Daddy is over there by that tree visiting Grandpa. We're going home in a little bit."

She told Zeke she lost her mother just a month ago and that she died while giving birth to a baby boy, who was small and frail. Angela was sad, but she wasn't complaining. She told Zeke that she wasn't angry with God or her mother, either. Instead, she simply stood by her grave and said a beautiful prayer, wishing that she would be happy wherever she was. She promised her mother that she would take care of herself, her little baby brother, and their father so she didn't have to worry from up in heaven. She had brought her mother's favorite flowers so she could smell them and be happy.

She turned to Zeke, "Mommy loved daisies. They'll keep her happy in heaven."

Zeke kept looking at this little girl. He didn't know who she was, but he knew she was there to teach him a lesson, to show him that he wasn't alone. There were other beautiful souls, other innocent children and lightworkers like him, who had to endure pain and loss. He smiled at Angela. "Don't worry, our moms are neighbors now. They'll look after each other."

The little girl looked up and smiled. "Really?" She took some of the flowers from the ones she had put on her mother's grave and placed them on Audrey's. "There, now they both have daisies."

That evening, the little angel he met at the graveyard taught him a very important lesson – a lesson in faith and patience. Pure souls, like him and Angela, have to learn to live with pain and loss because, as the guides of other human beings, it is their duty to rise above tragedies. Precious souls like them need to know how to transcend human boundaries. It's not the pain, but the way they handle it, that make them different from others, and thus Zeke was reminded of the fact that all beings of light return to the light, and hope for them is never truly gone. They become greater souls because they know how to handle worldly pains, losses, and grief differently.

Meeting Angela helped Zeke rise from his depressive spiral and return to his path towards achieving greater enlightenment. He realized that, even in the darkest time of his life, it was not fitting of a lightworker to blame anyone for his loss. He realized that he, himself, was the light he had been seeking. He was a beacon of hope for all others. He didn't have to blame God or his mother, nor did he have to wait for an external source of light to save him. He was his own light, and it was his duty to guide others who needed him in times of crisis.

After he went back home, he realized he had been selfishly engrossed in his grief and that he had overlooked the pain felt by others around him. In his own pain, he had overlooked what his sisters and his father had been feeling. Zeke decided to set his personal grief aside and become the beacon of light for his family's gain. Audrey's death had brought an end to the happily-ever-after the Tartal family had been living for the last year of her life. It had left them all shaken and broken.

Ben took Audrey's death harder than anyone could have imagined. It damaged him so badly that he started falling back to his old ways of drinking and staying away from home for days at a time. He was literally falling apart. Maya and Leia were also left heartbroken. Maya had only recently started to have a healthy connection with her family, and she had relied greatly on her mother's support as she was healing from her own trauma. She was trying to find happiness and joy within the family, and her mother had been her anchor. Now that anchor was gone forever.

Leia, on the other hand, had just begun turning her passion for car mechanics into her vocation, and she had chose to deal with her grief by diving into her work. With their mother's death and their father turning away from them once again, both Maya and Leia were left to fend for themselves, emotionally weak and vulnerable. All of them needed help. They needed Zeke.

Zeke often remembered his mother's counsel and advice. He treasured those lessons of love, patience, forgiveness, compassion, and empathy. Even in death, he couldn't afford to lose those beautiful values she had instilled in him. As a lightworker, she had been his first teacher, his first guide, and his source of light. He knew he needed to get his life back on track. He needed to be in charge so he could guide his family through this difficult time.

"Healer, heal thyself," one of his first lessons, came back to him. He began spending more time with his father again, trying to bridge the gap that had been formed after Audrey's death. He slowly guided his father with gentle words and even gentler feelings. Once Ben realized that he had done all he could and that his wife's death was the will of a higher power, he found the strength within himself to face his fear, guilt, and shame head-on. He needed to bear both the emotional and financial responsibilities of his family and be their support system, so they could learn to smile again. Leia needed him to be her mentor once again and to guide her back to her dreams, and Maya needed unconditional love, so she could heal the psychological wounds that she still carried.

It took Ben a lot of time and effort to learn what it meant to be both a father and a mother to his children, but he did learn eventually. He became a much gentler man, a kind man who loved his children more than anything else. Once he put his family on the path to betterment, Zeke could finally focus on himself.

The black cat still followed him. He saw it every single day, looking sad, dejected, and abandoned. Zeke launched a million accusations almost immediately after his mother passed, directing all his anger and frustration towards this poor, little creature like a scapegoat. From the time he lost his mother, he had begun considering the black cat a bad omen and blamed it for all his loss and pain. He needed to make things right. It was time for him again to correct his mistakes and heal himself.

One day, as he sat thinking deeply about it, he had a sudden realization that his feline friend had returned to support him. The cat had come to him in his time of need as a carrier of love and care, not as a harbinger of death and destruction. It was for his own good, even if it had come to warn him against a fateful event. The cat was a simple messenger, one who cared for him. Zeke now knew that it had come to him to give him the support he needed in his time of crisis, as it could sense an impending loss in a friend's life. He himself had a very strong intuition of pending doom for a while before the incident even happened, didn't he? He connected his mother's death to the horrible aura he had been sensing for months.

Zeke now understood that in no way the black cat to be blamed. Death was ever-present. Certainly, it was written, and thus it occurred. He could not fight it. The cat was just a friend, a true friend. True friends are a rare find, and they are meant to be respected and cherished, not dishonored or hurt. He knew how kind and loving his mother had always been to all that lived, and this cat was a gift from the universe. He could not turn his back on it.

He remembered his mother's words. "We should love and care for plants and animals just as we care for our children, the elderly, the underprivileged, and the disabled, for they are as much a part of our experience as anything. They are loved by Nature as much as we are."

Zeke needed to forgive his friend from the bottom of his heart once and for all. He couldn't live with regret or guilt any longer. He decided to spend an entire day with his one-of-a-kind friend, so he could release all the pain and the dark thoughts he was carrying.

He stepped out of his house, and sure as ever, the cat was sitting right by the fence, waiting for him. He opened the door and waved his hand, inviting the cat straight to his room. He fed it milk and leftover salmon with his own hands, sat beside it, stroked its back and tail, and genuinely apologized for his rude behavior. He did not know if the cat understood his words or not, but his sincere apology took a load of guilt off his own shoulders.

"I am sorry," he said, kneeling by the cat. "I know you wanted to warn me, to help me, and to prepare me, but I directed all my rage at you. Please forgive me."

That evening, he decided to visit Noah again after a long time. He wanted to go to his wise old friend and share his story of anger, frustration, and forgiveness. He also wanted to take his new animal friend along with him to meet his human friend. As he left his house, the cat followed him as it always did. Walking past the woods, he suddenly stopped once he realized that his friend had paused a little further behind him.

The cat stood there silently for a while as if thinking deeply about something. It then walked ahead of Zeke and turned its head, almost smiling at him as it pulled its whiskers up and called out one last time, "Meeeooowwww!"

It did not look back again after that and disappeared into the trees. Something inside Zeke told him that the messenger had left him the message it came to deliver. Its job was done. His friend had bid him a final goodbye and left forever, never to return. It took him a while to come to terms with it, though. He had finally asked for forgiveness from the bottom of his heart and had released all his grievances. Though he felt a little sad, he was still happy because he knew he had been forgiven.

When he met Noah that evening after such a long time, he was greeted with the same loving smile and a warm hug. "I know how difficult it must have been for you to lose someone as dear to your heart as your mother, my boy. I wanted to visit you, but I know what the pain of losing a loved one is. You needed to face that on your own terms."

Zeke told Noah about all he had been through. Noah listened and then he spoke. "Do you still remember the dream we shared of the underworld when I was feeling just like you — when was I trying to come to terms with the pain of losing my family? Do you remember the lesson we learned together, the lesson you helped me understand? There is nothing called death, my friend. It's a simple transition to another world, a better world," he said with the usual smile on his face. And Zeke understood. His mother was not gone. She was simply in a higher place.

He had lived through the darkest time in his life, and now he was a better person. He was stronger in both body and spirit and had become a better man. That night, Noah invited him to stay over, and he gladly accepted.

CHAPTER FORTY

GOD'S ARMY

Noah poured Zeke a mug of hot apple cider as he continued to give him advice. "Remember, you are a very, very special child, Zeke. You aren't meant to be a part of a pack, even if you sometimes wish it so. You are meant to be a lone wolf, destined to carve your own path and to always walk ahead of the rest. You are a guide, and you have to help lead humanity to its destiny."

Noah then went on to share stories of such leaders who had to tread extremely difficult paths before they could reach their final goals of truth, peace, and salvation. Most had to lay down their lives for a higher cause. "Do you know throughout history how many examples there have been of pure souls, guides, and leaders who have walked paths full of thorns? Persecution has been a common fate for those who have attained enlightenment."

Zeke paid great attention to Noah's words, as he always did.

"Whenever a lightworker, an enlightened being, has tried to speak about higher truths or to awaken people from their ignorant slumbers, their voices have been muzzled. They have always been held down by force. The powers that rule the material world and control human minds have always unleashed unfathomable cruelty upon these gentle souls. Yet, their message could not be stopped. Their resilience and strength have always broken through the silence, and they have ultimately spread their words to millions through love and sacrifice. Their names can never be erased from the hearts and minds of people. They will forever be etched in the collective psyche of humanity, shining brightly in the golden pages of history."

Noah narrated the lives of many who had spread the message of the light, those who had come to Earth as lightworkers before Zeke. "One, singular, awakened soul has the power to destroy the entire structure built by the millions who wish to control the human race. They are like live bombs that nobody can stop once they begin ticking, and when they go off, they change everything."

His eyes began to glow with reverence and pride as he spoke. "Jesus, our beloved Christ, was scourged, given a crown of thorns and crucified by the Romans for spreading the message of love. Galileo was pronounced guilty of heresy, stoned, thrown in jail, and persecuted by the Catholic Church for speaking a simple truth. He tried to teach that the sun was at the center of the universe, as opposed to the popular biblical belief that it was the Earth that everything revolved around. They faced such tragic fates simply because they were ahead of their times and very much ahead of the pack. Don't forget there is an eternal war between the conscious and unconscious forces governing the human mind."

Noah went on. "But do such inhuman acts of brutality stop the message of love from spreading or muzzle the voice of truth? No, my dear boy, they do not. Today, we all know the Earth and all other planets orbit around the sun, and the world witnessed the resurrection of Christ to learn the lesson that the physical body can be killed, but the higher soul can never be crucified. The voice of truth comes back to strike the human consciousness with a thunderous force and will continue to do so."

Zeke had read those stories before, but when Noah talked about them, he revisited those fallen heroes of the past, and for the first time in his life, he connected with their pain and loss and valued their contribution to the advancement of humanity all the more.

Just then, Noah abruptly stood up from his seat and smiled at him. "It's quite late. Sleep well tonight, kid, and do not forget, you are a lone wolf. You need to chart your own path." He smiled at him one last time as he turned off the light and left the room.

Zeke tossed and turned in bed for a while, and finally fell asleep. That night he had a dream, and like all his dreams, this one too was a sign from above. In his dream, he was dressed like a poor countryman and was walking through a field. He stopped as he saw a beautiful peasant girl working in the field and humming a beautiful tune. He hid behind a tree and kept looking at her as she happily sang and danced around the field. He stared at her until his dream shifted. He was now walking down a street when he suddenly saw a young boy being chased by a few men. Zeke immediately hid behind the ruins of a broken stone house next to the street and watched the whole scene play out.

The boy tried to run as fast as his tiny legs could carry him, but the men caught hold of him. They shackled him with iron chains and dragged him away as Zeke followed them. What he saw next shook him to his core. The boy cried and screamed for help, but nobody came to save him. Zeke tried to move, but his own feet were frozen, and he stood there like a lifeless piece of stone, totally helpless. They pulled at the boy repeatedly while he kept struggling to free himself. Suddenly his hair fell free, cascading down his back.

Zeke was stunned to discover it was the beautiful peasant girl he had seen earlier. He could now move, but as soon as he tried to help the girl, his dream shifted again. Now a group of well-built men dressed like soldiers was taking the girl to an open ground.

They tied her to a wooden stake. Zeke could clearly see that she had a cross clenched in her hand as tears rolled down her cheeks. The men laughed and hurled deplorable abuses at her, calling her names: witch, demon, charlatan. She shut her eyes, and from her expression, he knew she was ready to embrace death, but then she suddenly opened her eyes one last time, looking straight into his own.

Zeke felt as if she wished to tell him something, silent tears still rolling down her cheeks. He tried to scream, but his voice choked. As much as he tried, no one could hear him. She finally closed her eyes and whispered her last prayers as they burned her alive at the stake. He was reminded of the last words of Jesus as he silently watched her body burn to ashes: "God forgive them, for they know not what they do."

When he woke up, there was an excruciating pain in his chest, and his eyes were wet with tears. The morning sun kissed his face, and as he looked around, Noah was sitting by his bed.

"You were screaming in your sleep. I didn't want to wake you because you were so deep into your dream, and I knew you had to work through it, so I just sat here patiently, knowing you would come out of it soon."

Zeke sat up and wiped what was left of his tears. He shared his dream with Noah. "Do all lightworkers have to face the same fate? Are all of us destined to be hanged, stoned, or burned alive at the stake? Why do we always have to suffer and perish? She was such an innocent and beautiful girl. There was a divine light on her glowing face, a beacon of hope. How could they do that to her? How can human beings be so cruel and unkind to each other? She wanted to share something with me, but I couldn't be there for her. I couldn't save her, Noah. I just… I couldn't do anything."

Noah held Zeke's hands and sat beside him for a while. A few minutes later, he went to his kitchen and prepared some hot chocolate for them both. He came back with two mugs and handed one over to Zeke.

"So, you saw her in your dreams then! I wanted to share her story with you last night. I forced myself to stop because I thought you had enough stories of pain and sacrifice already, but it looks like she wanted you to remember her, too. The Maid of Orleans, Joan of Arc, was the epitome of a fearless soul, an extraordinary leader, and exceptionally gifted in her ability to lead. No wonder she inspired her troops enough to raise the siege of Orleans. She was practically the savior of France, but her strength and bravery came at the cost of her own life. The Duke of Burgundy sent his men to capture her. They caught hold of her at Rouen in English-controlled Normandy, tried her for such regressive charges as witchcraft, and violated divine law by dressing like a man, and finally burned her alive at the stake for heresy."

"Then what was the point? What was the purpose of her struggle, of all she lived through? Will humans ever learn to recognize their saviors?"

"Yes, they surely will. Joan was declared a martyr and bestowed with the honor of sainthood, you see. The French parliament even decreed a yearly national festival in her honor. Even though the gratitude and acknowledgment came some five centuries after her death, they finally had to concede and acknowledge her contribution."

"Don't you think the lives of spiritual beings, starseeds, or light-workers are designed differently from the time they're born — or maybe way before that, and isn't that unfair?" Zeke questioned.

Noah smiled and said, "There's an inspiring story of a light-worker from the East who wasn't charged with heresy, wasn't stoned or crucified, but was, and still is, respected and revered by the entire world. I'm speaking of Siddhartha Gautama, or Buddha, as you may know him. The title Buddha comes from the word 'Buddhi,' a Vedic

Sanskrit word for intelligence, or awareness. Cosmic intelligence downloaded constantly through his mind. You would do well to learn more about him," Noah said with a wink.

"This is fascinating, but also a hard act to follow!"

"As a lightworker, you must be prepared to face the thorns that will surely be laid on the path you have set out for yourself and others, my dear child. Remember, you are among the vanguard of God's army."

Noah's words took away much of Zeke's doubt. That night, he had the most peaceful, uninterrupted sleep. The next morning, he began a new journey. The evening spent with Noah and the day before resolved many important issues in his life. He learned that regardless of what he would have to go through, in the end, it was his destiny to propel humanity further towards enlightenment.

Zeke already knew that death wasn't as ominous as it seemed. It was a mere transfer, a shift, a simple transition from this world to another, just as we would board different buses or change planes to reach a certain destination. He had come to terms with his mother's death and accepted it, but he knew his life would never be the same. She was one of the pillars of strength that had kept him grounded in the physical world while allowing him to experience his meta-physical journey at the same time. Her support which helped him navigate his journey between his human and Lyran identity was now gone.

He had finally realized his mother's death was a marker between the end of an old chapter and the beginning of a new one. Thus far, it had only been a journey of his awakening to the other world, which had slowly and steadily unfolded, leading him towards higher consciousness moment by moment, day by day. He was a fully real-ized guide of humanity, but with his mother's death, this chapter of peace in his life was over, and now his duty had begun. Now it was time for him to realize exactly what he was meant to do. It was time for him to face all obstacles head-on and carve a path for himself and others, just as the others who had come before him had been doing for thousands upon thousands of years.

Institutions and structures weren't for him. There was no border nor bounds that could hold him. He needed to learn his lessons from a much larger campus called the world. His knowledge could not be confined to books alone, for books are only other people's interpretation of things – of knowledge, of life, and of experiences. He needed to observe and draw his own conclusions instead of blindly relying on others' inferences. He knew now that he had been born to break all the taboos and shackles that society had placed on itself, and breaking shackles is never easy. The task he had been assigned by the realm of God was not an easy one.

Zeke was very sure his path would be as difficult as the ones who came before him if not more so. There was a higher calling for him, and he knew it. His call to action was drawing near, and he could feel it with each passing day. Soon he would need all he had learned because something was coming his way. He didn't know what it would look like or when it would finally appear in front of him, but he was certain of its existence.

The only respite for him was the knowledge that this time around he wasn't the only one treading this path. He wasn't alone. There were other lightworkers across the globe walking a similar path, and they had not been chosen at random. Each one was a part of the Source. They all carried a piece of God's will, like Zeke, and thus were loved unconditionally by God himself. They were his warriors, spreaders of his light, the commanders of his forces of goodness and love. They were God's army, and Zeke was one of them. He was among the greatest of them.

CHAPTER FORTY-ONE

THE NEW WAVE OF CHANGE

A new and fresh wave of change hit Farley Street. Ben had been handling his garage business and his two teenage daughters quite well, and he was pleased. Yet, something inside of him was still restless and unhappy. He was a changed man and needed change in his life as well. He was seriously considering a career switch and wanted to take new risks and enter new territories.

He had a secret wish to become a chef and open a chain of restaurants one day ever since he discovered his extraordinary culinary skills. He didn't want to entirely shut down his garage and car dealer's business, though. His desire was to transfer the family business to his two capable daughters, but they were still young, just sixteen years old. He knew he had to wait until they were adults before taking the next step in his life. He was sure they would be able to handle his business eventually and thus fondly renamed his garage "Tartal and Daughters."

He shared his thoughts with his son, insisting that he would eventually want to shift to London and start life anew once all his children were settled in their own lives and he could have time for himself. Zeke didn't want to stop his father this time around. He himself had been waiting for something in his life to change, so he understood exactly what his father was feeling. As a result, he chose to be more of a silent observer, watching and enjoying the positive changes he could see in his house and around the Farley Street neighborhood. His sisters had become more mature. They had been through a lot and were well on their way to becoming reasonable and beautiful adult women in their own right.

Zeke also started to notice something new about his sisters he had never paid close attention to before. As they grew up, Zeke realized that they were looking more and more like their mother and reflected many of her personality traits. Maya had inherited their mother's perfect combination of grace and poise with a hint of her silent resilience. The care, compassion, and strength that their mother had was now showing up in Leia, and she wore it beautifully. The more he looked at them, the more he was reminded of her, and the more he missed her.

While sleeping one night, he saw his mother sitting by his bedside, smiling at him. It was a dream he did not want to end. He had accepted her death, but her memories kept haunting him. She was caressing his hair with all the love and affection she always displayed while she was alive. She softly nudged him and whispered in his ears, "Zeke, my child, wake up. Wake up, you have to move on."

"Mom? Is that really you? I miss you so much. Why did you leave me?"

"I never left you, my son. I just moved on, so you can move on, too," she replied, smiling at him.

"Are you happy? Where are you now? Tell me," he pleaded, unsure if he would even get a response.

She looked sad as she replied, "I could be happy if only you were happy, but you are in so much pain. How can I be happy when I can feel your pain?"

"How can I make you happy again, Mom? Please tell me. I need to know what to do."

"I'm bound by your pain, and I can't fly now. Once you release me from this cage in your heart, I can be as free as a bird. I can finally find my place. Death is not pain. It's freedom from the chains of this life, my son. When you wake up tomorrow, look up at the sky. Notice how happy the birds are as they soar high over the Mighty Mac, then you'll know how happy I can be."

The next morning, as he studied the birds gliding so effortlessly in the open sky, he whispered to himself, "That's how happy she will be if I let her go. I'm setting you free, Mom. I won't chain you or make you feel sad because of me anymore. I've received my closure. Promise me you'll always be my guiding light when I need you. Shine your light upon me, Mom. Shine your light upon me."

Just as he whispered those words, a soft ray from the sun fell upon his face as if kissing him and saying, "You have set me free, and I can fly high now, but I'll always be with you, my son. I'll always be with you."

The next few days were much happier for Zeke. He finally gained closure with everything in his life. He was a better man than ever before and would soon become even better.

· · ·

"Wake up, Mr. Tartal. Will you wake up, please? It's playtime!" A very familiar voice echoed through Zeke's room on a crisp, fall morning.

Zeke woke up in a state of shock as he saw a little, old friend doing somersaults on his chest. He squeezed his eyes and pinched himself to check whether it was real or a figment of his wild imagination. His foolhardy chum had returned, livelier than ever! Overwhelmed at the sight of Zag the Leprechaun, Zeke was about to jump out of bed with sheer joy when he heard another very familiar voice.

"How could you forget me, Mr. T? You can't forget me! Long time, no see. I do agree. But good old friends aren't we supposed to be?" Ziggy Bird was back again as well, tweeting from the window-pane. But his initial joy of seeing his childhood friends was soon trumped by the anger that slowly rose from inside of him.

"I forgot YOU? What do you mean??? You're the ones who forgot ME! You left me alone when I begged for your guidance. How selfish and insensitive could the both of you be? And now you're putting the blame on me?" His voice choked as he was really upset with his friends for not being there for him when he needed them the most. He was overwhelmed by the happiness he felt upon their return, but the pain of being abandoned by them was still lingering beneath it all.

"Ahem… Mr. Tartal, you got us all wrong. Old friends some-times need to give way to new ones to allow them to grow and evolve. Take my advice, sir, or let it be," Zag said prophetically.

Just then, Zag gave Ziggy a look, and off they went, back to their old shenanigans. It was hilarious for Zeke to see the two of his oldest friends running and chasing each other around his room again with the same zeal they once had. They brought back all the memories of the good old days. It was a brand new morning indeed. The three of them ran out of Tartal House playing around Farley Street as they had in the earliest days of Zeke's childhood.

"You still haven't told me why you both had suddenly disap-peared and for so long?" Zeke was adamant about receiving a proper answer.

"We left you to help you learn to let go and allow yourself to go with the flow!" Ziggy answered.

"Contrary to popular belief, there's no need to go against the tide. Life isn't a race you've come to win. It's a moment, albeit a lengthy one, and you've come to enjoy and experience it. We left so you could learn to experience life without us, so you could learn to let go of your dependence on us," added Zag.

"Yeah," Zeke sighed. "Letting go is pretty difficult, and I learned that lesson the hard way, but I guess at the end of the day, it was something that just had to be."

Zeke and Zag played hide and seek around the corn mazes the whole afternoon, while Ziggy tweeted from above. Then they visited the cemetery in the evening after the sun went down. Zig went back to a nest she had made in the old birch tree outside Tartal House to get some much-needed rest, and Zag went down to the cellar searching for moonshine once again. Zeke was left alone, but he wasn't lonely anymore. He sat on his porch looking up at the vast nothingness of the sky, stargazing again after a long, long time. It was a magical night with a sky full of twinkling little stars and a magically full, pink moon.

Suddenly an old and strangely familiar, cracked voice rang close to his ears. "My friend, you have finally woken from a thousand years of slumber. As I once told you, age is but a number."

Zeke turned around and discovered an old barn owl perched high on the branch of a tall and shady sugar maple, looking down at him. The large, pulsating moon created a strange and mystical halo around its head. Zeke recognized the owl in a heartbeat. It was the same one he had seen all those years ago.

It looked straight into Zeke's eyes and continued its rhymes. "You've got to go a long, long way. Your precious wisdom is here to stay, keeping your human ego at bay. It's now time to show others the way." Zeke wasn't scared of the owl's wise words this time. He smiled back at it with assurance and gratitude. His mission on Earth had already begun the day he'd been born. He knew his entire life up to this point was just a struggle to come to terms with it.

The next few days went by in a state of pure bliss. Zeke, Zig, and Zag revived the old days of roaming around Mackinaw City together. They spent a whole day at Mill Creek Park on the shores of Lake Huron, where Zeke had met Ziggy as a five-year-old child. They strolled the beach near McGulpin Point, where he had met Zag on Halloween night when he was ten, and they spent an entire evening watching the Northern Lights at the Dark Sky Park. The journey of Zeke's life thus far was replayed as they visited each of those sites one by one. He could organize and rearrange those memories like pages of a book. His old friends were back, and they were here to stay.

• • •

Zig and Zag became a part of Zeke's daily life again, and along with Noah Leitner, he had all the support and guidance he needed, but something was still missing, and it was time for that missing part of his life to come back, and so it did.

One September morning, as the soft rays of the sun fell upon his face, Zeke felt a soft pair of lips kissing his forehead and a gentle hand caressing his unkempt hair. It was a touch he knew. "You're taking your mission way too seriously. Just go out there and enjoy life. Who knows? Maybe that's your mission — just to enjoy life as it is," the soft and tender voice, filled with love, whispered.

Zeke did not answer. His eyes were still closed.

"You do not smile as often as you used to, my love. I know your mother's death hurt you terribly, but your mission right now might be to just smile the way you used to. Your smile had the power to make someone's day. Maybe someone simply needs to see your smile to sail through and forget the drudgery of life. Your smile has the power to lift pain and sorrow, the power to light up someone's life."

A blissful smile played on his lips and lit up his face. Zig and Zag's return had renewed his faith in the timelessness of friendship and love. He was sure his beloved would return in time, too. He finally opened his eyes only when the sun was shining brighter and stronger. Of course, he was still alone, and there was no one around, but he knew it was time — time for her to return.

• • •

It was a bright and sunny morning. After breakfast, Leia and Maya headed for school, and Mr. Tartal headed for his garage. Zeke didn't want to stay home, either. He spent the whole morning walking aimlessly around the city, enjoying the warm sun, and smiling at strangers on the street. He could feel the warmth being reciprocated. He could see people, even with sad and grumpy faces, being forced by an inner nudge to smile back. That was when, in a crowd of lively tourists, his eyes fell upon a face he had not seen in many years — the old Hawaiian healer. He had given Zeke his first lesson as a lightworker all those years ago. The old man was simply smiling at him. His eyes were glowing with pride and acknowledgment. Upon seeing the man, Zeke ran towards him, but he disappeared into the crowd, leaving Zeke confused.

Luckily enough, Gael had the weekend off from college, and Zeke decided to check in on his childhood friend. They went cycling together and eventually decided to stop by an ice cream parlor. Zeke wasn't one to reminisce about the past, but it was impossible for him to avoid nostalgia now as he sat with his oldest friend, talking about the life they had lived and the friends they had gained and lost along the way, especially Kai, who had still not contacted his parents or anyone in the neighborhood.

After dropping Gael back home, Zeke decided to visit Noah and spend the rest of the afternoon there. Even Noah could feel his infectious smile. His eyes were gleaming with childlike joy after a long time, and his warm smile was radiating the peace and happiness he felt within. It was literally brightening up the day for everyone he met.

Once he was back on the street, he was surprised to see the Hawaiian healer again. He was sitting on the bench across from Indigo Children with his eyes closed. "There he is!" Zeke shouted in his head.

As Zeke approached him, the old man opened his eyes and smiled. "A smile can heal, and you are healed. Your mission began long ago, young man, and today it grows into something more." Again, his words sounded like a prophecy, but Zeke wasn't scared or worried this time.

He smiled back at him and whispered, "Thank you. I still remember what you taught me: Ho'oponopono, a magical word indeed!" That was when he heard a voice. It came from inside his heart.

"You must have made someone's day. You are already on your mission, Zeke. Just keep smiling!"

Night fell, and as he tucked himself in bed, he heard a whisper, a sound he had been waiting to hear. He knew it was her. He could feel her around him the whole day. She was the reason he was smiling. She kissed his forehead and said, "Let's go on a cosmic adventure one last time before your true quest is revealed, my love. Shall we?"

He closed his eyes, but the smile kept lingering on his face as the greatest of his cosmic trips began.

CHAPTER FORTY-TWO

LOVE AND GOD

Upon opening his eyes, Zeke discovered a burst of dazzling colors in front of him. He saw powerful lights exploding like bombs in every direction. The colors were so bright and powerful that he instinctively shut his eyes. Each time he opened them, he felt a hypnotic pull from the spirals of color around him. It was as if they were trying to suck him in. He might have resisted had he been alone, but he was by no means alone.

Zoom had finally returned. She was once again by his side. They had been apart for far too long, and so much had happened to him during her absence. He had learned to let go of everything he had ever held dear, and his life had forced him to grow as a person and as a lightworker. The thought of seeing her again and the hope that she would one day return had kept him strong throughout all his trials. He had endured all that pain, and in doing so, evolved as a starseed to the point that he was now ready for his final lesson. Zoom grabbed his hand and pulled him out of bed for one last cosmic dance before the war he would fight for the rest of his days would begin.

It was an out-of-body experience, something he had felt many times before. He felt weightless, as if his soul had left his physical body behind, allowing him to glide across the stars with Zoom by his side. They flew past galaxies and nebulas as he saw time and space morph before his very eyes. It was overwhelming until they suddenly stopped. They had arrived at a blindingly bright light that stood at the center of a spiral of colors. It was the most magnificent thing Zeke had ever seen, and he had seen a lot.

He was practically speechless as he simply couldn't find the words to express what he was witnessing. "Wha... what's that?"

"That, my love, is the Source," she lovingly whispered in his ear.

"The Source, the source of what?" he asked, even though he felt like he already knew the answer.

"Of everything. We stand at the center of all creation. Welcome, Ezekiel, to the Cosmic Factory."

Zoom began dancing and running amidst the showers of divine light, as happy and as giggly as a little child, unfazed by the brilliance of the all-encompassing light that was before them. She floated and glided with ease in the eye of the storm, swam in the magnificent waters of the cosmic ocean as her wavy cascade of hair swung and rolled down her back like a wave crashing against the shore during high tide. He stood there for a while, looking at her cosmic dance with absolute awe, forgetting the fear he had initially felt when he saw the light of the Source. She took his breath away. She was the center of his attention, even at the heart of the universe. He ran beside her, stopped her, and softly held her hands.

"Zoom, look at me." He stared into her eyes. "We've been on so many journeys before, but tell me, why now? What is this place? What is the Cosmic Factory?"

The colors that spun around them immersed them in a light unlike any other in the entire cosmos as she told him the purpose of their visit. With a twinkle in her eyes she whispered, "Every trip across the stars before this had been a part of the journey and your quest to seek the ultimate truth. You needed to know where you came from, what your true identity is, and what your role on Earth is supposed to be. You needed to learn how the Earth evolved through millions of years and the connection the earliest human civilizations had with the people of the stars.

"All of that was a part of your evolution as a lightworker. It was all to help you on your journey to awaken humanity from its ignorant slumber. But, at the center of it all, you must learn the answer to a simple question: who are you, Zeke Tartal? Beyond Ezekiel of Lyra and Ptah of the gods, who **are** you? What is your immortal soul made of?"

"Come on, Zoom, isn't that all I've been doing for years? My whole life, I've been trying to figure out who I am and where I come from, and now that I have all the answers, you're telling me there's more? Isn't this enough?"

"You're not wrong. You're just missing one simple point, my love." She gently laid her hand on his cheek. "I know you've been through so much on this journey, and you've beautifully made it to the end. You have been to Lyra, experienced star systems, and learned about galactic wars. You have seen the Akashic Library, met God's angels, and passed through the Lion's Gate. But they were all different experiences from different dimensions, meant to open the doors to a metaphysical world beyond Earth, beyond your physical reality, where the mind can dwell, and so can the astral aspects of the human race. But where you are now, at this very moment, is beyond all dimensions. It's the place where everything begins, and everything ends — the place where all realities converge. You, my dear, are at the center of the universe!"

Zeke listened to her, and though not much of what she said made sense to him, she continued as she always did, in her natural flow. "This is where the non-physical turns into the physical, where nothing turns into matter, and that which exists dissolves into the non-physical. There isn't any distinction between you or me or anyone else here. Where you are now is the beginning and the end of everything." Zoom was as mesmerizing and mysterious as she had always been. "This, my love, is where time and space are born, the origin of all things."

"I still don't get it. Why call it the Cosmic Factory? Does this place make everything like some machine in a factory?"

"In a way, this place makes nothing. It only reshapes everything. This is where everything becomes nothing, and nothing becomes everything! All that exists in the universe eventually merges into one and then disintegrates into infinite things once again. This is where the formless takes form, where light is shaped into life, and life draws back into the light once again. The energy that escapes the factory scatters everywhere; it goes as far as it can from the Source, and it makes galaxies, universes, and dimensions, down to every last little thing you can touch. While at the same time, the realities and universes are pulled back here to a great nothingness at the center of creation, and from their destruction, the energy of creation is realized once again.

"This constant emergence and re-emergence are like an eternal cosmic dance that takes place here, where you now stand. Does that make any sense to you, Ezekiel? This is where the eternal energy of good merges with the eternal energy of evil. They call it the Yin and the Yang in many cultures. This is where the inert cosmic force merges with the flowing fluid of mass and matter."

"Then, is this place… heaven? The same heaven where we all end up after we die, where everything goes to be remade? Is this what we call God?"

"Maybe, maybe not." She smiled as mysteriously as always with a twinkle in her eye. "Ezekiel, I have brought you here, to the center of the universe, to show you how creation comes into being. As much as human beings would love to believe, God isn't really a kind, old grandfather sitting on a throne, waiting to grant all their wishes — a celestial version of Santa Claus or Father Christmas as he is known in other cultures. Most human wishes and desires are nothing but an unnatural need to satisfy and feed the ego anyway. Contrary to what they believe, God is a force, an energy that is the source of creative love." Zoom held his hands and whispered, asking him with the eternal twinkle in her eyes, "Do you wish to see the magnificence of God and what you know as heaven?"

He nodded, curious to experience what every human being wishes to see, if even once… HEAVEN!

In the blink of an eye, everything changed. Zeke looked around and realized he was at the center of the storm, where everything was calm and serene. As he looked down, he realized he was standing on what looked like a transparent glass surface. Through it, he could see the entire cosmos under him. From the greatest of universes to the smallest of worlds, everything and everyone on Lyra and on Earth, it was all crystal clear to him. At that moment, Zeke was omniscient; he could see all of existence at once."

"I don't know if you can bring yourself to accept what you see now in front of you as you stand in the place of God. Humans have extraordinarily strong notions about the nature of God. I know you have your own understanding, but can you at least try to comprehend the fact that this is how God works." She was still holding his hands through it all. "Throughout the infinite universes, there are these swirling matters that beget creation. God is simply the first principle that creates, dissolves, and recreates. God is the eternal generator, operator, and destroyer. All these swirling matters you see before you are in different phases of creation, and that is how God loves to work. Creation is, thus, a constant and ever-evolving process."

Zeke felt overwhelmed as he saw the source of all creation and reached a new understanding of God. Then Zoom took him further to the other side of the Source, to heaven. It looked like paradise, indeed. It was full of joy, peace, and love, with angels and other celestial beings flying around. The holiest of all places looked magical and beautiful. He looked hard for his mother, and a part of him knew she had to be there. She was the purest of all souls he had ever come across. His eyes desperately searched for her as he walked around this ineffable place. Zeke and Zoom were roaming around trickling streams and beautiful gardens, walking hand in hand, when he suddenly felt something. It was a sense of power, the presence of something beyond his comprehension.

"What in the world…?" Zeke could not understand what was happening, but then he realized that the spirit of God had fallen upon heaven and everything around him had stopped. Every single entity, every flower, every blade of grass, and every drop of water bowed down in reverence to God's majesty. Angels and the heavenly choir began singing out in jubilation. It was so magical that no words could ever describe the feeling he experienced in that moment. Along with everything and everyone, he, too, bowed deeply in reverence.

He wasn't sure how long he stood there in a state of trance, but that ecstasy was broken by a soft whisper in his ears. "God is an experience. You don't need to define God. You just need to *feel* God."

As he raised his head, he looked around in awe of everything he was witnessing. "Your mother is right there, see?" Zoom pointed her out at the other side of a garden. He saw a much younger version of his mother giggling and laughing with other heavenly beings like a little kid. It brought a smile to his face. She watched his eyes light up as he kept looking at the childlike joy on his mother's face.

"She looks much younger than when I last saw her," he proclaimed.

"That's because the soul lives in a perfect state — youthful, healthy, and vibrant," Zoom answered prophetically.

He looked deep into her eyes, held her hands, smiled, and whispered softly with the deepest gratitude, "Thank you."

She winked at him and smiled back. She took him to a quieter corner of the garden so they could be alone and talk. "Humans have always been taught to keep pursuing extravagant, material *things* throughout their lives that always leave them wanting more. They are never satisfied. It's never enough. It's called greed. These teachings come from a dark source. You and I have both faced that source of darkness before."

Before she could say anything else, Zeke uttered, "Draco…"

"Yes," she confirmed. "Draco was a manifestation of the darkness, and he still is. He is on Earth, and he is still corrupting the hearts of men. Humans are supposed to be beings of light, but instead, because of the influence of the Reptilians, they keep focusing on winning and losing, success and failure, life and death. They always want to make sure things happen just how they wish, and in the process, they miss the whole point. They can't even accept what it is they're really looking for.

"Just look at what the darkness has done to the young minds of today, Ezekiel. They are so caught up in chasing the perfect idea of success that they no longer understand the greatness of failure.

Nobody is open enough or willing to think about the true meaning of failure. Failure is our greatest teacher. It teaches us accountability, patience, resilience, humility, and charity. We learn things about ourselves that we would never have known otherwise. We learn what we are good at and what we need to work on. It is the burden of all true masters – masters like you, Ezekiel Tartal."

For the first time in his life, he didn't feel confused. His mind was free from all human limitations in heaven. Thus, the wisdom of all his past lives returned to him. "You're so right, Zoom. The human race needs to understand that failure is inevitable, just like death. Our perception of death and failure is what the Reptilians have distorted and thrive on. Failure is as inescapable as death. Humans need to be reminded of their relationship with both death and failure and what they mean for the survival of their race. Yes, failure is indeed the greatest teacher!"

She nodded, "And this is where you come in. Now that you know it all, the truth about the minds of the human race, you must free them from the holds of Draco and the evil his people represent. You need to teach today's youth, and all of humanity for that matter, the importance of failure and liberate them from their fear of death."

"You know something, Zoom? Death has been something that has bothered me all my life. Every time I thought I understood and came to terms with it, another challenge was thrown at me – another death and I would crumble all over again." He had no shame in admitting his own faults because he had risen above the holds of the human mind. "But thank you once again for showing me the ultimate reality."

"And just what is that reality?" She was curious to know.

"Nothing matters. At the end of it all, nothing really matters. In the Cosmic Factory, matter disintegrates into nothing, and nothing just turns back into matter. I'm not scared of death anymore, my love, because I know that it's simply the beginning of a new life. All I need to do is just be. I simply need to exist and accept that I am human. All that matters is the creation and re-creation by Source, which naturally creates progression and evolution." He stopped to look at her reaction. Even he himself did not know where all this knowledge was coming from.

She looked at him with pride in her eyes. "Go on," she said.

"Nothing matters but the truth, and the truth is that we all come from nothing and turn into nothing. Simply by accepting that, by accepting our integration and disintegration, we automatically realize there's nothing called death. It's simply a name we give to something between two states. It's like being on a musical scale going from one perfect note to the next. We have to pass through discord. If only every human being could witness the Cosmic Factory, we would so easily know we would all ultimately merge into one, and there would be no separation or death. We are One with Source, we are Source in Form, we are God in Motion."

She looked at him, remembering how he used to be in his past lives as she was brought to the verge of tears.

He noticed her tears and stopped. "Oh, Zoom, please don't cry. Did I say something wrong? Do I not make sense?"

She smiled back at him. "You've never made more sense than this, my love."

He laughed with all his heart as he went on with his revelations. "If we, as the human race, could all experience this journey of creation and realize how we have emerged out of nothing, and how fantastic and magnificent a creation we are, we could all become God — just by being, because God just is!"

Zoom held his hands and said, "All human beings have an easy way to access and experience this, Ezekiel."

"What is it? What is the way?" He was eager to know.

"They must learn to be still and declutter their minds by spending time in self-reflection and self-examination, asking themselves, 'What could I have done today to make the world a better place? What could I have done in charity to make someone's life better? Where did I fall short? What can I work on for tomorrow?' They must use each and every day, each and every experience as a gateway to delve deeper into themselves. If they try to peel one layer at a time from their egos, if they try seeing and being their true authentic selves and just allowing their souls to guide them instead of their corrupted minds, they will be able to see and experience the Cosmic Factory. The center of the universe is inside of them, for they are the universe!"

Zoom held his hands and said, "Ezekiel, take my hand, close your eyes, and concentrate on my words. We are going back to experience the Cosmic Factory one final time, and then you must return to begin your mission in its truest sense."

He closed his eyes, held her hands, and focused on her words. They flew by an unseen force out into the cosmos until they reached the cosmic cycle's epicenter. The unstoppable force of love drew them and pulled them into this great magnetic field.

Just before the finale of the grand cosmic show, she whispered, "Ezekiel, when you return, just remember you were created out of nothing to experience everything that comes your way. You ultimately merge back into this great nothingness, so just enjoy the flow of being. Appreciate and celebrate every moment of that being. Always remember the great nothingness that awaits you. You'll know that being and flowing and experiencing life in physical form, created out of this great cosmic energy just for you, is the ultimate miracle. Nothing else matters but you being you. Enjoy the miracle that you are. Just enjoy being!"

Zeke felt himself and his beloved being turned into two huge and magnificent lights, as if they had been at the beginning of it all, at the genesis of creation. Their lights merged into one big flare of cosmic light and were then slowly sucked into the pool of light inside the magnetic field. The lights finally dissolved into the great void and became one with Source Energy, the center of ALL THAT IS.

CHAPTER FORTY-THREE

THE FAR END OF FARLEY STREET

Zeke woke up hearing the sweet sound of birds chirping outside his window. As the morning sunlight filled his room, an intoxicating fragrance of some unknown wildflower filled the air, and a timeless melody from the 1930s was being played on a piano somewhere down the road. He remembered it from *The Muppet Show*, an old-timey song called "When I Grow Too Old to Dream." The lyrics always reminded him of his relationship with Zoom.

It was the beginning of a magical spring unlike anything Mackinaw had ever seen before, and a lot was about to change on Farley Steet. Zeke looked at the little clock staring at him from his nightstand. It was just past nine in the morning. He left his bed feeling calm and peaceful, with no worries and nothing to care about, because he knew the truth. All he needed to do… was to be.

The loud giggles of his happy sisters and their exciting conversation with their father over cars, business deals, and clients at the breakfast table had also reached his ears. He brushed his teeth, freshened up, finished his chores, and joined them for breakfast. They had just started a family conversation about what Zeke was planning to do with his life when they heard someone knocking at the door and calling out the whole family by name.

"Yoo-hoo!" Ben? Zeke? Are you there? Maya and Leia, my twin darlings, can anybody hear me? Is anybody home?"

The Tartals couldn't believe what they were hearing. It was an old, familiar, and beloved voice — one all three of them recognized at once.

Leia rushed to the door and threw it open. "Mrs. Braganza… is that you? I can't believe it!" She jumped and gave the old woman a hug.

"Oh my God! How did you get here?" Maya shouted.

"This is the best surprise ever! Are you okay? Do you need help?" Zeke added.

"I'd like you to meet my son Tiago who brought me all the way from Portugal," she proudly stated as she presented him to the Tartals.

"Hello everyone. I feel like I know you already! I've heard so many wonderful things about you. Please excuse my English. My mother was helping me practice on the way here."

"The pleasure is ours, Tiago, and you are most welcome here," as Ben offered his hand for a hearty handshake.

The three bombarded her with a barrage of questions, unintentionally forgetting to even invite her to come inside.

"Children, children, at least allow this poor, old lady to come in. Give her some water and some rest before she can speak. You haven't grown up a bit. You still act like little monsters!" She scolded them as she had when they were young. It only took her a few seconds to return to the loving and nurturing role she had played at Tartal House for many years. Almost as soon as she sat down, the children noticed that she looked much younger than she had when she left. It was as if she had aged in reverse.

"What happened to you, Mrs. B? Did you find the fountain of youth or something? You look so young and healthy. How?" Leia was the first one to openly express her amazement.

"This is just wild!" Maya exclaimed. "How *did* you do it?"

"You look quite fetching, Eleanor. I must say, this is a remarkable change — nothing short of a miracle. You've got some explaining to do, young lady," Ben chimed in with a playful wink of his eye.

Zeke noticed it too, but he refrained from adding to the excitement. He just smiled. He understood that life was indeed a miracle, and nothing was impossible over the course of all he had learned.

Mrs. Braganza seemed to show no interest in answering any of the questions thrown at her. Instead, she kept blabbering nonsensical things like how unclean and messy the house looked and how frail the girls had gotten. Just then, something completely unexpected and magical happened. As all four Tartals were focused on Mrs. Braganza, Coconut silently snuck into the room and parked himself behind the chair where she was sitting, as if he was hiding behind her, hoping to surprise the children. As soon as they saw him, all hell broke loose.

"Coconut!" Zeke shouted.

"No effin' way!" Leia cried out, stunned in disbelief.

"This has to be a joke," Maya echoed back.

The girls erupted in shrieks loud enough to shake the walls and ran to hug their long-lost pup. Ben just stood there with his mouth open while Zeke laughed heartily, watching it all unfold. He laughed because he understood how the universe worked. The wish he made to have Coconut and Mrs. Braganza back in his life had finally come true. It had taken so long, but the universe had not forgotten his prayer. It was only waiting for the right time.

Zeke merely lifted his eyes to the heavens, smiled slightly, and silently whispered, "Thanks, Tony."

This was the first miracle he witnessed after his return from the center of the universe. This was the perfect example of how amazing the Cosmic Factory worked and how wonderful God is. God brought these two extremely important figures back into Zeke's life. But how did all of this happen? How did Mrs. Braganza make it back to Tartal House from Portugal so late in life, at an age when her own death was so near, and where on Earth could she possibly have found Coconut? How were they together? How did they both age in reverse? There were so many of these unanswered questions, but none of them mattered to Zeke. He learned to simply accept the will of the universe. But his sisters wanted answers, and so did Ben. These answers were way simpler than any of them had expected them to be. The explanations for all these occurrences only reassured Zeke's faith in the fact that to fulfill the will of the universe, even the most absurd of events take place quite naturally.

Mrs. Braganza loved the Tartals as much as they loved her. Back home in Portugal, all her children had married a long time ago, and they were all busy with their own lives. Her husband had been dead for almost a quarter of a century, not long after the couple had moved to America. She eventually decided to go back to Portugal because she believed she wasn't going to live much longer and wanted to be with her children before her time finally came, but it never did, and she felt lonelier than ever. It wasn't like her children and grandchildren didn't love her. They all loved her very much, but they all had their own lives, which she hadn't been a part of for a long time, so she felt like a stranger in her own family — something Zeke could absolutely relate to. The fact of the matter was that she had grown used to life in the U.S. and didn't feel as comfortable readjusting to the ways of village life in Portugal anymore.

The most important reason for her return, however, was Tartal House. She realized that she loved and missed the three little troublemakers and the cute little Coconut far too much to be away from them. She used to wake up in the middle of the night, having vivid dreams of either Maya and Leia crying for her or Coconut looking for her in the streets. She missed them terribly and finally came to the understanding that Tartal House wasn't just a place where she had worked — it was her home. It was where her soul belonged.

She had developed some health conditions that the local doctors couldn't diagnose, and one day, one of her sons convinced her to visit an alternative healer to help her deal with them. The therapist was an old Chinese woman married to a Portuguese man. The couple lived in the same village as Eleanor's family. They had no children and had been living there for almost half a century. The Chinese woman had been all over the world and carried with her the knowledge and wisdom of many healing techniques from the East. She slowly introduced traditional medicines, herbs, alternative healing, and other holistic practices to the villagers and was almost considered a miracle worker. The village folk called her "Old Mother," and she looked after them.

Eleanor desperately wanted to heal, and Old Mother helped her with a combination of rare Chinese and Indian herbs. Old Mother also taught her yoga and meditation along with fasting, cleanses, and other known remedies from the East. Eventually, many of her age-related health issues receded or even disappeared, and not only did she begin to feel healthier and stronger, but she was also noticeably younger.

She turned to Ben. "I received the letter you sent me about Audrey's passing. If only I had come back sooner," she lamented. "My medicines could have saved her. Oh, Audrey. She was such a lovely woman."

"Thank you, Eleanor. She thought the world of you," he replied.

Zeke put his hand on her shoulder and said, "She's gone now, Mrs. Braganza, and trust me, if that was how it was meant to be, you couldn't have helped her. It was her time to go. I had to learn that the hard way."

"My, my, Master Zeke. You have certainly grown into quite the Renaissance man."

"Well, I've been woodshedding in your absence," he said with a wink and a smile.

• • •

As a beautiful and thriving spring continued to roll along in Mackinaw, Tartal House was livelier than ever. They were a beautiful family again, and that made Zeke very happy because he knew that his mother was smiling at them from up in heaven. For the next few days, the Tartals were on fire. The whole house was in a state of grand celebration. Mrs. Braganza was pleasantly surprised to meet the new version of Mr. Tartal, who was now a warm, caring, and compassionate man. Coconut found his doghouse waiting for him the exact same way he had left it. Mrs. Braganza headed straight to the kitchen to make her famous Bolo de Mel cake. When it was finally in the oven and its heavenly scent began to fill the house, the kids went wild.

"Oh, Mrs. B, how we longed for this cake! No one can make it like you do," Maya proclaimed.

"I have to admit, Eleanor, it's the best there is. You're going to have to teach me and the kids how to make it so we can continue this yummy family tradition," Ben added.

Mrs. Braganza was finally home. She finally had a place to belong, but this was not the end of her story. The universe had more in store for her.

Not long after her arrival and Tiago's return to Portugal, Mrs. Braganza realized her stock of herbal medicines was about to run dry a lot sooner than she had hoped. The little suitcase she brought all the way from Europe could only hold so much. She needed her herbs to stay healthy and fit. One day, she went out in search of those rare herbs so she could prepare the formulas she had learned from Old Mother.

It was late afternoon and there weren't many people out on the streets. She didn't know where to go or what to do. Mackinaw had changed a lot in the few short years she had been away. The only way left for her was to ask people she met. On her way, she came across a few shops and asked the storekeepers if they could lead her to any herbal medicine stores in the city. Nobody had any clue about a place that would have the kind of herbs she was looking for. Many of them had never even heard of such things.

"You would probably have to go to Traverse City or visit a local witch in the woods for that stuff," one shopkeeper joked.

"I guess you could only get those online," another told her.

Eventually, she found her way to a unique store in town, a place where she was told anything could be found. It was Noah Leitner's store Indigo Children. She went into the store searching for her Chinese medicines but ended up meeting the most amazing man she had ever come across. Two lonely, aging people with similar likes and interests became friends instantly. Noah knew all about the herbs and medicines she was looking for. In fact, he had some of them in his own garden. He gifted her some herbs and promised that he would ask around and find her exactly what she needed.

He brought her all the herbs she needed, and she eventually convinced him to start taking them, too. He initially had no inclination whatsoever to take special care of his aging body, but she was the only friend his own age he had made in a long time, and he just couldn't turn her down. He began a holistic regime and many of his seemingly complex problems began to disappear as a result. Eventually, Zeke found out that the two seniors had become friends, and to him, this was another sign of the fact the universe worked in many mysterious ways. Both Noah and Eleanor were also surprised to learn that they had a connection through a young man they both loved dearly — Zeke Tartal.

The two slowly began meeting for an hour-long practice of breathing exercises and Tai Chi every morning by the lake or inside a park. Coconut remained a constant companion. What they did not know was the fact that Zeke, Leia, and Maya were the ones who had engineered these meetings in the hopes of getting the two lonely folks to fall for each other.

"You know, Mr. Leitner, you really should try all that yoga stuff Mrs. Braganza knows. It would really help you. Why don't you ask her to teach you?" Zeke said to him one day.

"Oh, no, no, no, Zeke. I…"

"What's the matter? Do you have a problem with her?"

"Oh, no. Of course not! I think she's wonderful, but I don't want to bother her."

"Oh, come on. I'm sure she thinks you're wonderful, too! She'd love to help you out."

"You sure about that?"

"Oh, yeah!"

As Zeke convinced Noah, his sisters made sure Mrs. Braganza was also on board.

"So, I hear Mr. Leitner from the woo-woo emporium is looking to get into yoga," Leia remarked in a waggish manner one morning over breakfast. "You know a lot about yoga, don't you, Mrs. B?"

"What? Noah never told me he wanted to learn yoga. I would be more than happy to teach him what I know."

"Oh, that's cool. Tell me, Mrs. B, what do you think about Mr. Leitner as a person?" Maya added.

"Well…" she lightly blushed. "He is one of the kindest and most generous men I have ever met, and he most certainly is the wisest."

Both girls looked at each other from across the table and giggled. "Looks like someone has a crush," Maya playfully announced.

Eleanor's face turned as red as a beet as she scolded the girls for teasing her. "Don't think I don't know what you two are doing, you little yentas. Do you really think I was born yesterday?" She pretended to storm out of the room, but then she stopped for a second and smiled, realizing Leia and Maya truly had her best interests at heart.

One day, Noah offered her a unique kind of partnership. He would provide all the herbs and ingredients she needed for her concoctions, and she could sell them from a small counter in his shop. That way, she could have a source of income, and the people of Mackinaw could find alternative healing through the teachings of the old Chinese Mother.

One evening, almost a month later, Zeke decided to visit his old friend at Indigo Children. It was only when he entered the store that he realized how much it had changed. There was a funky, New Age dispensary in the back corner where Mrs. Braganza set up shop with Coconut by her side, selling all kinds of lotions and potions to the locals and tourists alike. Indigo Children had gotten a makeover with Eleanor adding a feminine and a Portuguese touch, and it was now better than ever. Zeke was also happy to see how close they had become, and he was proud of himself for helping put their relationship into motion.

That summer and the months to come brought the two seniors even closer as they began to rely on each other for emotional support. They would spend hours at a time talking about the long and fruitful lives they had both lived. They often watched old movies to-gether, and even cooked for each other. Sharing and caring for each other kept them young, healthy, and happy. When autumn arrived in Mackinaw, the two enjoyed evening walks in the park, the scenic drives, the hayrides, the cider mills, and the pumpkin patches. They walked hand in hand by the lakeside as if they were two teenagers in love. Their stories may not have had the happiest of beginnings, but they finally had their chance at a happy ending.

• • •

There were more stories yet to unfold on Farley Street that year. Ben announced to his children that he would finally be leaving for London when his daughters turned eighteen the following spring. He felt content leaving his business to them, partly because he knew they would have Mrs. Braganza and Mr. Leitner to watch over them. He had been talking to a friend he knew from London for a while now and had finally received the green light from him. He had shown interest in partnering with Ben and helping him find proper locations to build a restaurant, which they could later develop into a chain if Ben could convince him with his business plan.

He had been to London once, many years ago with Audrey for their honeymoon, and had always felt a natural pull towards the city. That was why he had originally wanted to move there years ago when things were not going so well for him. His original decision had broken his wife's heart and created even more distance with his children. He had been a selfish, cold, and unemotional man who was only concerned about his own happiness and didn't care for the future of his family, but he was a different man now. He loved his children dearly, but he had a new ambition that he needed to pursue. He decided that he would alternate between Mackinaw and London if needed, or at least until his daughters were completely set up with the dealership. He also decided that he would not immediately sell Tartal House until all his children were financially secure.

Time had changed him, made him the man he was today, and now it was time for this man to get what he deserved. The universe was listening to him now. The dream he had held for years, the dream of having a small chain of cozy restaurants in London where people could just come and relax, be free of their worries, and enjoy good food, wine, music, and laughter was something only a kind man could have thought of.

Investing all his savings, all his time, and all his emotions in this venture was definitely a big risk, but in the end, it was all worth it. It was all for the sake of a dream, and dreams are always worth the risk. He would be leaving his home and the comfort of his family behind, but he had learned that a family doesn't need to be together to be connected. On an emotional level, he had nothing left to lose. His children were all grown up. Zeke was twenty-one, the twins were soon-to-be the legal age of eighteen, and his wife was dead and gone. He was a free man in every sense of the word, free to finally chase his dreams. Even though he still wasn't going to permanently move away for a while, he took the measures needed to sort things out for his kids. He made the girls the legal owners of "Tartal and Daughters" on their eighteenth birthday and fairly divided what property he had among his kids.

Knowing that he was going to leave next year made every moment bittersweet for them. They had spent their whole lives emotionally distant from their father, and now that he was finally a part of their family in its truest sense, he was leaving. Maya and Leia had started to love their father with every fiber of their being, and even Zeke, who had once detested the sight of him, now relied on him. The Tartal family was not going to be the same without the man who had learned to be both a father and mother to his children after years of neglecting both responsibilities. They all wanted him to stay, and somewhere deep down, he wanted to stay, too. But nothing ever really stays the same. Change is inevitable, and change eventually came to Farley Street as well.

• • •

Ben's departure from Mackinaw and from the family business would change the neighborhood dynamic in many ways. Zeke had already made it crystal clear that he wanted no part in the car dealership or the garage. He had other life ambitions, though they weren't clear to him just yet. Gael, on the other hand, was now studying business management at an online university and had tired of the lawn care business. He wanted to branch out. Under Ben's supervision, he started working at the dealership. Ben knew he was a good kid, and he wanted to leave Maya and Leia with someone they could rely on.

When he suggested that they work with Gael, both Maya and Leia gladly jumped at the proposal. They had both grown up with Gael and saw him as a member of their family. The three of them would spend hours sitting in the garage, making plans about expanding the business. They all had big ideas and ambitions. They wanted to make "Tartal Brands" a global enterprise. Leia wanted to design cars, Maya wanted to sell them, while Gael was there to hold it all together. It was a big dream, but they were devoted to it, and Zeke was happy for them. Together, the three of them were a force to be reckoned with.

Zig and Zag still visited Zeke, letting him know that he had a connection with cosmic forces beyond his human existence. But their visits were rare, reminding Zeke that he was a grown man now and that he would have to carve his own path soon enough.

The magical period of stability and happiness on Farley Street was coming to an end, and more change was on the way.

• • •

It was the beginning of August, and around the Lion's Gate, another revelation shook the hood. One evening, Maya, Leia, and Mrs. Braganza were watching TV. They came across a promotion for a new fall sitcom, one that everyone was sure would be a success. That is when they saw him. A familiar face just flashed across the TV screen, startling everyone at the same time. As it turned out, a fresh, new face had burst onto the American television scene, and for the residents of Mackinaw, this face wasn't new at all. One of the actors left everyone speechless and overwhelmed, not because of his handsome, dreamy looks, or what they could gather of his talent, but simply because of who he was. It was Kai Copeland!

The reaction was decidedly mixed. Initially, it was a feeling of joy and pride, seeing him alive and thriving, and yet a sense of pain and hurt to know he never bothered to return or let his family and friends know what he had been doing for so long. For Zeke, it was a sense of relief. Seeing his old friend on the small screen offered him some closure to their relationship, and so it was a welcome sight.

Soon, everyone became aware of Kai's imminent success. His name and face flashed all over TV and in popular news magazines. He became a local hero in the town of Mackinaw. Nobody in their wildest dreams had ever guessed Kai Copeland would end up in Hollywood instead of studying business at Harvard. He was a headstrong guy who had never given up on his dream of achieving success. His roles were limited to television and some commercial work, but he was a success regardless. He was the talk of the town for months, but no one really knew how he had ended up on TV instead of Harvard. No one except Zeke, that is.

One night the previous spring, he received a call from a number he did not recognize, and to his surprise, it was Kai. They talked for a good hour. Kai told him how the guy he was supposed to stay with in Boston had backed out of their deal, and he was left helpless. He had barely been making a living doing odd jobs when a talent scout from New York noticed him and told him to go to an audition for an off-Broadway play in Manhattan. He won the role with virtually no acting experience because he was simply right for the part. Unfortunately, the show only ran for two months and then closed. From there, he started taking acting classes and going to auditions during the day while working at a restaurant at night. He was lucky enough to win a role for a TV pilot in Los Angeles that sold, so he moved to California. He was now a stable, working actor with a number of opportunities lined up.

Zeke felt tremendous relief knowing that his friend had been doing so well, both financially and emotionally, but when he asked Kai to talk to his family, he learned that there were still some unresolved issues underneath all that success and recognition.

"Why don't you call your mother, Kai… or Gael? Why not call them? They all miss you so much," he asked him over the phone.

"I… I don't know how to Zeke, I really don't. I feel like I abandoned them. I don't think I can face them, at least not yet. I'm not ready. I'll come back to Farley Street someday, maybe soon, but for now, I don't think I can face them."

Zeke understood his friend's pain, and he understood that Kai still needed time. "I won't force you to talk to them, Kai. Take your time. I know it can be hard to look past the kind of pain and guilt you're feeling, but one thing that you must remember is that they're your family. They'll always care about you, but don't take too long. We both know from experience that life is just too short."

Zeke could hear the emotion in Kai's voice as he spoke. "You know, Zeke, you always were the smartest of us all." He and Kai talked many times after that, but Kai never did come back to Farley Street, at least not while Zeke was there.

• • •

Meanwhile, in late September, Noah brought a wave of great happiness by proposing to Eleanor in full rom-com movie fashion by the lakeside. Of course, he had help from Maya and Leia, who had helped him pick the spot and the ring. When he knelt down, she yelled, "YES!" before he could even ask the question. Everyone erupted in laughter and applause.

A late October wedding was planned. "At our age, long engagements don't make sense!" Noah proudly proclaimed. So, on the auspicious day of their wedding, Noah Leitner and Eleanor Braganza promised to be with each other as man and wife "till death do us part." She permanently moved out of Tartal House and moved in with Noah, and Coconut naturally went with her. Coco had gotten so used to running between the two houses that nobody even bothered to follow him when he did.

Just after the grand October wedding of Mr. And Mrs. Noah Leitner, the call to action that Zeke was waiting for finally arrived, and it was unlike anything he had expected. It was the morning of Halloween. Zeke, Gael, Maya, and Leia all went out to spend a day in the corn fields like they did when they were kids. After running around all day, Zeke was exhausted, and when he finally laid down to rest, he fell asleep. That was when it came — the darkest dream he ever had.

In his dream, he saw a man ominously smiling at him with his eyes closed. The man had a charming face, but something about it made every hair on Zeke's body stand straight on end. It was a face unlike anything he had ever seen, and yet it was strangely familiar. Just as he was about to move towards the man, he opened his eyes, leaving Zeke terrified. The man had the slit eyes of a lizard. It took Zeke only a fraction of a second to understand who the man was. He had felt his dark presence before, in other lives and in this one, too.

"Draco!" he shouted in utter shock and recognition.

The man said nothing. He simply stared at Zeke with his cold, dark eyes.

Zeke spoke again, with bravado in his voice and a conviction like never before. "You're Draco, aren't you? ANSWER ME!"

The man still did not speak. He only continued to stare at him, his Reptilian eyes locked with Zeke's human ones. Then he opened his mouth, revealing his slit, snake-like tongue. He licked his lips and spoke in a raspy, blood-curdling voice. "I've been waiting, old friend. I'm glad you're finally back. Now we can begin our little dance. Oh, how I've missed a good challenge. I will wait for you, Lightbringer. Come find me," he pompously asserted as he slowly backed away.

Zeke instinctively felt a burning rage, and he sprinted towards Draco. But as he pounced, the image of the man instantaneously turned to dust, and from behind that dust, an older, much more saintly man appeared. He wore a long, brown robe with a rope belt and had a soft, glowing light emanating from his face, one that made Zeke feel much more collected and at ease. He looked at Zeke and said, "You have seen your enemy, young man. Now you must go after him."

Zeke felt obliged to listen to the old man, but he also needed answers. "Where… where do I even begin to look for him? And who are you, wise one?"

"He is everywhere and nowhere, in the east and in the west, in the air and in the earth. He never stays in the same place. You must find him and end him. That is your duty." The old man said no more. He turned away from Zeke and started walking. Zeke continued to call out to him, but no answer came. Then, just like that, the dream was over, and he woke up.

Zeke had received the final call he needed. It was time for him to bid adieu to Farley Street and begin his journey. He knew Draco and the Reptilians were out there, and now he had to hunt them down. He had to liberate human minds from their control. He needed to travel and to travel solo. He knew he needed to go all over the world, and for that, he needed money. So he talked to his sisters. The three of them sat together, and they eventually found a way to fund his journey, but that would prove to be unnecessary as he would soon learn that the universe was on his side once again. Out of the blue, a large sum of money appeared in his bank account one morning because of an accounting "glitch." But Zeke knew what it was. It was the universe helping him on his mission. Even when he tried to question the money, the bank insisted the deposit was legitimate.

And so, on his birthday, December 25th, 2021, he packed his bags, ready to embark on an unknown journey towards his mission — towards the face in his dreams, the embodiment of darkness itself. Where would he look for the Reptilians first — Egypt, India, or China? Where on Earth could Draco be hiding? He didn't know, but something told him that he needed to go east. There were answers waiting for him there.

He also needed to find Zoom again or wait for her to find him. Zeke didn't know if she knew of Draco's existence on Earth, but he knew that some twisted force had bound the three of them together. Their fates were one. He did not know if his actions would lead to another war between the Lyrans and the Reptilians, nor did he know what kind of effect they would have on Earth and on humanity. All he knew was that he had to go east. He had to follow the call. His mission to save mankind had begun. Where it would take him, only the Source knows. But one thing was for certain: even though he was leaving Farley Street far behind, Ezekiel Tartal's journey had only just begun.

The End

Are YOU a Lyran Starseed like Zeke and Zoom?

Lyran Starseeds originate from Lyra, a small constellation sometimes visible in the night sky. The most famous star in this constellation is Vega, which is also one of the brightest stars visible from Planet Earth. The stars form the shape of a lyre or harp which gives the constellation its name. You'll note the Lryan symbol on the crown of the old High Council head and remember Zoom sported a Lyran tattoo on her earthly visit to Mackinaw City.

Known as the original keepers of ancient knowledge, Lyran Starseeds are highly intelligent, evolved beings from Vega. Rather interestingly, it's highly unlikely that first-generation Lyrans exist anymore. Their civilization is considered ancient. It's the galactic equivalent of Earth's ancient Romans or Egyptians. The majority of the original Lyran population was believed to have been wiped out during the Draco-Lyran war, an energetic battle against greed, power, and control. The surviving Lyrans decided to flee their homeland, entering reincarnation cycles in other star systems such as Pleiades, Sirius, and Orion.

Many Lyrans have volunteered to reincarnate on Earth to help awaken humanity and evolve the collective consciousness. They are needed now more than ever to guide humankind through a crucial transition to a higher-dimensional existence. As such, they love the chaotic nature of Earth life and the undeniable freedom that comes with it. Lyran Starseeds exude extremely high vibrational energy. People always notice them and feel drawn to them. As intergalactic explorers, they spanned the entire cosmos acquiring a level of knowledge and experience no other starseed can match, and thus they deeply impact people around them.

Lyrans feel a deep connection to felines like lions, tigers, or cats as they often have subconscious memories of being feline humanoids. Lyran Starseeds show paradoxical traits and are thus often misunderstood. They are sociable yet loners, dynamic yet lazy, extraordinarily loving and endearing yet can easily lose their temper. They're not meant to be a part of a pack because they are already ahead of the pack. They love refinement and sophistication, are highly spiritual, extraordinarily soft and sensitive, but emotionally very strong. They love to lead but can't be led. They are extremely loyal, yet they come across as unattached and commitment-phobic when it comes to human relationships.

We know they existed at some point, but now only descendants of their bloodline carry on. Could you be one of them? If you believe so, be sure to proudly display the Lyran symbol all around you! You can find Lyran and Farley Street merchandise here:

www.zanezubin.com

ABOUT THE AUTHOR

Zane Zubin is a recognized indie author from Florida but calls the world his home. He has written several creative pieces in the course of his lifetime and this is his first-ever fantasy fiction novel. Farley Street was inspired by his dreams, meditations, out-of-body experiences, channeling sessions with his spirit guide, his wacky, fantasy-filled imagination and, naturally, his love of the space opera genre.

He currently is writing the sequel to Farley Street, BEYOND FARLEY: THE HUNT FOR DRACO, and is developing a video game centered around the characters. If you love the story, be sure to spread the word!

Write to Zane at contact@zanezubin.com